"A highly compelling drama . . . Writing in fluent, energetic prose . . . Wolff succeeds in combining the psychological subtlety that James pioneered in his novels with the stark fable-like symbolism he so often employed in his shorter tales."
—Michiko Kakutani, *The New York Times*

"A book about the past, as it was lived, and as it is (sometimes willfully) mis-remembered; it is also, of necessity about self-fulfillment and self-delusion. Wolff perfectly renders a sense of the texture of the town's life, the web of moods and motives that becomes more complex and contradictory as its citizens and their children grow older."
—Ron Carlson, *The New York Times Book Review*

"Wolff . . . skillfully lays bare a world of rueful adults, even children, whose memories are rife with ache and bitterness—a bleak, amoral place where no one can move fast or far enough from harm."
—Paula Chin, *People*

"A well-considered novel . . . Wolff has displayed a magnanimous sensibility and strong heart."
—Gail Caldwell, *The Boston Sunday Globe*

"An adroit and engrossing chronicler of lives gnawed raw by futility and defeat . . . Wolff's sober fury, simmering just below the surface, sends currents of tension and depression streaming through his narrative. We embrace the anguish when it arrives even as we realize more will be coming."
—Margaria Fichtner, *Miami Herald*

"Wolff's enviably constructed novel moves swiftly to a dramatic and surprising climax. . . . It will take your breath away."
—Carol McCabe, *The Providence Sunday Journal*

"Touching, chilling . . . *The Age of Consent* benefits from a prose style that's straightforward (almost sweetly so) yet resonant with suppressed emotion, plain and almost breezy at times yet fervently cutting close to the emotional bone when necessary."
—Frederic Koeppel, *The Memphis Commercial Appeal*

The Age of Consent

Geoffrey Wolff

The Age of Consent

Picador USA
New York

Picador® is a U.S. registered trademark and is used by
St. Martin's Press under license from Pan Books Limited.

Library of Congress Cataloging-in-Publication Data

Wolff, Geoffrey
The age of consent / by Geoffrey Wolff.
p.   cm.
ISBN 0-312-14081-9
1. Community life—New York (State)—Fiction.
2. New York (State)—Fiction.   I. Title.
[PS3573.O53A74   1996]
813'.54—dc20   95-46790   CIP

First published in the United States by Alfred A. Knopf

First Picador USA Edition: March 1996
10   9   8   7   6   5   4   3   2   1

For Priscilla

The Age of Consent

Then Was Then

Gravity

He'd have forever to remember hauling himself from the water, slumping on the stream's mossy edge, his pockets puffed with wet gravel. He whacked his ear to clear a bubble, swiped at deerflies. Ted was thirteen and his gestures were willfully unexcited. He was drowsy. He had spent a late night helping his neighbors build a float for the parade, and this Independence Day morning he had marched with his neighbors through town and uphill to the bandstand. Now the noon heat was breaking records. Here in the shade of a quaking aspen, with a breeze rustling the leaves, with his feet in the water, Ted rubbed his eyes. The Raven Kill was sluggish; the winter runoff was long gone to Lake Discovery, and this little river had been more than a month in drought. Lethargic trout were said to have collected in the deeper pools near the swimming hole, but Ted felt too lazy to search for them.

Above, on a ledge jutting from falls petering down a sheer granite headwall, stood his sister. The swimming hole was crowded today—the heat and holiday had brought them out, townspeople and visitors. But Maisie was alone up there, looking down, her hands on her hips and one knee imperiously cocked. It struck Ted then that his sister, washed in dappled midday light, was lovely. Her long black hair glistened wet against her pale shoulders. Until a year ago skinny-dippers had the run of this lush green place. They lined the banks and dozed on the warm rocks midstream. Last spring some local old-timers, determined to retrieve their town from the clutch of outsiders, had made such a fuss at a town meeting that the sheriff was provoked to enforce antique ordinances outlawing public indecency. But even during bygone summers of pure license, there were limits, and a teenaged girl would wear a bathing suit. Maisie's was a black one-piece, the color and style she had settled on as a child. But when Ted rubbed his eyes again, his sister had made a quick, slippery move, shedding her suit. She was naked.

He felt along the damp bank for his glasses. Where they lived, citizens didn't show off, yet his sister seemed nonchalant as a queen. It was difficult through his blurred vision for Ted to read her expression, whether she was smiling or sneering. Maisie was fifteen. Ted, bewildered, wondered whether to call out to her. She seemed to be arranging herself for something weighty. He remembered years past, watching her turn cartwheels on the pebbly beach below the falls when she prepared for each performance with ferocious deliberation and execute her upside-down trick with strict grace.

Ted thought that for his sister gravity didn't apply. Rules didn't. Now the world stirred. People lined the banks, gossiping and eating sandwiches and laughing beside the water sucking gently at the banks of the Raven Kill gorge; Maisie's schoolmates and their parents and her parents, citizens and tourists, all looked forty feet up at her. Human noises stuttered and fell. Above, a glider soared the thermals, diving like a raptor in a tightening loop; Maisie glanced up, must have heard the rush of air over its great fragile wings. She assembled herself, as if gathering reserves for a medal event, degree of difficulty extreme. Ted could see her feet were together, her arms at her side. He put on his glasses as she came off the ledge in a layout dive. Her takeoff was stylish, with her legs locked together straight and her head back and her back ecstatically arched. He adjusted his eyes as she swung her arms out like wings, out from her shoulders, the maneuver for a swan dive. Ted waited, frozen, for her arms to rotate forward, for her hands to break her fall. But just before she hit the shallow pool beside the trickling chute, she swept her arms back along her sides and plunged in headfirst, a clean entry.

No one applauded. No one spoke, cried out, looked away. They'd remember the components of this act, this calculated process, how suddenly it was finished. Mosquitoes hummed, scavenging whiskey jacks called to one another from the high branches in a low-pitched serene whistle, and the trickle of water ran down. Then came speech: Maisie's mother—*"my baby!"*—and her father and her brother. And all these friends and neighbors who knew this girl, and all those gawking strangers who didn't, what could they make of this?

She was down there, somewhere in the vortex of the swirl-scoured pothole. Spectators, many now, moved to help. They were diving in, tangling their arms and legs in an effort to rescue the girl, or making a show of making an effort. Suddenly one of them, Doc Halliday, cradled her in his arms. Her neck was slack, arched too far back. Her face was bloody, and Doc held her with theatrical tenderness as he arranged her naked body faceup on the mossy shore. He said something, and several young men took off running. Now Ted was astride his sister, covering her breasts and belly and thighs with towels, moaning, "Don't don't don't, Maisie, *don't!*" Doc Halliday gently pushed the boy away, said to leave her be, and lowered his face and breathed into her mouth. Maisie's mother said, "She's dead; you did it." "She's okay," her father said. "Please, Doc," Ted whispered, "please do it right." And Doc breathed into the girl's mouth, and she was inert as ice, all grace gone, and blood in her eyes, on Doc's face.

Time must have passed. Now the rescue squad moved through a knot of sightseers who gave way easily. The people collected at this pacific place this soft summer day stood in a semicircle around the girl and the man breathing into her mouth and the girl's little brother and her mother and her father. Doc was just his nickname, and so he backed off when the professional saviors arrived. The onlookers didn't crowd in. They didn't know what had happened or why. And later Ted would understand that many didn't want to know, and who could blame them?

Ted

That summer he tried to go crazy. No dice. As a nutcase, he was a nonfinisher. He tried to take pride from his mother and father's struggle to stay sane, but that wasn't in the cards either. He simply didn't know what to think or believe or do. The Jenks family would sit together in Maisie's hospital room, staring at her or at one another or at a magazine, rearranging the flowers on her sill and bedside table over and over.

After the surgeons had done their high-tech best in Albany, she'd been returned north to the hospital in Lake Placid, an easy reach from home. Bedside, Ted's father settled into a routine of talking to his numbed daughter, and Ted recognized the languid cadence of Jinx's monologue as his long-distance telephone voice. Jinx gossiped to Maisie about the neighbors, gave opinions about politics and foreign affairs and the environment, now and then punctuating his rap with a question:

"What do you think, sweetie? So what do you make of that, Maisie?"

Ted tried to give his father the benefit of the doubt, and

understood that it was consoling to pretend that Maisie could hear his voice. But whenever Jinx asked Maisie for a response, waiting patiently for her to reply, Ted would feel the ground roll beneath him. "She can't talk, Dad. She can't hear you."

Then his mother, combing Maisie's greasy hair, would say, "We don't know that for a fact. We don't know what your sister knows."

When Jinx finally tired of talking, Ann would read to her. A year or so ago, Maisie had found her way to poetry. Ann searched her daughter's anthologies for pages that gave evidence of having been read and she'd say the poems aloud: John Donne and Emily Dickinson and Andrew Marvell. Ted liked to hear her voice; he didn't understand the poems, exactly, and didn't know whether his mother did either, but he understood that whatever else was happening while Ann turned those tissue-thin pages, she was trying to figure something out.

But then Ted would remember where he was, where his sister was, how she got there. Ann might as well have been reading to a sackful of hammers. Watching his mother touch Maisie's hair was worse. He'd flash back to how that hair, black as a crow's wing, glistened so wet when his sister posed herself above the falls. He'd remember her with her friend Helen, not so many summers ago, the two of them taking turns braiding each other's hair, weaving their hair together in a common plait while they giggled about some secret, whispering into each other's ears so Ted couldn't hear. Now, in the hospital, when he couldn't bear another instant of the sanity charade his father and mother were acting out, Ted would steal into Maisie's bathroom and lock the door and shriek silent shrieks, contorting his face so that he looked, he could almost believe, like that picture Maisie had showed him, Munch's *The Scream*. But then he'd catch a glimpse of his face in the mirror, laboring to give up control, and he'd lose it, slip away from himself, feel flooded with light, smirk, choke back laughter.

Ted had come to believe that his dad was deaf to other people's voices, but his mom would hear him in the bathroom, assume he was crying, and talk softly through the bathroom door, saying words she must have supposed were comforting:

"It's got to come out okay, Ted. It's not fair. Don't cry, baby."

Then he'd make himself hold his eyelids wide open for a minute or two without blinking, till his eyes turned red and wet, and once his appearance satisfied the teary occasion, he'd open the door. She'd hug him and he'd hug her, and his father would look up and say, "What's going on?" Clueless.

Dinners at home were as painful as the sessions at the hospital. Ted's father was so steadfastly cheerful in the face of the crushing facts that Ted wanted to drown him. Hit him with an oar. Push him off a mountain. Put a scaling knife in the back of his neck. Set his beard on fire. Mr. Jenks had a reddish brown beard then, just a lot too peppy for the family's circumstances that July and August. He'd promised not to shave until Maisie came back to them whole. He also had freckles. Ted began to resent that he was called Jinx, and he decided that his father looked too young to carry the weight that had been put on them.

"Look at it this way," Jinx said. "It could be a lot worse."

"How would that work?" Ted asked.

"She could be dead."

"She might as well be," he said. "She could die tomorrow. Maybe she's dying right now, while we're helping ourselves to seconds."

His mom said, "Don't you ever ever say such words again, young man. And you haven't touched a thing on your plate. The squash is from Maisie's garden."

Ted wanted to explain he'd said what he had because he

couldn't stand watching his father put that piece of lamb in his mouth, seeing the juice grease his lips and beard. But how could he? So instead, he said, "Mom, you've never ever ever ever called me 'young man' before."

"I don't think I can stand much more of this constant talk," she said.

"We've hardly said a word all day," Ted replied. In fact, words had passed between his father and mother, a choral exchange of blame and defense under the general heading of being a dreamer versus being a realist. "We never talk," he said.

"Now Ted," his father said. "You know we're always here for you. If you want to talk, we're here to listen."

Well.

When Ted was young, when Maisie bugged him, when he felt he couldn't bear more mocking, when the blood flushed his face and neck, when this made Maisie laugh out loud, his mom would advise him to take a deep breath, hold it, count to a thousand, and then he'd be okay. It wasn't till this summer that he learned he was supposed to count to ten. That's what the rest of the world's mothers had taught their sons. When he asked his mom at Maisie's bedside if she was trying to kill him, she tugged at a strand of hair and said, as she often did that summer, "What are you talking about?"

"Joke, Ma, just a little joke."

"Of course, Teddy. What did you just ask me?"

Her son answered with his answer to most questions those days: "Nothing."

Instead of holding his breath and counting while he waited for providence to make up its mind about his sister, he chose to remember how they had arrived at that summer, how they were passing through it. He wanted to believe he could be certain of something, and then if fury was his lot, he wanted to know why he was furious, on whose behalf, by whose fault, to what end.

Before this summer he didn't like to go to sleep angry. Now he didn't want to wake up. His anger was new to him. The people he'd grown up among, his neighbors and his family, described him as a sunny kid, and even though he valued composure and reticence, what he called cool, he was glad to be known for a warm heart. If his mother and father had had their differences before Maisie's dive, he knew that others had worse troubles. At least his parents were together. They were a tight family. They hiked the nearby mountains on autumn weekends, and in summer they would take a couple of canoes down Lake Discovery from its source at the Raven Kill. These canoes were antiques, from a J. Henry Rushton design, built at the turn of the century in Canton, over west on the Grass River. These wood canoes—*Alacrity* and *Vivacity*—had been bought derelict at a fishing camp and bait shop in Alexandria Bay by Doc Halliday and Ted's dad; the two friends had made a gift of them to the community of Blackberry Mountain. Under Doc's supervision, Ted and Maisie had put in hundreds of hours restoring the cedar lapstrake planks clenched with copper tacks and brass screws over elm frames. They'd finished the delicate canoes bright, with coat after coat of spar varnish, smoothing with pumice between coats.

During their lake excursions, Maisie and Jinx would paddle one of the delicate featherlight canoes, Ann and Ted the other, camping on the shore below the dove gray cliffs of the fjordlike chasm. The next day it would be Maisie and Ann, Ted and Jinx, mixing and matching day after day for maybe a week. At night, Ann would tell jokes and recite limericks, or call to the loons. Jinx would lead them in corny songs, doing Irish and Scottish songs in his high warbly tenor or folk songs in his flat nasal whine, singing about the hard luck of hobos and sharecroppers in Arkansas or the Indian Territory, lamenting the death of a cowboy in Laredo. Ted grasped, without putting words to it, that these ceremonies were formal. Ann always brought lamb stew to heat and reheat, and they always managed to catch perch to fry on an iron skillet and they always argued about which star was which. Until now, Ted had been wise enough to recognize these family rites as reassuring rather than staged. Now everything seemed different, shaky and treacherous.

The facts were plain enough. Maisie had suffered a concussion. What this really meant was Maisie had cracked open her head, and a neurosurgeon down in Albany had trepanned her skull to relieve the pressure that was about to kill her. What that really meant was a mechanic with many college degrees had drilled into her brainpan to create an exhaust valve from which fluid could leak. Also, his fifteen-year-old sister had broken her neck. What that really meant was she was frozen in a body cast, paralyzed—not that she knew any of this.

But what had really happened? Why had she stepped out of her bathing suit, putting herself on display to everyone who mattered to her? Why had she aimed herself headfirst into a shallow pool? She wasn't saying, and they couldn't, or wouldn't, guess out loud. And the weird thing was, Ted didn't even try to guess. He knew they should be turning questions this way and that way, holding them to the light, but he didn't ask. The why wasn't uppermost, then. Maybe he was afraid he'd discover why.

Of course the why and where and how mattered to others. A weekly paper from a sullen manufacturing town nearby explored his sister's nakedness, how she'd "exposed herself for all and sundry to see" before she sent herself off that ledge and down into the Raven Kill gorge. The reporter dug into clip files from the late sixties and early seventies for editorials crying shame upon the morals and family arrangements of the "homeless hippies" in the Jenkses' neck of the woods; of course he mentioned the settlement on Blackberry Mountain, referring collectively to the people closest to Ted as "trust fund socialists." When Ted asked his mother what the newspaper meant by this, Ann laughed a laugh rare for those days and said, "That's an old story, from way before your time."

Maybe she'd wake up; maybe she wouldn't. Maybe she'd move again. Maybe she hadn't suffered brain damage. Sweating it out, Ted would catch his mom's eye and she'd shake her head or nod in bewildering recognition, as though they were tuned to some common understanding; if they were, he wished he knew what it was. Ted would catch his dad's eye and his dad would blink or glance away.

Maisie's eyes were swollen shut, at first. Her head, angled above her heart on the reclining bed, was bandaged, and some of her face, but they could see the bruise spreading down her face like an oil slick. The doctors claimed this was only natural, explained that the blood seeping beneath her skin was responding to gravity. Ted knew it was natural, too, that friends and neighbors would ask every time they saw him how his sister was coming along, shaking their heads in pity and distress even before he'd say, "About the same." Nonfamily weren't invited to visit, but they'd watched his sister grow up, or had grown up with her, and they didn't have to fake their affection, except for a few Ted could name who didn't appreciate Maisie's rough way of teasing. He believed he'd never understand how so many people he thought he knew could pretend that the unluckiest thing that ever happened to Ted's family was merely the way of the world, as though it was an old Independence Day tradition in the Adirondacks to stand forty feet above a crowd, peel off a bathing suit, and dive headlong, perfectly, into a shallow rock-bottomed pool.

Sitting in Maisie's room, watching her machines live her life, Ted asked his parents how their friends could carry on as usual, as though what had happened was only a setback, like having your dog clipped by a car.

"What do you want them to say?" Jinx asked.

"Something different," the boy said.

"Maybe they need to pretend this was an everyday thing," Ann said. "Maybe they need to pretend they live in a rational universe ruled by sensible natural laws."

"Maybe they don't know what to say," Ted wondered aloud.

Raven Kill, where the community of Blackberry Mountain voted and paid taxes, convened an emergency town meeting the second Tuesday after Maisie's dive. Ann and Jinx wouldn't attend, but Ted asked Doc Halliday to take him. The four selectmen and a selectwoman each delivered an oration about how their thoughts were with Maisie in her hour of need and with her family. One of them, Mr. Drover, put his hands together and requested a moment of silent prayer, and Ted pretended to pray. Instead, he thought about Maisie, about what he should say to her now. He wanted to talk to her and hear her talk back.

After speakers had their say on the powers of positive thinking and prayer, after they voted by a show of hands to cook casseroles and bake cakes and deliver them to the Jenkses' house, after they asked Ted to rise for a round of applause, as though he'd won a ski race or a spelling bee, after they agreed that all were deeply indebted to Doc Halliday, who once again had proved his ingenuity and community spirit and heroic willingness to jump in where he was needed, after all this, the citizens of Raven Kill got down to business.

"We have to consider our exposure here," said Mr. Brinker, the Commissioner of Roads. Maisie had played a trick once on his boy Seth. Seth was twenty-five then, maybe thirty, and Maisie was in sixth grade, and Ted and his sister and their gang were horsing around, dawdling down the hill from school to the Emporium, past the town's road-machinery shed. Seth Brinker was out front, fiddling under the hood of a brand-new Caterpillar grader, as vividly yellow as the maple leaves that October afternoon. Snow was getting ready to fall, and a hard frost had been forecast. Sounding interested, Maisie had asked Seth what he was doing. Seth explained he was preparing it for winter, adding that it was tricky and that it cost an arm and a leg to fill the huge radiator with antifreeze. Maisie said he didn't need to buy antifreeze, and Seth said she must not know her Cats, that without seventy dollars' worth the engine block would freeze and crack. Then she told him he could keep that money for himself and fill the radiator with springwater. Had Seth ever seen a spring freeze up? "Think about it," she said, and the kids left him to it. When Ted learned at school what Seth had done, or hadn't done, at first he thought it was funny, then he was scared, and then he felt sad. At first, Maisie tried to act tough about it: "Tough shit, he's a moron." But when Ted asked why she wanted to be mean to a moron, Maisie blushed and said she didn't want to be mean to anyone, she was only fooling around. Ted said it was his fault, too. Maisie said no, it was all her fault. And when their parents found out what had happened and Ann told her children that Seth had almost lost his job and Jinx said he wanted them both to apologize, Ted knew that his sister had already told Seth she was sorry, but she wouldn't admit this to their parents. Sometimes, many times, Ted just couldn't figure her out.

Now Seth's father said, "It's obvious to anybody with a brain that we're not liable for some show-off teenager who decides to commit suicide in front of the whole town, but that damn fool plunge aside, our swimming hole's an accident waiting to happen."

Ted's face flushed like sunburn, blood drummed in his ears, and his heart hammered against his chest. Doc Halliday didn't look over at Ted, but he put his hand on Ted's leg to still its furious shaking.

"Waiting to happen? Some wait," old Mrs. Clarke said from the front row. "We've had three drownings in that gorge during my short life, and I can't count the close calls. It's a wonder no one's sued the pants off Raven Kill before now."

There was much approval of Mrs. Clarke's disapproval, and during the next half hour schemes were devised to bar the falls to swimmers. A chain-link fence was proposed (too expensive), filling the pool with boulders (even more), exhorting the Army Corps of Engineers to riprap the embankment or alter the course of the river. The Corps of Engineers, despised by right-thinking townspeople for straightening gorgeously chaotic streams and rivers to resemble interstate highways, had this to commend it: its work didn't cost taxpayers a bit of money.

Doc Halliday sat still beside Ted. Ted was conscious of his stillness because it was so uncommon for Doc to sit at all. He even ate standing up, pacing back and forth, doing: banging nails, planing, bulldozing, mowing, blasting, grading, liming, seeding, pickaxing, chainsawing, assembling a table or designing a house or a July Fourth parade float or a float for the lake or a toboggan for the toboggan run he'd cleared, digging a hole or filling a hole, picking berries, splitting wood or stacking it, shooting baskets, spiking a volleyball or swinging a croquet mallet, drawing a plan in the dirt, in the dust of a car's hood, on the back of his hand. He thought out loud, so that when he was inventing something, and he was always inventing something, they'd hear the whole process: *How about if we built the cross-country ski lodge into the side of that cliff, but how would we get to it? We could string a cable down from the upper pasture and run a car right into the lodge and the cablecar could be cut from the body of a VW camper. Hell, it could run on a VW engine. . . .* But at the meeting he'd been quiet, till now. He cleared his throat, stood, unfolded his arms, and started talking:

Doc Halliday's speeches were famous, at least up on the mountain. Ted's dad called him a visionary, and Ted guessed that he was. Doc was a big-picture kind of guy, but the picture was composed of details radiating from smaller pictures, and so on back to some picture source in Doc's incomprehensible fancy. His notions would bubble out of his thoughts in a stream of talk. Just before Independence Day, he'd argued that Blackberry Mountain should apply for a license to cultivate and market marijuana once it was legalized. By now grass was no big deal; the years of mind bending as political platform or as spiritual metaphor were long past. This was practical, an agricultural opportunity. It didn't seem to occur to Doc—thus to any of his neighbors, always excepting Ted's mom—that dope might never be legalized. He'd made a study, told them what kind of soil the crop best responded to, and inside that lecture gave a short course on organic gardening (by the way, did they realize that waste processing could be made to produce, as a by-product, orchids?), then detoured to a lucid presentation of the pros and cons of crop subsidies, summarized the history of tobacco in the New World and Old Europe. His voice was friendly and warm. He didn't run down opposing opinions, and this might have been his secret. He didn't recognize opposition, so he talked to his neighbors then as though all people were cheerleaders or teammates, and that was how he was talking to Raven Kill now.

He began with a theory of community, how that swimming hole was their town pump, how it served the same sacred function as theater festivals in Periclean Athens, how free access to such a central place was a mark—maybe *the* mark—of civilization. He gave the etymology of the word *civic*, talked about free access to water, and examined water as a political and mythological concept. Then—Ted couldn't have specified how this made sense, but it seemed to—Doc spun on a dime and attacked civilization, quoting Huck Finn on Aunt Sally, saying that she'd tried to civilize Huck, tame him, bar him from the river, so he'd lit out for the territory ahead of the rest.

Ted watched Mr. Brinker listening to the spiel and was surprised to see that Lutheran dairy farmer, owner of the valuable land that abutted an ambitiously developed ski area, a shrewd old Dutch uncle (according to Ted's dad) who refused to sell out low or even high, who had so recently called Ted's almost-dead sister a "show-off teenager," get all misty-eyed listening to Doc Halliday's sermon about a human being's irreducible right to run risks, even at the price of "God forbid, worst case, a civil tort." And then, maybe sensing Ted lean forward in the seat beside him, Doc said, "I mean, we're not going to have a death here. Believe me, you can take my word on that."

Then Doc paused, and Ted knew he was cranking up for another assault on the town. "Listen up, people. When climbers die on Everest, does the Himalayan town council put a chain-link fence around the mountain and post a guard at the gate? Swimmers are sucked out to sea by undertow every summer day, but—correct me if I'm wrong—no one has proposed to plant razor wire around the rim of the ocean. Untrammeled access. Unrestricted choice. Free will, my dear friends. We should use this sorry occasion to honor Maisie's great spirit, not to build a brick wall around our inalienable rights. I'm telling you . . ."

Doc said more, and still more, and as his voice began to rise in volume and his pitch climbed to a mesmerizing singsong cadence, the citizens of Raven Kill began to nod their heads and, once or twice, interrupted his words with applause. To be polite, Ted clapped his hands, but he didn't like it that Doc had dragged Maisie into his speech, even if the meeting had been called expressly to discuss a response to her swan dive. Ted was as inspired by Doc as anyone. He'd worked as his apprentice, followed him around like a puppy; he sat learning at Doc's knee, and wanted to live as he lived. But there was something out of whack about the way his mentor had just used Maisie's name. Ted couldn't put his finger on the right word for his discomfort, but hearing Doc talk about "us" and "we" made him wonder if maybe we aren't more alone in the world than the man beside him claimed.

In fact, he'd been wondering this for some days now, ever since he'd discovered a sheet of paper busy with notes his dad had jotted a couple of days after Maisie plunged off the ledge. Ted didn't want to be a snoop, but he wanted to know as much about his sister's story and hopes as anyone else, and he had begun to understand that facts were being hidden from him. The paper was on a clipboard his dad used to calculate costs and rates of amortization and prospects for profit in his building enterprises. The previous April, Jinx had tried to teach his boy how he reckoned risks and rewards, but balance sheets were beyond Ted's grasp. In fact, until the smashup, Ted had remained in awe of his dad's mastery of numbers and his vision for their community. He guessed that it was natural to be in awe of his father, and then he found that sheet of paper. At that moment, the certainties in his family life that hadn't already trembled began to slip downslope. The reason was printed neatly in Jinx Jenks's hand on a legal notepad:

MAISIE'S MEMORIAL SERVICE

1 / For he shall be as a tree planted by the waters, and that spreadeth out her roots by the river, and shall not see when heat cometh, but her leaf shall be green; and shall not be careful in the year of drought, neither shall cease from yielding fruit.

2 / Many waters cannot quench love, neither can the floods drown it.

> *3 / These are the thoughts I often think*
> *As I stand gazing down*
> *In act upon the cressy brink*
> *To strip and dive and drown*
> *But in the golden-sanded brooks*
> *And azure meres I spy*
> *A silly lad that longs and looks*
> *And wishes he were I.*

#1 = Jeremiah 17:5–8 (see Bartlett, p. 34)
#2 = Song of Solomon 8:7 (newspaper clip about floods in India)
#3 = A. E. Housman: "A Shropshire Lad" (Berger Evans, Dictionary of Quotations, p. 668, maybe change "lad" to "lass" and "he" to "she"? Or maybe better just to read the 1st 4 lines?)

Check out Bartlett and Evans and Magill's Quotations in Context under "water" "dive" and "drown."

There was also a speech. What Ted couldn't figure, maybe didn't want to know: Did people really act this way? He'd

heard of politicians who walked around with abridged obitu-
ary speeches folded in their wallets just in case the President
died, or the Pope, or Bob Hope. But this was Mr. Jenks's
own daughter hanging on. Ted wondered whether his mom
had seen that sheet of paper, and in case she hadn't, he tore
it in quarters, balled up each of the quarters, and pitched the
pieces one by one into the composting toilet.

So maybe Ted should have forgiven himself for feeling a
tug of resentment when Doc Halliday traded on Maisie's
name. Ted's sensing mechanisms were so overamplified those
first days and weeks that they picked up every stray signal,
and it was tough to make sense of what he heard through
the static or saw through the hard glare, or to respond to
friends who hugged him, patted his head, shook his hand.
Anyone's touch, however well-meant, was unwelcome. Every
gesture of sympathy came to him distorted. He suffered from
binocular vision. One eye saw every emotion as humbug and
the other saw his neighbors' sympathy as genuinely felt but
impossible to convey with simple accuracy of sentiment.

Ted had always counted on Doc to tell him what was true,
and to tell him nothing if he didn't know the truth. But now
when Doc sermonized about Maisie's beliefs, what Maisie
would want them to do, Ted knew his mentor didn't know
what he was talking about.

Ted had heard the story of his father's first meeting with Doc,
freshman year at college, many times. His dad would run
through a set of anecdotes, sanded and varnished in the retell-
ing, whenever he tried to explain the wit and power of his
old friend. They had been thrown together in a four-man
suite at Columbia. John Jenks and two classmates from a
progressive Manhattan day school had arrived early, and
young Jenks had staked out a bed below a window overlook-

ing a narrow sliver of the Hudson River. The three city-wise friends were unpacking and setting up their sound system and hanging posters on the wall when Doc blew in from Oklahoma with a flattop crew cut, wearing a mustard yellow rayon shirt buttoned to the chin and a Lord Jeff V-necked yellow sweater; his brown sharkskin Haggar slacks rode low on his skinny hips; they were cinched with a slim black leather belt buckled off to the side. Doc carried a bag of golf clubs and a battered wooden toolbox—accessories not indigenous to the Upper West Side of New York City. This was still the age of cool, and the first thing Ted's father realized about his new roommate was that he was not cool, or not by any standards he understood. Doc smiled and was affable; years later he claimed not to have noticed that Ted's dad and his school friends gave off an urban chill in their perfunctory nods and crabby handshakes.

"Well," Doc said, opening his toolbox, "let's get this room rebuilt."

Ted's dad confessed he couldn't reliably remember what he or his schoolmates had replied, but it must have been something like *Say whaaat?* Doc then made his design clear with hammer and saw, taking furniture apart to remake it, stacking beds on top of each other to build double-deckers. By the end of the day, John Jenks lived in the oddest room in college and had somehow been moved from his prime window location to the top berth of a bunk built into a closet. From that day forward he was Doc Halliday's intern.

They roomed together all four years. Ted's dad was a psych major and Doc studied fine arts, with a minor in philosophy. Even though John Jenks was a private-school product, he sported a ponytail and a wispy mustache, as was the fashion, of course. In his Tulsa wardrobe, which he made no effort to replace with tweeds or army-surplus gear or bib overalls,

Doc looked hopelessly square on that venerable campus, but in fact he was out on the edge, way beyond bohemian, light-years past hip, and nobody who knew him wasn't convinced that he was marked special, going places.

He made a reputation as a practical joker, although *practical* was an odd word to associate with Doc. Ted's dad liked to tell how Doc had handled a group of boarding-school boys who lived next door that first year. These young nabobs made a show of smoking cigars in their room after a bad cafeteria dinner, for which they dressed in jackets and ties, sometimes in suits. After they dined, one of them would say, "I believe a *digestif* would be in order, gentlemen." They would then "repair" to their "suite," where they'd roll Armagnac in snifters held over a cigar lighter, rotate cigars between their fingers, and look through the smoke at one another as if lost in profound thought, the *Goldberg Variations* spinning away on the turntable. Anyway, the music, the sound of clubmanlike snorts, and the aroma—these were a red flag to Doc Halliday. So one day he adapted a vacuum cleaner to suck down a rack of six cigars at a time and then blow the smoke out an extension tube. After dinner, once the young squires were settled in their overstuffed club chairs and were commencing to yawn and harrumph, why ye Gods!—someone began to beat on their door. More precisely, someone was nailing their door shut. Doc was, and then came the extension hose, insinuated through their mail slot. Then the high hum of a vacuum cleaner was followed by the god-awful stink of a couple dozen White Owls gassing the room.

Sometimes, Jinx would run through these anecdotes in front of Doc; he'd wheeze and gasp telling them, breaking himself up with the audacious cleverness of his college roommate and best friend. At such times, Ted would study Doc, noting his thin smile. Doc would dismiss the tale, act puzzled by its significance, and claim not to remember the cigars or the vacuum cleaner—but "it must've happened or Jinx wouldn't say it had." About this, too, Ted wondered.

His dad made this much clear: You had to love Doc Halliday. He was fun to be with, fun to talk about. But fun was the least part of it. Dreaming up a trick was fine, but his bigger dreams amounted to fresh ways of seeing, understanding, living. Doc's trademark question was, "How about if . . .?" Better: "How about if *we* . . .?" Put something in his path and he'd tip it arsy-turvy, but cheerfully. He never got mad at anyone and nothing seemed to impede him. He claimed he could redesign human nature, natural law, whatever. He was the guy who named things: anointing John Jenks "Jinx" within an hour of meeting him, and it fit.

Jinx *was* a screwup. The best stories he told were on himself, and he told them well, shaking his head and grinning: "Boy oh boy, did I ever piss in my soup on that one. Wow, did I screw the pooch or what?" Ted was disarmed, once upon a time, by his father's tales of fuckuppery, but Jinx's was a charm that required youth for its full effect, Ted's youth and his father's.

Ted understood that Jinx was to Doc what you'd call a sidekick; he wasn't sure sometimes that sidekick wasn't what you'd name what he himself was to Maisie. Ted didn't enjoy understanding some things, and this was one of them—the calibration of the unequal force fields that envelop people, the gravitational pull of some but not of others. He knew that his father was in awe of Doc, and he couldn't fail to notice that Doc wasn't in awe of his father.

Ted learned from his mother that in the men's early years as friends, if Doc was the master in their companionship, cooking up games and adventures, well, that was what Doc did—he led. He seduced Ann and Jinx to Blackberry Mountain, where Ted was born. Until Maisie's crash, Ted didn't take an interest in why they lived where they lived. But while she lay in the hospital, there were so many specific questions he dared not ask that he pumped Doc and his parents for explanations of first-principle puzzles, beginning with the why of their where.

Ted was working with Doc on a new project the day after the town meeting, trying without much success to forget what Doc had said about Maisie. Ted knew his sister hadn't thought one second about access to the Raven Kill once in her life, and he had a compelling hunch that her first words, if she ever came awake, wouldn't be, "Hey, you guys, what about that free public access to the river?"

He and Doc were installing a windmill beside the lake. That is, Doc, aloft, was installing it; Ted was climbing up and down the tower to fetch the bits and pieces he called for. The windmill was meant to serve two purposes—as almost all of Doc Halliday's big ideas did, which was why he could usually sell more than one person on them. The outcome of this particular brainstorm would generate electricity for the Boathouse and Pool Hall, including free juice for the video games, pinball machine, and electric shuffleboard, and neon lights Doc had collected from antique shops wherever his construction work called him. Moreover, the windmill's surplus power could be fed back into the local power utility grid, in theory and in fact running the meter backward.

The local power utility had been sold on experimental give-and-take notions ever since the oil-shortage crisis, back when Ted was in kindergarten. Although time and cheap oil had calmed the panic of that earlier time, alternative energy remained a theoretically respectable enterprise, which explained why Ted's dad was at that time sort of in the windmill (and

solar-panel and wood-chip) business. Jinx had made a dynamite pitch of the reverse-power-flow notion, Doc told Ted,
and he'd lectured the board of the power utility, claiming
that here—at last—was the free lunch they'd all been hungry
for. Ted's mother, noting during the celebration barbecue
after the windmill tower was raised that the generator, less
blades, had wholesaled for eleven big ones, higher than the
price of a good used Wagoneer, questioned aloud if that free
lunch wasn't pie in the sky served up by Doc and Jinx, "our
revered blue-sky artists." Ted wondered, Where was the trouble with blue skies? What was amiss with artistry?

Ted regarded his mother's gusto for common sense as an
exaggerated offset to his father's unreasonable enthusiasms.
This push-pull between the adults had become a family habit
conditioned by persistent exercise. Playing a four-handed
game of hearts after dinner, Ted would hold back, scheming
for a low score, while Maisie angled frankly for the jack of
diamonds. Jinx could be relied upon to try to shoot the moon,
and Ann to baffle her husband's design. The upshot of their
opposing wills favored Ann, of course. The four would have
failed to notice what they revealed in play had not Jinx, after
a time, stymied so regularly by his wife, not shown such
extravagant hurt.

Now Doc was putting a wrench to the hub nut on the
windmill. "I do believe this generator will fuck up their television reception," he said, referring to the beavers who had
built their elaborate lodge at the foot of Lake Discovery, fifty
yards down the beach from the windmill. This was common
land, like the pastures and woods and boathouse owned by
the community. The beavers had made a wasteland of a stand
of paper birches nearby, and last month they had killed a
neighbor's dog, who'd impulsively chased one into the water
near its lodge. Once upon a time, long before Ted could
remember, the depredations of those beavers would have pro-

voked an emergency debate on ethics. To "control" the pests, to shoot or poison them, would have been out of the question, naturally. To trap them in a Havahart and remove them to someone else's agreeable lake or pond might have won adherents, but most likely the back-and-forth of hip neighbors then would have centered on who owned the land—men or beasts?—on what we mean by *own*, and on the spiritual properties of the beaver in Seneca and Mohawk and Algonquin legend. Now all the hipsters had left or had stayed and grown up to become carnivores with a lively regard for the fences dividing common land from their own. The residents were students of metes and bounds, recorded on deeds as neatly as any Dutch burgher could wish, locked in a Chatworth safe in the Raven Kill town clerk's office. Nowadays, when Ted's neighbors left for a business trip to New York or a vacation in Eleuthera, they didn't trouble to change into suit and tie in the Albany airport or pack the luggage in the trunk of the Saab under cover of night so the tribe wouldn't notice the golf clubs. As to the busy loggers, Ted knew it was live and let live. Jinx and Ann had explained that after the beavers felled the last birch nearby, the animals would leave that part of the lake.

"This thing will generate a little juice and a lot of wicked noise," Doc said, his legs clamped around the tower, greasing the hub's spindle. "Our toothy pals have had their last night of untroubled sleep in this neighborhood. Our infernal machine'll scare 'em off. Don't you think?"

"Doc? Why do we live here?"

"You're kidding," Doc Halliday said. "Is there another place to live?"

"Dad's from New York, Mom's from Pound Ridge. People say nice things about Seattle. My best friend from school just moved to Sun Valley."

Ted's signature was research, a persistent curiosity about

how things came to be as they were. Why was the sky blue, of course, and what caused thunder to roll, lightning to burn? His mother wouldn't offer offhand answers to these. His father seemed never to be at a loss; if Ted wondered how far the moon was from the top of Blackberry Mountain, Jinx would never say, "Huh? Beats me." He would say, "Two hundred nineteen thousand five hundred and six miles, give or take a few feet." When he was younger, Ted was amazed by the range of his dad's knowledge, but by now he regularly tested against his common sense the accuracy of any fact retailed by Jinx. About facts, Ted was a prig.

He was the family historian, felt compelled to establish sequences and causes. He'd ask his mother how she had met his father, whether she fell for Jinx all at once—bingo!—or whether he crept up on her. ("Crept up," Ann said, without needing to meditate.) How did they decide to marry? ("*Decide* isn't the word for that kind of thing," Ann said.) Did they consider marrying other people? ("No comment," Ann said. "Ask your dad." Ted was relieved that she'd smiled when she said "No comment.") Were they glad to have kids? ("Well," Ann said, "learning Maisie was on the way came as the *best* news. Now you, what can I say? It was okay till we saw you." "*Ma!*"—which was Ann's cue to laugh.)

Maisie didn't ask such questions, either because she believed she knew the answers or because she didn't want to know and didn't care. Ted couldn't imagine why his sister wouldn't care about these things.

Ann and Jinx had moved up here from New York City in 1968, when Maisie was a sweet little baby girl sucking her thumb and going goo-goo at the wind chimes jingling above her cradle. They made the jump a few weeks after Martin Luther King was murdered, congratulating themselves on the boldness of the move; whatever regrets they might have developed later, each showed pride in the other's blind nerve. When they quit their city jobs and left for an uncertain future in a sweet wilderness beyond the back of beyond, Ann and Jinx agreed that they were recoiling from the violence and intolerance of urban culture. In fact, as Ted guessed, his parents' motives for fleeing one life and homing in on another, on *his* life, were personal, fuzzy, difficult to tell. Ted's mom said, "Let's leave it that I had my reasons for chucking it all down there and coming up here." Well, Ted wanted to know, what were they? "Good reasons," his mom said. But, Ted asked, what were they? "Search me." (But with a grin, with a wink.)

Ann liked to tell her son that his father was a "romantic" and a "utopian." The way she said the words changed with her mood, sometimes dreamy and sweet, sometimes nasty. Ted was proud of his dad's idealism, his fantasies and devotions. Jinx talked and behaved as though pretty soon everyone in the world would come around to his way of thinking, but because his way of thinking changed so frequently, there was an atmosphere of inclusiveness in his faith. The family liked to tease Jinx about the particulars of his enthusiasms. In the early days, when Ted was a baby, the boss passions of communards were solar energy, organic agriculture, waste-not/want-not composting, the Sachem wisdom of sweat lodge and longhouse. But like his neighbors, Jinx had moved on from those hip conventional wisdoms. Now his fires were lit by sparks that fell helter-skelter onto his imagination. This year, for instance, he kept bees, and he couldn't imagine why anyone in the world would choose not to keep bees. Apiculture was the way! He'd sell honey and beeswax. He'd rent his hives to pollinate crops. He'd ferment mead. Mead was better than beer, tastier than wine, the *best* drink. Last year he'd bred rabbits, and three years ago the hills were alive with the music of ill-tempered angora goats, for the government mohair subsidy. Ted put blind faith in his father's whimsies, but his mother's sense of humor seemed to be approaching a limit. Used to be, when Ted said, "That's a nice idea Dad's got," Ann would smile and shrug, What can I say? Now she just shrugged and shifted the subject.

His mother and father had first visited this valley in the early sixties, when Lake Discovery had begun to lose many of its skiers to Vermont, to Stowe and then Mad River and then Sugarbush. Ann was at Barnard, the same class as Jinx, but they didn't know each other until they met on the Outing Club ski trip during a winter reading period their junior year. Ted and Maisie knew by heart the story about how their parents literally bumped into each other on a run called Harm's Way. Ann was skiing too fast for the conditions, which hardly surprised Ted. His mom's way of attacking a headwall was just to do it, point the tips down and dive, as though being *up* pissed her off so bad it hurt, and only down could comfort her.

Anyway, their first day on the slopes, Ann banged into Jinx, who was traversing the steeps, which were a little over his head, which was Jinx all the way. She didn't hit him hard enough to stop and apologize, but she hit him hard enough to give him a hairline fracture of his fibula. When she learned later from her friend Doc the hurt she had caused, Ann sought out Jinx in his ski-dorm bunk to apologize. He was a good sport, laughed through his pain, hobbled on crutches to a party that night, and cadged a ride home to New York the next morning. Back at college, Ann began to hang out with Doc and Jinx, and that spring the three friends hiked the mountain trails near Lake Discovery. Now it was Ann's turn for bad luck. She sprained her ankle trying a shortcut on a steep path, and Doc and Jinx had to help her down the trail to a warming hut. Doc was quick to wrap Ann's ankle and volunteer opinions about the nature of her injury, but he seemed impatient, resentful to be used for support. Jinx did the heavy lifting that afternoon, cheerfully. Ann said later she'd never experienced such a sunny disposition, and years later she remembered to mention her husband's kindness. That night something happened between them. It wasn't like Ann to explain to her children what that something was, but it was entirely in her nature not to care how it looked that she took a guy to her bed. Even though this was the 1960s, it wasn't really the *sixties*: not yet much dope being smoked, and for sure no sexual revolution. Ted knew his mom went her own way, no matter what the spirit of the age. If she'd been born the same year as Queen Victoria, she would've shared her bunk with anyone she wanted. It was from her mother that Maisie got her grit. Ann's way was Maisie's way: If you don't like how I do things, screw you.

There was a blank time after the three friends' outing in the Adirondacks, or nothing that Jinx and Ann wanted to make into a story for their children, but Ted knew that Doc Halliday figured into the story somehow. Ted doubted it was a triangle kind of thing, but who could say for sure? For Ted, his parents' history picked up when things "got heavy," as Ted's dad put it. Ann was writing music reviews and political commentary for the college newspaper, hoping to break into big-time journalism, and Jinx said she had a shot; senior year she was a *Times* or *Herald Tribune* hopeful. "Hopeful is cheap; hopeful's a dime a dozen," his mom said later, and Ted caught her meaning, but still. Whenever they got to the girl-reporter part of the story, Jinx would quote Brando: She coulda been a contenda. Ted never liked the sound of this, recognized it as unfeeling the first time his father said it. So what happened? Ted wondered.

They married. Jinx said it was a whirlwind romance, that Ann had had her doubts and then she didn't. Ted's mother would turn quiet when Jinx told that part of the story— *thoughtful*, Ted thought. He knew there was more to their courtship than that, and sometimes he suspected there was no such thing as a story there wasn't more to. His mother seemed less than a hundred percent sure she understood what had happened, or why, or to whom. Ted wondered if marriage was always like that. If someone always scratches her head afterward, how did this go down? Where was the fork in the road?

It wasn't a controversial marriage. Their parents approved. Jinx's mother had died when he was a baby and he'd been raised by his father's parents while his father busied himself spending his late wife's small fortune on a high-minded and low-profile career in reform Republican politics. Mr. Jenks fought the good fight on the pitiless battlefields of New York City elections, getting nowhere fast until John Lindsay had his day and a half in the sun. Whatever Mr. Jenks sacrificed in achievement, he repaid himself in reputation. Ann's mother approved of Jinx, and so did her father, a well-heeled Democrat, a partner at a Wall Street law firm with a Republican President among the names featured on its letterhead.

These were Jinx's descriptions of Ted's grandparents. Ted's mother disliked what she called "résumé shorthand." But even she would concede that it was hard for their parents to work up a good case against either of them. It was hard for Ann, too. Jinx was ambitious and friendly, a "good-time Charlie," he called himself. Jinx said he fell for Ann because she was smart and direct, even if this made her easy to flim-flam because she couldn't say less or more than she meant and couldn't imagine why anyone else would want to say less or more than he meant.

Ted told Maisie once, just weeks before her awful Independence Day, that he'd heard someone out by the lake accuse Ann of being cold, of not being "cuddly." He could see that Maisie didn't know what he was talking about, didn't even understand the nature of the report. "Why the fuck should anybody want to be cuddly?" she said. Maisie admired her mom's directness extravagantly. She didn't seem to mind Ann's indifference to gestures of affection.

Back then, as now, Jinx was handsome, and so was Ann. Ted liked to study their wedding picture, and even in black and white he could infer the high color in his mom's cheeks. Now Jinx was on the hefty side and Ann was too skinny, but they still made a show of an enviable couple. Ted's dad had an honest face. People mentioned this about him. To see him was to trust him. Maybe Ted had some snob in him, but he was proud that his father had a Yankee face, lots of thick, unruly hair, a beakish blade of a nose, bushy sand red eyebrows. Ann said he looked like a boarding-school headmaster, that he had the deep voice and ironic laugh of someone used to talking down to the boys during morning assembly at St. Whosis. Sometimes Ted couldn't tell if his mother was proud of her husband or critical. Jinx wore kooky clothes: not with ducks and whales on his pants, but everything in wild colors, bright reds and greens and oranges and yellows, jackass pants. He had flair, was quick to laugh at himself.

Ann had class. Her bloodline wasn't anything notable, she said; she was middle, "well, maybe upper-middle, like your dad." Dignity oozed out of her, and she couldn't tell a lie if it would put out a fire in her bedroom. Ted measured movie stars' faces against his mother's broad forehead, her pale blue eyes and sultry, expressive mouth. The actresses came up short. Ann wore her brown hair parted in the middle and with a barrette. She worried out loud that she looked preppy, but that was crazy. To Ted she didn't look like anyone. And even though when he was in grade school he wished she'd dress like their woolly-vested and appliqué-bloused neighbors—instead of wearing khaki or plaid skirts with solid-colored shirts and navy blue shetland sweaters—now it was fine with him how different she looked. It had always been fine with Maisie, who dressed the same way.

Ted didn't know much about their life in New York after they got out of college, except that Jinx was in real estate and Ann worked as a reporter for an alternative newspaper that looked down on the *Village Voice* as reactionary. For a while his dad wore a hilarious Afro—he liked to show off the snapshots—and his mom's work got them free tickets to amazing concerts: they heard the Stones, Simon and Garfunkel, the Grateful Dead, Janis Joplin, the Buffalo Springfield, all the greats. Maybe it was enough to say that they were on the cutting edge, like almost everyone was once upon a time. Not long ago, at dinner, Ann had recalled that she used to feel so strongly about the world's troubles that she'd find herself walking down a midtown street weeping. Jinx, hearing her tell this to her children, laughed and said, "That was the dope, baby." But Ann wasn't laughing. Her eyes were red. "Maybe," she said. "It certainly would be easier to believe it was just the dope." She missed how she felt then, Ted realized, but that was probably true of every grown-up looking back. Besides, from Ted's point of view, his mother cared too deeply about injustice, greed, falsehood, human error. Not that he was willing to sign on to Jinx's complaint that his wife was a "hanging judge," but he did know it was too easy to make his mom sad, make her believe she wasn't up to the challenge. Unlike his dad, Ann didn't like to laugh at herself.

During those first years after they all finished college, Doc would shuttle between Raven Kill and the city, where he'd crash on Jinx's sofa bed. By senior year, Doc had scraped together enough cash from rich college friends to take an option on Blackberry Mountain, a few miles along a dirt road cul-de-sac from Lake Discovery Inn—a semiprivate fellowship favored by East Coast gentry, who brought their children and grandchildren to the Adirondack camp summer and winter for wholesome patrician canoeing and hiking and ice-skating parties. By the 1960s, the inn was a sad anachronism. Ted and Maisie knew only that the resort had been ruled by snobs, whatever those were. The policy of ethnic and religious restriction, extending beyond clientele even unto busboys and dish-washing staff, doomed the inn during that militantly democratic time. It had been built at the turn of the century to afford robber barons a wilderness experience 'neath the balsams and within earshot of loons. Fresh air provoked healthy appetites in these transient patroons, who ate often and well, who needed—bare minimum—a sound night's sleep in comfortable pine-pole beds on clean linen, who must have snow removed from their path in winter, who required anything that popped into their minds to hanker after. The inn was service-intensive and, from its beginning, had been Raven Kill's most important business, hiring the town's sons and daughters to cook and serve and clean, to clear trails and work as lifeguards. In the early 1960s, after the Eisenhower recession waned, the offspring of Raven Kill began less and less to suppress their contempt for the rich softies who paid them little and called them by their first names. The inn's guests had accustomed themselves to ingrained devotion in its Caucasian help, so when deference flagged, well, there was always Sun Valley, not to mention Sea Island.

Ted and everyone else on Blackberry Mountain knew the

details of their community's founding myth: Doc was shrewd enough to recognize that he might pick up one of the inn's marginally developable hinterland parcels at a desperation sale. Of course he had a rough idea what he wanted to make of it, but he didn't use the word *commune* to describe his reverie. If many of the settlers and squatters in the early seventies were conventional counterculturists, reflexive opposition had never been Doc's ruling principle. He took no interest in the theory or practice of capitalism, except as a useful fuel to power his dreams. With a few of his architect and builder friends, he plotted to raise one monster ski palace on speculation, sell it for a monster profit, and use that money to finance experimental houses in a community where he and his friends could work and play together. Ted had heard his dad name this plan a parallel universe, and he heard his mom describe it as a space capsule, before she began calling it a pipe dream.

Right out of college, Jinx worked for a makeshift private enterprise he described as "sort of like the Peace Corps," providing decent housing for poor people. He was in a partnership of some kind, and he and his colleagues used his father's political connections to raise money to invest in low-interest mortgages that financed renovations, mostly in Brooklyn. After a year of this, Jinx suddenly quit and went into commercial real estate—because, he told Ted, "cynical interests" had worked themselves into the project and had found a way to exploit his vision. The turning point came when he overheard a colleague yammering to his doubles partner on the tennis court, describing their business as "packaging niggers," and from then on, Jinx said, he felt soiled. So he got in on the ground floor of a new concept, selling airspace above office buildings already in place, and in no time at all he'd made what Ann described as "a killing." When Ted asked his mom what "a killing" was, she said that it meant different things in different circumstances, although it always meant that someone took for little effort what someone else had put great effort into making. Anyway, before long, Jinx's ponytail was gone, though he kept the beard for a while, and then that came off, and after a while the mustache, too. Since then, Jinx's facial hair had come and gone several times, so that Ted, imagining his father, could never settle on any one picture to fix in his mind's eye.

After the killing, with discretionary cash in their poke, and after Doc and his colleagues had finished whacking together the huge ski house they named the Seraglio and had put it on the market for a price nobody seemed willing to pay, Ted's parents house-sat the place during the August of the year they finally decided to move up for good.

Now Ted was sitting cross-legged beside the lake, facing Doc at the base of the windmill; the machine spun benignly, its blades fluttering as the warm breeze surged. Doc tore a chunk from a loaf of oatmeal bread, opened his jackknife, cut a slice of cheddar, and offered him the rough sandwich. Ted stared at Doc's fingers, splayed paddles, dark with grease, calloused, split and scarred from chisel cuts, bruised from hammer mishits. Doc's hands—put to such headlong work—were awesome. The windmill squeaked as it turned on its rudder post, jittering to face the wind.

"I'll grease it," the apprentice said.

Doc nodded. "How's she doing?"

Ted shrugged.

"She'll be fine," Doc said. "She's a tough girl."

"I don't know." Ted shook his head. "I don't know what to think."

"How are your mom and dad doing?"

Ted shrugged.

"This is the hardest thing that could've happened to them, have one of you two suffer in an accident."

"What accident?" Ted asked. "She didn't fall. She took a dive."

"Watch it," Doc said. "You shouldn't talk that way about Maisie."

"What way? It's the truth, isn't it?" Ted was surprising himself. His words were coming out too loud, as if he was angry—but why at Doc, or Maisie, or his parents?

"You should ease up on them," Doc said. "You've always been a sweetheart, so don't try to be a hard guy."

Ted felt his throat tighten, and he knew he might cry. He hadn't cried even once since Maisie went over the edge, and here he was about to bawl like a baby. It was because he knew Doc was right. Doc was brave, hot to climb a roof or a tree, take a kayak over the falls, test the ice before they skated. Ted's mom called him a "he-man" when she was mad, but Ted knew Doc hated macho. No bluster in him, just resolve and zip. And now, when Ted thought he needed to be tough, Doc was teaching him to be soft. Doc was never what Ted expected. Doc's normal way of talking was machine-gun fast, bursts of incomplete sentences hectoring, pleading, arguing. He usually talked as if he was running out of time. But today he was deliberate, studying Ted's face and listening to every word.

Maybe Ted was about to weep because he loved Doc. Ted was old enough and had sufficient sense of himself to understand he didn't want to trim his words to suit the conventions of sorrow and piety. But the worst curse he could imagine, after the curse Maisie had visited on them all, was to lose his place under Doc's wing—Ted's mom sometimes said under his thumb, but what did she know?—to become one among many, a mere citizen in the democratic state of Doc's routine affections.

"Tell me again," Ted said, "how my parents moved up here."

Doc brightened. He cut a wedge of apple and passed it to Ted. Then he reached forward, plunged his hand into the lake, and fished out a bottle of birch beer, snapped the cap with a pair of pliers, took a long slug, and offered the cold, wet bottle to his companion. "Finish it," he said. "Your folks were basically flatlanders."

"But they'd been up here in the mountains," Ted said. "They fell in love someplace around here."

Doc made a dismissing gesture. "Sure. It's easy to love the north country visiting in winter. You know how pretty it is with snow on it, and a chairlift can ease you right to a comfy view of things, Saddleback and Lake Champlain to the east, islands scattered all over hell's half acre, no end in sight to nice. They plow the roads in to Whiteface, and even the dirt roads are easy driving when they're frozen. But your folks were still flatlanders."

"So were you, right?"

"And how!" Doc said, laughing. A loon called from the opposite shore of the lake, only a couple of hundred yards across, and Doc cocked his ear. "I'll never get used to that sound," he said. "No loons back in Oklahoma. Now that's *flat*. No, I mean your mom and dad got misled by this place, mistook the part for the whole. And August up here can do that. Look, it's almost August now, and can you imagine an easier life? Warm enough to swim during the day—"

Ted flinched.

"Come on," Doc said, "I can't talk with you if you've laid a minefield, okay? I can't worry about every word."

Ted nodded.

Doc snapped shut his knife and gazed up the windmill. The blades were still now, and a mosquito had settled on his arm. Ted watched it nestle down in the tangled black curls of Doc's forearm; mosquitoes were skimming the water's surface. He thought about brushing Doc's arm, but he didn't want to change the subject.

"Did I ever tell you about my cat, Mickey?"

Ted shook his head. He wished Doc hadn't changed the subject.

"Mickey, full name Mickey Mouse. I thought it was real witty back then, but now I'm not so sure. What do you think?"

"I'm not that crazy about cats." Ted considered Doc's question seriously. "Mickey Mouse is a pretty good name for a cat."

"He wasn't the smartest dude in the animal kingdom," Doc said. "He was a manly guy, had a mighty set on him." Doc made a weighing motion with his hands, as though hefting a pair of grapefruit. "Old Mick was stubborn, knew what he liked. Thought he knew what he liked. He liked the girls, of course, which was why I had to lock him up in my Range Rover with the windows cracked a little for air. This was the summer before I moved up here, when I was scouting around." Doc looked up at the humped mountain, lush, with a vertical ribbon of a far-off waterfall reflecting the sun. "It was hot this time of year, this time of day, afternoon doldrums. I figure he must've smelled another cat, or maybe a nuthatch had perched on the wing mirror. Whatever, Mickey wanted out, and he squeezed through the crack in the window, and out he got. And he took off. Jesus, he must've thought, what a hoot! Where has this been all my life, man? Where have *I* been? Think of it, Ted, the soft nights, crickets to play with, overfed birds to stalk, toads and voles. Fat city, don't you think? I mean, after the real city? Then, one late August night, September it could've been: first frost. Hmmm, Mickey thinks. Hmmm! Son of a bitch, Mickey thinks, this air is showing me some serious nip. So then he finds a barn, but it's full of cats who run the barn. 'Hi,' Mickey says. And those country cats kill his tender city ass. Don't you suppose that's how it was?"

Ted wondered what it would have felt like to be Mickey. To realize without realizing he was realizing it that this was not as anticipated, that the cold has teeth and uses them. "You were talking about my parents," he said.

"Man alive! They didn't have a clue how it would be. Nobody knows who wasn't raised here, like you were. You know; Maisie knew—I mean, Maisie *knows*. I mean, you know? It's not just the cold. It's October, after the leaves flare and go down like shot birds. When the sun switches off and the Jeep's radiator freezes, if you're smart enough to own a Jeep. And the pipes freeze, the roads even, the ground. The sky shuts down on the earth like an iron lid on an iron kettle."

"I've heard Dad describe November like that."

"Well," Doc said, "we both stole it. It's from a poem by Baudelaire. You ever read him?"

Ted shook his head.

"You should. I gave Maisie a book of his poems. Maybe it's in her room. If it is, take a look and give it back to me when you're finished. Okay?"

"Sure," Ted said.

"Let's get back to work," Doc said.

"Okay."

"On second thought, let's not get back to work. Let's play." Doc stood up, stole out of his clothes like a snake shedding skin, and dove into the lake. The water parted for him and

Ted watched his old friend slip in slim-hipped, shimmery as an eel. Then he undressed and went in, too, and the golden water, soft as honey, swallowed him.

They stretched naked on the canvas-decked float, flat on their stomachs, looking down through the still water at weeds rocking subtly in the invisible spring-fed currents beneath them. Ted trailed his hand in the water, remembering lying this way with Maisie so many summers past, saying anything that seemed right to say. Without ever discussing it, Ted and Maisie had taught each other that anything they said out here was privileged. They could risk being so solemn that they sounded foolish. Here Ted expected Doc to say only what he meant.

"Doc?"

"Uh-huh."

Ted waited. "Nothing," he heard himself say.

He angled his head, looking into the late afternoon sun toward the Jenkses' house. The pointed tower, his dad's office on the fourth story, was forty feet up, a huge bird's wing tipped on end above a white pine that stood behind a grove of paper birches sandwiched between the house and the lake. The tower had a 360-degree view: of the lake; of the slate-roofed cedar-log boathouse on Lake Discovery, down the path from the inn; of meadow livid now with Indian paintbrush and ready for mowing; of the valley— where they skied cross-country under a midnight moon— falling sharply away, and of the mountain. The copper roof of their tower was domed with a Plexiglas bubble; at night, when Ted was little, he liked to lie on the floor and look up at the sky, at the stars, at the moon shining down on his family. It was as though the moon were looking at them, looking out for them.

Ted felt chosen, as they all did. Weren't they? When it

snowed, they trained an outdoor floodlight on the sky above the tower, and sometimes all four of them would lie two by two beside each other, the couples toe-to-toe, and they'd watch the huge flakes fall, swirling. Jinx would fill them in on what they were seeing, like someone jabbering in the movies, "Look at those flakes. Are those crackerjack flakes, or what? I've never seen flakes that big. . . ." Ann would say, "Shush, be still." Maisie would lie with her eyes wide open, staring straight up; Ted couldn't tell by looking at her whether she loved the falling snow or hated it, but he knew she felt strongly about it one way or another. He figured out that she was staring so hard, concentrating so fiercely, because she wanted to rise right out of their house, fly off into the snow. She wanted to be the snow; she wanted to be everything; he couldn't explain it.

"It's not a bad house," Doc said.

Ted shivered. The sun was low in the valley now, the breeze had come up again, and the windmill was creaking. Ted heard some of their friends, his age and Doc's age and all kinds of ages, hollering over behind a band of aspens, where they'd set up a volleyball net.

"Feel like playing?" Doc said.

Ted shook his head. "Who really designed our house? Dad?"

"Well," Doc said, "*design* isn't exactly the word. Mostly your mom and I brainstormed it on the backs of napkins. Your dad had some ideas— what he said were fundamental needs—that weren't in my design book."

"I heard you had a fight about our house."

"This is the peaceable kingdom up here," Doc said. "We don't fight."

Ted considered Maisie, and he knew that wasn't true. They'd had some beauts, and if that wasn't fighting, what was? Maybe Doc was too busy to notice, but he'd seen plenty of fights. He was listening right then to some pretty rough talk over by the volleyball game. "Do you like our house?"

"I just said, it's not bad."

"But do you *like* it?"

Doc ran his hand through Ted's hair. "What is this? Cross-examination?"

Ted knew the answer, anyway. His father had had to bring his plan to a design-review committee. The meeting—with Doc at the head of a roundtable, so to speak—hadn't gone well. Jinx wanted to soar. His neighbors wanted him to hunker low. Doc's house was the model for hunkering, a rambling white stucco affair set lakeside, impossible to notice from the back screened by a thick stand of evergreens. From the lake, it blended with the pale rocky shore. Ted had heard the story many a time, how Doc had gathered forty friends—Jinx and Ann were there—and framed up his house in a week.

Doc said, "I think it stuck in your mom's craw to have to submit your house plans to friends. Not that your mom and dad actually had any real plans, but there had to be an approval in principle. Your mom has a lot of pride."

"How did Dad take it?"

"Take what?"

"Having to ask your permission to build his house."

Doc shrugged. "Having to ask *our* permission." Then Doc laughed. "I remember he quoted Le Corbusier at us, like it was some kind of revelation 'A house is a machine for living,' right? We maybe gave him a hard time."

"How did he like that?"

"You know Jinx," Doc said. "He's easy."

In the end, Doc had thrown himself into raising his old roommate's house, and it soared, and had internal jokes, like bar stools made of tractor seats. The sinks were wood. Even the toilets were specially designed by Doc. The house had been built ad hoc, with Jinx scratching his head, Doc solving a problem, figuring out to extend a beam here, raise a wall there. Ted had seen photographs from that summer, a hell of a jamboree.

"Tell me again who worked on it."

"Oh, Ted, a gang of folks. Musicians, a lobster fisherman, a woman who claimed she was in the Weather Underground, on the lam. Too cool for words, that lady, turned out she was FBI. She was wasting her time up here—nobody had anything much to hide—but she banged nails real good. And for free. Or for free food and dope. Your father was a genius at getting free labor out of people."

Ted didn't like what he thought he was hearing. "My dad pays his way, doesn't he?"

Doc stared at him. He blinked. "You've got the whim-whams, pal. We all do. Chill out."

"Did my dad ever borrow money from you?"

Doc stared at him. "Cool your jets, man." He took Ted's nose between two of his middle fingers and made as if to twist it off, then stuck his thumb between his fingers to make Ted believe his nose was there in Doc's hand.

Ted might have thought he was too old for a trick like that, but in fact it was a private thing between them, like a secret handshake, and he pulled the same stunt on Doc sometimes. But not now. Now he said, "Did Dad ever try to borrow money from you?"

"I don't think so. I can't remember that he did," Doc said. "Let's get back." He rolled off the float, let himself sink, and moved deliberately toward shore, underwater. Ted followed.

Standing on the mossy shore, struggling into his jeans, Ted turned his back on Doc. He knew that Doc believed something was fatally flawed in the Jenkses' house, that it was too pushy, pushed up too high. At the same time it was too conventional. Posters and paintings hung on the walls of Ted's house. He knew that in his neighbors' houses paintings didn't hang on the walls. Those walls had been decorated with murals, bright enamel parodies of Soviet hero-worker fables and Greek myths and Christian transfiguration scenes, all populated by the people who lived up here.

But this much at least seemed indisputable, from the evidence of scrapbooks and home movies: building the house where Ted lived had been fun, and on Blackberry Mountain fun was the champion virtue. While his parents and their friends were framing the house, from sunup to sundown both sides of the summer solstice, volunteers would mix up a kettle of chili, or roast a pig on a spit, or put together a clambake, digging a deep pit, filling it with stones from the lake and seaweed trucked in from Maine, and then steaming the Maine mussels and native corn. Life was a series of topping acts. Ted had witnessed the building drill many times and become part of it. Some folks built, and those who didn't cooked. This cut across gender lines, age lines. Hell, there were no age lines, which was why he was lying now on the grass next to his friend Doc, which was the only name he grew up knowing to call him.

Now Doc was lying on his side, his elbow on the grass, resting his head on his hand, studying Ted.

Ted felt uneasy. He was wondering something he'd often wondered about: how it was that Doc and his dad came to look sideways at each other sometimes, as though one was trying to solve the riddle of the other. "Did you try to put the kibosh on my parents' design?"

"No, that wouldn't have been right. I'd talked them into coming up. I wanted them to be happy here. They insisted on having a big view. Your dad called it a 'commanding view.' Commanding wasn't my bag, so I tried to talk them out of it."

"But you didn't command them to build low," Ted said quietly. He supported himself on his elbows and looked along the lake at Doc's house. It seemed like the mouth of a cave. You'd want to explore that cave. It was cool in there. It could stoke up in Ted's house, with walls of glass facing the sun. Jinx didn't seem to notice the heat, but Ann did. Last summer they had come home after a canoe passage up the lake, to find *Sergeant Pepper* dripping off the turntable, like a Dali painting. This meltdown occurred beneath an oval sheet of Plexiglas installed to collect heat in the winter, and it collected more than you could believe in the summer. "Did you get mad about the kind of house we live in?"

"I don't think so. It never occurred to me. But my God your mother was stubborn! I wasn't much used to people saying no. There was no such thing as not getting what you wanted."

"Maybe that's how they felt, too."

Doc stared at Ted. Then Ted heard someone running from the direction of his house.

"Ted! Ted!" It was his father. "She's come awake!"

Doc mumbled, "How would that work?"

Ted looked at him.

"Ted!" Jinx yelled. "Can you hear me?"

Ted climbed slowly to his feet. He wanted to run, but his legs were numb.

"I mean," Doc said, "is this good news?"

Ted stumbled. He thought his legs would fold under him, and he staggered toward Doc.

Doc put up his hand, not to catch the boy's fall but as though to ward him off. "I mean, sometimes, after a coma like that . . . such an injury . . . I mean, who knows what crazy thing might come out of her?"

Ted managed to stand, his legs shuddering. "I don't understand," he said.

"Ted?" his mother shouted. "Teddy!"

Doc stared at him as he trembled. Ted couldn't stop trembling.

Coming Out

The family hovered around the bed, leaning over her. They stood at an awed distance, looking over the shoulders of a bearded doctor talking to the girl in a steady hush. On the other side of the bed a young nurse from intensive care, as painstakingly absorbed as a bird nourishing a fledgling, fed Maisie chipped ice a piece at a time. Ted's mother approached her daughter, took her hand, squeezed it. Maisie didn't squeeze back. Her face unfroze by almost intangible degrees. She twitched her nose— was that a smile? Every tic, alive with implication, was noted. The onlookers, struggling to comprehend the quiddities of this mystery, caught one another's eyes. Maisie's eyes had been open half a day now; Ted never believed he'd see this. Now he tried to believe that they'd all been rescued, that the shipwreck of his family had bobbed safely ashore. He knew better: he knew they were in deeper water than ever, and what happened to them now would happen glacially, relentlessly, at dear, dear cost.

They'd all been entertained by hospital scenes on television, and they must have noticed that this was different. The patient, the heroine, had been cleaned but not prettied. Her hair was snarled; her skin had an underlying gray pallor, blackheads stippling her forehead; she drooled and her breath was bad. Nothing that had happened to them this past month struck Ted as deeply as his sister's appearance. Her scrubbed, blush-cheeked beauty—her freshness—had been an invariable quality. He'd heard it so often he didn't even register the words, take pride or offense: Your sister's a real babe, where'd she get that gorgeous skin, hair, those cheekbones, legs, eyes?

"Please." She said a word. They leaned toward her. Please *what*? They asked her pleasure, tell us what you want, say the word, Maisie, and it's yours. The bearded doctor raised his hand like a traffic cop: Stop, listen, shut up. He'd warned them that performances would not be as they seemed; her words, if words came from her, might not mean what they seemed to, might mean nothing, just sparks in the darkness, neural short circuits, random bolts of lightning flashing across the girl's synapses. They recognized that the doctor would not overpromise, but "Please"—now "Please please please please"—had his interest.

"She wants more ice," Ted said. "Please."

Her eyes seemed to light on her brother. This might have been a misinterpretation; nothing was certain today. But when the nurse dropped another chip of shaved ice between Maisie's cracked, swollen lips, she blinked. Ted took this as a sign; he felt something join them, a connection fine as her hair, fragile as filament. "She'll come around," he said.

"Of course she will," the nurse said.

"We'll have her back," Ann said.

"She'll be good as new," Jinx said.

"Please," said the girl. "Pretty please."

Maisie

Maisie had doctors for this, specialists for that. The synergy was a bitch: neurologists did their road-mappy thing from a distance, in wire-tangled Manhattan labs, squinching their eyes staring at CAT scans and graphic readouts in order to fine-tune statistical auguries (memory recovery and muscular twitch rates) for the girl; physical therapists at Maisie's rehab center upriver on the Hudson were up close and personal, bluff tough-lovers who took the long view (Maisie couldn't accustom herself to their uninvited touching, the therapists' emphatic lack of interest in her wishes, their extravagant regard for her mechanisms). She was poked, pricked, tickled, and hammered; lights stabbed her eyes and ears. Some young staff doctors, from forward-looking medical schools that re-quired courses in humane patient care, must have taken to heart the role-playing group demonstrations they'd been obliged to attend: they spoke to the girl and her family with exaggerated sympathy in low voices, person-to-person, lock-ing in solid eye contact. Maisie was called by her first name; she was called Miss Jenks; she was called Ms. Jenks. She was patted on the head at the beginnings of examinations, tapped on the soles of her feet at the end. She was grilled, warned, exhorted. One specialist judged her to have a fair shot at a hundred percent recovery; another specialist said offhandedly she should thank her lucky stars if she got back half of herself.

After swimming out of her coma, after rising through successive levels from stupor to agitation to mere confusion, she'd been installed in this clinic set beside the Hudson, an hour north of New York City. Here she learned more than a young girl should have to know about neural pathways and her ascending reticular activating system.

Here, too, she was exhorted by doctors to apply herself to the task of recovering what was lost from her memory of the events and circumstances leading to her plunge off the lip of that Raven Kill waterfall. It didn't escape Maisie's notice that her mom and dad seemed to be of two minds apiece regarding their daughter's mission of repossession and salvage. They showed her photographs, recollected birthday parties and camping trips and school plays: they urged her to recall these experiences accurately, and to recall them fondly. Or maybe, she wondered, they hoped she'd adjust her memory's lens, call forth her previous daily life with simple pleasure. Her brother was wary about her effort to rescue her past, seeming to prefer a clean slate. How could she figure out their motives? By blind hunch, by their shrugs, smiles, frowns. Sometimes, walking alone on the banks of the Hudson, seeing from the eastern shore the chalky palisades, and beyond them hills on fire with turning leaves and then dark with naked branches and then yellow going to green, Maisie felt like a baby, attentive, reliant on inference, scrubbed clean.

Supposing she was willing to jar loose what was locked tight: How would she? How could she? There were schemes aplenty. Maisie's "problem"—not a word she used to name the constellation of anxieties and aches, sometimes edgy and then again numb, that ringed her memory—was interesting.

Neurologists and nurses and psychologists and therapists were making careers for themselves studying how to solve Maisie's "problem." The consensus was that she write down everything she remembered. Maisie didn't get the point. Her problem wasn't the life she knew she remembered. It was the life she was told she had forgotten. What she did remember was bristling with snags, but they weren't complications she would commit to a journal or to rap sessions with the soft-spoken therapist she met twice a week, the woman punctuating her exclamations over each repossessed memory—"I see, I *see*!"—with the eraser end of a number 2½ Dixon Ticonderoga tapped so insistently against her front teeth that Maisie would drum the beat with her fingers against the desk, until the therapist would whisper, "Maisie, if you please?"

She remembered plenty. When she was alone with herself, she wondered what she had lost. Really. Did her brother know what he didn't know? Wanting to be thought a good girl— grateful, eager to collaborate in her repair—she tried to write an account of her facts, even though typing her report was almost too hard a chore. Not the remembering part, but the physical act of hitting keys one at a time. When she'd taken piano lessons, she remembered that her teacher—Mr. Blanchard?—told her, to encourage her, that she had strong hands, a "man's hands." She remembered that Mr. Blanchard instructed her to compose those hands with dignity, not to horse around with fancy hand dances, curled fingers, rhythmic taps. Maisie had no idea what music she'd played or whether she'd enjoyed it, but she could hear her tutor instructing her to bend her fingers at right angles to the joints and feel how they felt when they cramped. Like now.

It was weird what she knew. She knew it was a "near miracle" she could use her hands at all, that she could walk, see, talk, turn her neck, bend over. She guessed it would be a full miracle if she could tie her shoes, thread a needle, run, ski, dance, walk without a limp. In the journal she shared with her therapists, she wondered, "Will I ever swim again? Will I dive?" After these questions she added, in parentheses, "Joke! Lighten up, guys."

Maisie was a wiseass. Some people liked her sass; others didn't. Some might laugh with her sarcasm and irreverence at one moment, then wish to wipe the smile off her face the next moment (her brother, for example). Maisie knew she was taken two ways but didn't know what to do about it, or whether to want to do anything. She wanted to have character, yet she didn't enjoy being a character. A few nurses at the rehabilitation center smiled when they told her she was spunky. Her favorite doctor, Dr. Meadows, whose bushy white eyebrows and droopy lids covered his serene eyes like a cartoon of sadness, taciturn and exact, efficient with his penlight and rubber hammer, told her, "You're a King Kong pain in the ass," as though the words were fundamental to his diagnosis.

"But I'm not *in* pain," Maisie said without smiling, responding to a question he'd asked the week before.

"Good," the deliberate doctor said. "That's good."

In truth she wasn't in much pain, except for her muscles and joints, and sometimes her head ached, and her eyes were sensitive to bright light. But not much longer than a year after she woke up, she'd just taken a morning walk along the Hudson, watching the little speedboats pass close to shore under the bluffs and the leaves beginning to turn color. Her sight of this world was so brilliant and clear that she had to sit down and pull herself together.

She knew she was lucky. Some of her fellow patients believed nothing was wrong with her. Well. She'd been told that she'd suffered less atrophy than most TCVs. (Her dorm mates used the nickname the way Raven Kill high schoolers called themselves Catamounts: TCVs, traumatic coma victims.) Of course she was lucky. Maisie knew that Dr. Meadows had rewired her noggin almost up to code. She could read, add and subtract, and she was relearning the multiplication tables; she could get the punch line of a joke, and she could tell one. She wished she could shoot pool—she saw double when she focused up close—and win at Ping-Pong. She thought she used to beat Teddy, but if she asked him and he knew she couldn't remember, where was his incentive to tell the truth? He'd claim he always cleaned her clock. This was the kind of meditation that went in Maisie's private journal, public to anyone at the rehab center who wanted to see it.

She tried to be a good sport, count her blessings as she was told. But much of the time she wanted to slip off to sleep, and couldn't say why. When she thought about home, about her mom and dad and Teddy, she wanted to stay right here, though she couldn't say why. She liked the rehab center's impersonal nature, that it was in the service of the abstract principle of restoration rather than heedful of *her*. If its staff studied her, instructed her, cared about her, told her what was best for her, it was easy to imagine this was nothing personal. Maisie liked this about the place.

She figured she'd miss home at this time of year, in autumn. She recalled the crow's nest on the top floor, how she'd climb the ladder the first week of October and look every which way at the leaves copper and bronze and platinum and purple and pale gold, the colors on fire up on Blackberry Mountain. The light would have a scary clarity, and she could pick out individual leaves across her meadow, unless the wind was blowing them. When the wind blew, the crow's nest swayed a little, sometimes a lot. Outside her bedroom window stood a twenty-foot birch, and every morning she'd count the leaves on one of its branches and try to guess the day the last would fall, but there was always one that stayed put right through the winter, and somehow she came to imagine that her own life was connected to that leaf and that when it fell, so would she. When she told this to the soft-spoken therapist, the woman tapped her pencil against her teeth and asked Maisie to remember where she'd read the story of falling leaves equaling the diminishing days of one's life. This rattled Maisie. She'd believed the analogy to be original to her, or perhaps to her mother, and now she wondered if she could rely on anything that seemed solidly in place in her system of belief.

The tree was real enough, however, and she could see it in her mind's eye. They all warned her that there'd be voids in her memory, not craters so much as pinholes. That's how they felt, but how could she be sure? How could she remember what she couldn't remember? She understood that the people interested in her recovery believed they knew more about her life than she knew, and of course she resented this, felt messed around with. And how did she remember that idiom, *messed around*? How did she know what an idiom was? She couldn't recall. Could her therapists? Maisie knew that a big part of the "minor miracle" they all kept bragging about was that she could use words, talk, write. But how could she know that she was using them accurately? These were tiresome questions.

To rest her mind, to let it tick over like a tuned engine idling at a stop sign, she reconstructed her house. She'd been instructed to perform this exercise systematically, in the hope that it might train her memory; that even if the holes could never be plugged, the process would help prevent new cracks from opening along the seams. Maybe, if she reconstructed and furnished her house, she might try her family. If that worked, her community.

(She just looked up *autobiography*. She'd used it but didn't know what it meant. It made her squirrely to use words that seem to have floated in from outer space. She couldn't imagine how or why she'd ever have used *autobiography* before the thing they said she did on the Fourth of July. She was fifteen, for God's sake, and now she was sixteen. How much was she *supposed* to know?)

Slow it down, Maisie. See it again, ground floor first. Maisie's house didn't have a name or a theme. This was a strange thing to recall about it, she realized, the absence of something. How many houses do have names or themes? Well, up on Blackberry Mountain, most did. There was the Trestle House, because you had to cross a hundred-foot trestle built above a thirty-foot gorge to reach it. There was the Lift House, which you approached by aerial tramway. Tree House was supported by trees, bark, leaves and all.

Maisie's was set on a concrete slab, and coming through the door the first thing you saw was an Italian oil furnace. This was displayed like a piece of sculpture in a museum. Someone—probably Doc—had seen one in Europe and told Maisie's dad, who had sent off for a catalogue and got a Boston importer to bring it to America. Was that recall or what? The furnace made an impression on Maisie because it was knock-your-socks-off pretty: Ferrari red, with polished brass and copper pipes leading in and out, stainless-steel latches, and big dials that looked like a racing car's tachometer and oil-pressure gauge. It even made a *whooosh* when it lit, like a jet engine coming up to full thrust. The Jenkses' house was one of only two on Blackberry Mountain that wasn't heated with electricity. Doc had a theory that nuclear power—cold fusion was right around the corner—would produce electricity too cheaply to make it worthwhile metering. In Doc's view the power companies would say, any day now, Help yourselves, folks; the juice is on us. Maisie's mom didn't believe him and insisted on the oil furnace.

The entrance hall was lit by an antique black tin lantern hanging from a cord. This had little holes poked in it that threw strange shapes—like Maisie's memory?—against the barn-board walls and terra-cotta floor. The Jenkses stored firewood in the entrance hall, until Maisie learned at school that carpenter ants and powder post beetles could hitch a ride on the birch and maple. She brought this bad news to her dad, who phoned around to spread word of a new danger. Even then Maisie thought that it was an unfavorable sign that all those good pioneers dressed in wool pants and suspenders and work boots and checkerboard lumberjack shirts had to learn from a grade-schooler where to store their firewood.

Her dad put a lot of thought and care into his woodpiles. In the north country, instead of pink flamingos and glow balls on the front lawn, people showed off their woodpiles. Maisie knew about glow balls and pink flamingos because Doc had one of each at the entrance to his driveway, either as a snotty joke or because he enjoyed them. Maisie remembered that she liked to look at herself in the glow ball, to see herself all different colors and in pieces. Did this make sense? Their woodpiles certainly did. Jinx chainsawed and split the wood, and Ted sorted it by size so that each row had kindling twigs on the far left, medium pieces in the middle, and hefty logs on the right. Neighbors judged one another by the tightness of the symmetry, as if it were a stone wall, and by how much wood had been put by. Plenty of wood was a sign of industry and prudence; it showed that you weren't an asshole in the summer, lying around sucking sunbeams with your eyes shut, clueless about what was in store after all those green leaves came off the trees. They all stacked firewood, except for Ann, who said she'd spend her first thousand discretionary dollars on a face cord of Duraflame logs at the A & P that she'd stack at the front door for all the world to see. Sometimes Ann made Maisie feel two ways: She wished her mom would get with the righteous program, and she was proud she wouldn't. The glad part had to do with her mother's willingness to give the world the finger. But when Ted once told his sister that Maisie gave too many people the finger, flipped them off too quickly, she understood where he was coming from. There was a lot of her mom in Maisie, except that Ann had better manners.

A half flight up from the entrance hall, with a wall of glass facing the meadow, you'd find a bedroom and a big room known first as the playroom, later as the music room, and finally as Maisie's place. When they were little, she shared the bedroom with Ted, and neither of them minded that arrangement. It was fine after the lights went out, when they'd lie in the dark and talk—that is, she'd talk and he'd listen—until she tired of her own voice. Then she'd get him to tell her the kinds of things she'd never have told anyone. Ted talked about anything at all. Maisie understood he wasn't a motormouth, because the first thing people noticed about her brother was how quiet he could stay. Still and calm. Patient. This was why he was such a terrific fisherman: patience. Maisie wasn't known for her patience, and she couldn't remember how many times her mother had told her to slow down, to take it easy, what was the big rush? But Maisie could always get Ted to talk about the damnedest things, as long as the lights were out.

When she was in the fifth grade and Ted was in third, a couple of years before their parents put them in separate bedrooms because Jinx said that it wasn't "appropriate" for them to sleep together anymore (and Jesus Christ, who ever said things like "appropriate," except behind closed doors?), she asked him how he liked his teacher. She asked because when Maisie had her in homeroom, she thought Ms. Champion was witchy; even though she was in her twenties, Ms. Champion had steel-wool hair. She wore long gold hoop earrings and dark red lipstick, and she gave orders in a whiny, angry voice. Maisie thought it would be a hoot to lie in the dark and rag on that bitch, because she knew she could get Ted laughing. He had this whooping, out-of-control laugh when he let go. He'd chuckle, then make honking noises into his pillow, and finally, when he couldn't breathe, just let 'er rip, so loud that their mom would come down to see if the children were fighting. Ann would say, "Teddy? Are you guys at it again?" And Ted would say, "No way, I just had a funny dream was all."

Now, lying on her bed, watching the last of the sun bruise the Hudson orange and violet, Maisie slipped into her memory of that night beside her brother, not especially different from other nights except in its vivid presence. She remembered asking Ted what his line was on Ms. Champion.

"She's magic," he said.

Maisie said, "Huh?"

"She taught us to disappear from the world."

"Cut the bull," Maisie said.

"She did. She taught us to meditate."

"Oh," said Maisie. "That old baloney. All the teachers after third grade are into meditation."

Remembering, Maisie disappeared from her bed, from her body and her troubles as if into a cloud; she could see nothing to the sides or above, but looking down she had the illusion of knowing where she was. Ms. Champion had been flagrant in her meditation techniques: "You are getting very sleepy; now, you are falling under my spell; you're thinking about the softest cloud, a cloud made of feathers; you are falling into that cloud gently, gently. You are disappearing from the world, from my classroom. . . ."

This had always made Maisie giggle, but Ted claimed it worked fine for him. He'd shut his eyes, thinking of this hole in the ground, and then he'd imagine *easing* down that hole, feet first—Maisie explained that anyone who had the slightest acquaintance with *Alice in Wonderland* knew where the hole and the falling came from—and there he'd be, in this living room with Bob and Babs Lamb, Shep the collie and Tom the cat. Mr. Lamb was puffing a pipe and reading a book out loud to his wife, and when he noticed Ted slide down the hole from his third-grade classroom, he looked up and said, "Hi, Edward, pull up a chair and join us, I'm just reading to Babs from my new book about aviation."

At this point in Ted's account, Maisie had wigged out, but she managed to ask him what he meant exactly by "aviation."

"I don't know exactly," Ted said. "I'm not an expert on aviation, I'm just telling what happens when I go down the hole."

It seemed that Bob Lamb was wearing a lambswool cardigan sweater, and Ted didn't know what a cardigan was, either. So he was down there with this perfect family unit, where there was an endless supply of hot cocoa with marshmallows, and Babs had always just finished baking brownies. Everybody was going, "Gee, Edward" this and "Don't mind if I have another one" that, and Shep was wagging his tail and Tom was purring. The furniture consisted of normal chairs and tables, no built-ins, and Bob never had to stoke the fire because the wood was never green and there was never any blow-back down the stovepipe.

Maybe Maisie's brother was a little reckless in his candor. The girl was human, after all, and pretty soon on the school bus and in the school cafeteria and at Little League, when she was playing and he was watching, she'd get on Ted's back. She'd go, "Edward, old sport, why don't you pull up a chair and let Babs give you a little blow job?" Or, "Good afternoon, Edward. Getting much lately?" Ted would blush like he did, shake his head, and say nothing. It got to be a drag ragging on him, except the time he said, "Try to be nice." They were at the bus stop, and Maisie had to chase him and stuff snow down the front of his pants, but that just made him laugh. It came down to this: Ted wasn't all that much fun to be mean to.

And even after she gave him the business about Bob and Babs in their perfect little underground abode, she could still get him to confess his most secret thoughts. She didn't know why he trusted her. Because he did, he sometimes made Maisie feel puny. From time to time she thought it made him a better person, but she'd snap out of it and tell herself they were just different. Even so, Maisie wondered then about herself, and about Ted, how the four of them fit together, where they'd come from, how they got to be the way they were. She never would've told him her most secret thoughts. But she could ask if he believed in God, and he'd be quiet a bit, then he'd actually answer. *I don't know, but there's a lot out there we can't understand any other way.* And Maisie's response would be, *So ask me a question, I'll tell you why things are the way they are.*

He wasn't a moron. Even so, he'd tell Maisie what girl in fourth grade he had a crush on. Whoever he said, Maisie said she was an asshole. She even said *Helen* was an asshole when Ted said he had a "thing" for her. No girl was good enough for her brother. She meant it. She didn't like how she'd felt then and now she still didn't like it. What it boiled down to was: If she met Ted at school, or sunning on the float at the lake, or hiking in the mountains, she *knew* she'd like that boy and want to be his friend. She wasn't so sure he'd like her and wasn't at all confident—lying on her bed, staring at the black rectangle of her dormitory window, listening to Sam Cooke's "Another Saturday Night" drift from another patient's boom box—that he should. She was certain only

that she was alive, and wanted to be. For now, that would
have to do.

She had been remembering jealousy. Maisie used to try to
talk to Ted about their mom and dad and Doc. She had this
theory that Ann was jealous of Doc's power over Jinx. Maisie
knew there was more to it, but she wouldn't put her finger
directly on what that more was. Her dad would hang on
Doc's every word and at dinner quote from Doc's Book of
Wisdom. He'd get going on the problem of rusted cars and
lecture about salt on the roads being contrary to nature's
design, so the smart play was to go down to Reedman's in
New Jersey every other year and trade in your rusty old Jeep
on a late-model used Jeep driven on salt-free roads. This was
Doc's solution, but Maisie had trouble with the logic of
it—like, how did her dad know he wasn't buying Doc's
Jeep? Jinx would quote him on animals—"The only good
pet is the pet in your freezer"—or point out for the zillionth
time how standard bathroom sinks were installed too low,
that they were literally built to the lowest common denomi-
nator, the kids, and he'd say how proud he was that his sink
was higher, so he—and Doc, coincidentally—didn't have to
stoop as far to grab a mouthful of water from the tap. Ann
would roll her eyes, and Maisie couldn't figure out whether
her mom got hot under the collar because Jinx had so few
ideas of his own or because she was bored with Doc's
wisdom.

It wasn't Doc's fault, Maisie believed. He was a genius.
She seemed to remember this now, even though she couldn't
recollect what kind of a genius he was. She knew she should
want to remember because everyone had told her, even her
mother, that he'd saved her life. But when she tried to write

down what Doc was like, exactly, she grew tired and slipped away to sleep.

After what they called the "tragedy," what Maisie called the "thing I did," she never fell asleep without flashing—like the green fireball at sundown—on an engram from the dark, the sight of Ted humped in his pajamas in his bed beside her, the sound of his voice slurry from fatigue, refusing to join in a bull session about their parents. Maisie was on her own there: Ted wouldn't pitch in with theories about Ann, their parents' marriage, or agree that their dad could be a jackass. Jinx was like Doc in public, demonstrative in his affections, hugging and kissing everybody and laughing at their jokes. Doc didn't really laugh at jokes so much as he laughed at everything, but Jinx even laughed at bad jokes. He tried to please people, and sometimes this was so obvious that Maisie was embarrassed and would show her disdain. Her dad could be just too much. People said Jinx had a huge heart, but what Maisie had wanted to talk to Ted about was something else; she wanted to hear if he agreed with her theory that their father had a huger heart in public than in private. The thing was, Maisie wasn't sure if this was just her experience or if Ted had felt the same chill come off their father. Baby brother wasn't saying.

Today Maisie was sitting with her back to the window of her therapist's office, looking past the gentle woman's shoulder at a framed poster of a stylized locomotive, black and enormous, with an engineer looking quizzically out its window and an abstract clock face in the background reading 10:52. The poster, terrifying or monumental, was like either a nightmare or a dream of grand invincibility, relentless power. It was titled *Exactitude,* and Maisie took that word, given her present circumstances, as a challenge and a reproach.

"What is your earliest memory of a place?" the woman asked in a whisper.

"That's easy," Maisie said. "I can say with exactitude."

"Pardon?" the therapist asked, holding her pencil like a cigarette between her fingers.

Maisie wondered if her therapist shared this office with others, if the poster meant less to her than it did to Maisie, if two people's notions of consequence could ever square.

"I remember Doc's workshop."

The therapist busied her pencil against her teeth, and Maisie took a deep breath and spoke in a dreamy monotone about the place where she learned how things were. The smell of glue and sweat and sawdust. The dangerous whine of a planer. A saw tearing a cross-cut into oak. Maisie understood as a toddler that this wasn't the place to learn by making mistakes. There was an oil-drum stove into whose mouth Doc fed scraps of dry wood so combustible that the stovepipe roared with a kind of fury and glowed crimson in the late-afternoon darkness. Children were welcome in Doc's workshop on the understanding that they kept eyes in back of their heads and walked as though the floor had been seeded with razor blades. There were no cautions, no lectures about safety. For this reason and others, Ann didn't like her children to hang around, but of course they did.

That workshop was the happening place for sure. Brainchild Central. Neighbors and visitors from all over hell's half acre would show up to talk and drink frosties at all hours. Maisie would drop by after school and find a wizard from MIT or maybe a boatbuilder or a wild-haired inventor who talked fast and loud about his scheme to plant a windmill farm off the Maine coast or to feed the world with seaweed. If the notions were spacey, the workshop itself was substantial, maybe forty feet by thirty, with Plexi-bubble skylights. It smelled of walnut and cherry, coffee and marijuana. Serious power tools took up most of the floor space; on the barn-board walls hung hand tools, and the ones Maisie could see most clearly in memory's eye were a set of cherry-handled chisels, a Japanese backsaw, a French smooth plane, and a lignum vitae mallet, smoothed black with the sweat of Doc's hand.

It was a serious place, but what happened there seemed more like play than work. Work—as generally defined in the civilian world—was the least of the activities performed in Doc's workshop. By the time Maisie was in sixth grade, she'd heard Doc come up with every excuse in the book for why such and such a project hadn't been finished by its deadline. He'd always answer the phone the same way: "Duffy's Tavern, Duffy speaking, Doc's out of town." A routine, he told Maisie, from an old radio sitcom. He'd pull faces—cross his eyes or wiggle his ears—while he got scolded by one client or another whining about a Bauhaus birdhouse promised last month and still undelivered or a table that hadn't been built in time for Mimsy and Buff's tenth anniversary party. "Oh," he'd say, "I know, a thousand pardons, sir. All things fall under this name, fuckup and delay." It was a principle that Doc never finished anything on time. He said yes to every-thing, which Maisie loved in him. Bring him a broken-legged chair or a broken-winged bird and he'd *work* on that immedi-ately, in a kind of frenzy of mending, so long as the mending interested him.

But his contempt for deadlines and for honoring promises and for apologies was rock-hard. Even Maisie's dad got the runaround. Jinx had inherited a heavy old mahogany desk chair that had belonged to his grandfather, a lawyer. That chair was partly covered with cracked dark green leather, and Jinx had mended and refinished it, reglued it where the joints were loose, but a complicated carved piece was missing from the backrest. One morning, watching Jinx sit in it, Doc

offered to "whack out" a new piece and fit it where it belonged. "Magic," he said. "Good as new, presto-fixo." So
they managed to lower that chair from Jinx's tower office,
using a block and tackle attached to the roof beam extended
out for that purpose "in the custom of the Amsterdam Dutch
housesmiths," Doc said. Then he and Jinx had to sweat it
over to the workshop through the snow, and Maisie tagged
along in case she was needed. But before they got to work
on the chair, her dad and Doc decided they needed to pound
a couple of cold ones, and then they listened to jazz on Doc's
awesome stereo, with its huge speakers rigged in the lumber
loft; Doc claimed they came from Fillmore West, the world
capital of rock and roll, and many people—Maisie, for one—
believed him. Then the phone rang, and Doc busied himself
doodling a caricature of a guy with steam coming out his
nose and ears, about to blow his top, while a pissed-off client
of the moment shouted at him, and then it was time for
dinner, so they all went back to Maisie's place and Ann
cooked cheese fondue. As he was leaving for the night, Doc
said he'd have that chair good as new by breakfast, cross his
heart. Well, that didn't come to pass. A week did come to
pass, and winter and spring, summer, fall, another winter.
The chair almost disappeared under sawdust. Whenever Jinx
visited the workshop and saw the chair, his lips would tighten;
for her part, Ann made more than a few mentions of this
controversial furniture.

Maisie's dad, meantime, bought a gray metal swiveling
desk chair. Then, well over a year after Doc had promised
to fix the chair, Maisie caught him staring hard at it. Now,
she thought, he'll honor his promise, presto-fixo, do it. But
instead, he rigged a rope to it, led that rope through a fairlead
attached to an overhead rafter, and hoisted that chair way
up to the roof, out of sight. "I can't look at the damned thing
anymore," Doc said. "I've got to get it beyond my field of

vision, Maisie. I can't handle the pressure; your father's chair is hassling me to repair it, or return it unrepaired. It's so freaking binary. You know what I mean?"

"Did you?" Maisie's therapist asked, waking the girl from her recollection.

"Did I what?"

"Understand what your father and mother's friend meant by his response to responsibility."

"Huh?"

"Tell me, if you can, what bothers you most when you remember your home life."

"My whole life was my home life."

"Your mother and father, then. Tell me what it was like living with them."

"Okay," Maisie said. "I'll try," she lied.

Maisie spun her therapist a fairy tale of a dwelling and its inhabitants not much different in its furnishings and sentiments from the fanciful underworld home of Babs and Bob Lamb. Maisie's therapist did not say *I see* as she listened, didn't tap her pencil eraser against her teeth. She studied Maisie, whose thoughts were back there and back then.

Maisie could remember that when she was eleven or twelve she tried to sneak up on her mom and dad and catch them doing it. She told Ted she'd caught them in the mercenary position, but he said she was sick and was probably lying, and what was the mercenary position, anyway? Maisie said it was too kinky to describe, that normal people did it using the fireman's position. Back then Maisie lied for fun. She might tell Ted that their mom and dad were getting a divorce, just to make him cry so she could comfort her little brother. Was she an asshole or what? She knew she should feel ashamed, but the way she saw it then, the craziest stunt any kid could dream up wasn't half as hurtful as what grown-ups did to each other every hour or so. Doc had told Maisie that, but she couldn't recall the exact context.

The one time she really did hear her parents talk about splitting up, she kept it to herself. They were making lunch together, standing between the tiled kitchen counter and the cooking-and-eating island. The island was accidentally on purpose irregularly shaped, calculated to look like a mistake in measuring. This, Doc claimed, was according to the same ancient design principle used by the Japanese in their rock gardens, when they carefully rake the pebbles to and fro, then leave some little glitch, some irregularity to remind the looker that nature isn't symmetrical. "Ah, the inscrutable East," Ann would say, laughing, whenever Doc or Jinx brought up the subject of master artisans trained in the Oriental mysteries of craft. That was the kind of lore Maisie grew up on. The afternoon that Maisie heard her parents discuss divorce, she was hot from playing baseball and had come in to grab a glass of lemonade, and they hadn't heard her. She knew right away they were arguing, which they had a rule about not doing in front of company or family. Maisie sat on the wicker couch, where they couldn't see her, and pretended to read *Architectural Digest*. They were making omelettes, which was her dad's *specialité*. Ann was doing the drone labor, dicing onions and green peppers, shaving cheddar off a big chunk.

Now, telling a fable of amity to her therapist, who didn't seem to believe a word of it, Maisie remembered with awful confidence the loops and layers, the tonal shifts and haphazard pulses of that real conversation.

"I need more onion. Listen, I don't know why you have to climb on my back every time I hit on a good idea."

"We're out of onion," Ann said. "Look, someone has to protect you from your cockamamy double-or-nothing schemes."

"I can take care of myself, thanks very much."

"Take care of *us*, then. Shouldn't you fold that now?"

Jinx said, "It's not ready. Have I ever fucked up?"

"Have you ever fucked up? What kind of question is that? I don't have to go back further than last week. What about the 'done deal' financing for—"

"I mean fucked up cooking an omelette. And I haven't ruled out that financing. The Belgian guy's conservative. They all are. The frigging Belgians. Jesus, try to get one to smile. It figures—his name is Maeterlinck. Okay, get your plate, it's ready."

Then Maisie heard them eating and talking quietly between bites.

"I bet I could get a smile out of him. You make him nervous. The truth is, Jinx, you're just a blue-sky artist, and I don't know how much more of it I can bear. . . . Ummm, that's good. You've outdone yourself."

"It's the paprika. I also added a taste of curry powder. You've got to be part of the dream or you're part of the problem."

"I can't taste the curry. Oh, come off it! Part of the solution or part of the problem? I can't believe you said that! That's such an old movie!"

"I said *dream*, not *solution*. And what do you mean you can get a smile out of that gloomy moneybags? Pass the bread, will you? Let me put it another way: The train's leaving the station and I've got a great seat reserved for you, but if you try to hold that train back, it'll just run over you."

"That's Doc talking."

"Me and Doc both."

"Was that two eggs apiece or three?"

"Three."

"We've got to cut back," Maisie's mom said. "Can't you hear yourself talking? You're like a broken record, playing

Doc's tired old tunes. You've got the 'I've got a dream' speech and 'wave of the future' routine, and all that ever comes of any of it is this awful dissipation of resources, of *other* people's money. Mine, for instance."

"In case you didn't take Econ one-oh-one, that's how capitalism works."

"Did we come up here to be capitalists, for Christ's sake? I can be a capitalist in New York, where I don't have to hack ice off my windshield with a double-bit ax. There's no mud season in New York, no cluster flies to swarm through the heating vents and buzz my hair while I'm trying to sleep, no deerflies to chase me and the deer I'm chasing out of the garden."

"In New York? What garden? We'd be chasing burglars off your fire escape."

"Come off it, will you? I mean, you're talking here to someone who knows you! You're talking about investing in airtight woodstoves, in windmills, solar panels, pie in the sky."

"Is there any of that chocolate cream pie left?"

"I can't take any more. I'm warning you, I might have to go down the road on this one. Are you *listening* to me!"

"Not really," Maisie's dad had said.

Right then, she didn't blame him. She had thought his question about the pie was pretty clever. She wondered what it was between her mom and Doc. Everyone knew he was the most important thing that had happened in their lives; how could her mom not know it? And if she knew it, why did it make her so angry? Maisie snuck back downstairs, and she hoped they never knew she'd heard them.

Now Maisie's rickety memory led her by a steep ladder up to the crow's nest. Her dad dramatized the hardship of getting to his aerie, explaining that he needed to "earn his way to the top." Ann told Maisie that when she and Jinx dreamt up the house design, they agreed it should scrape the stars. When Maisie asked, Ann said, "No, it wasn't to defy Doc. Caves have their place, I guess, but we came up here to come *up*, to see far and wide." But somewhere along the line, Ann had become irritated with Jinx's crow's nest and began calling it his "tree house," his "pint-sized private club."

Maisie knew there was something to this. The kids had their own secret hideaway, and in fact it was in a tree, a huge Norway maple tucked away on the edge of an abandoned sugar grove. Maisie's gang learned early how to nail together an interesting shelter, and they knew where to scavenge building materials. Sometimes they made building materials fall off the back of the lumber truck when it climbed the hill for a delivery. They'd wallpapered their tree house with photo spreads from *Playboy*. A neighbor, Guy Watson, subscribed, and this pissed off his old lady, Jill.

Maisie's therapist interrupted this reverie. "You called adults by their first names?"

"Sure," Maisie said. "We were supposed to, I think. I never thought about it."

"Is that a fact?" The therapist smiled. "Would you prefer to call me by my first name? It's Dorothy."

Maisie said, "I don't know about that."

"Whatever," the therapist said, tapping her teeth. "Please go on."

The Watsons' son, Jumbo, would steal the magazines after they'd been in the house a few days. Mr. Watson wouldn't say anything, probably figuring his wife had given the magazines the heave. During a visit to her grandparents in New York, Maisie's best friend, Helen, had picked up a deck of dirty playing cards, and even though she lived down in Raven Kill—in a cottage set beside her mother's store, the Emporium—those were her membership cards to the Blackberry Mountain Gang. She told Ted and Jumbo and the guys that she'd picked them up with some "personal items" in a "sex boutique," but she confessed to Maisie during a sleep-over at Helen's that she'd found them in her granddad's sock drawer. When she told Maisie this, she cried. Maisie understood why this discovery might make her friend cry, and she never teased Helen about her secret, which in this rare case was safe with Maisie. Anyway, to see Helen in the tree house, smoking a stogie she'd copped from her mom's store, playing five-card stud with four naked guys and gals showing, you'd never put her down for a weeper. Maisie, though, had the toughest mouth in the tree house. While Army would read from the wallpaper—"my favorite hobbies are sitting by the fire on a bearskin rug drinking champagne, or curling up with a good book and my boyfriend, or riding naked on horseback"— Maisie would say, "Ride her, Army, break that filly bronc!" She loved to hear her friends laugh. Where was the crime in working for a laugh?

Ted's best friend was this kid Army, who wore Coke-bottle glasses, all bony knees and elbows. You noticed the knees and elbows because they were always bandaged. Army had a gentle voice, but he was a roughneck, always up to something risky. He got ribbed a lot for his name, of course, which was a little martial for local tastes. His real name was George Armstrong, and when his friends learned in school about George Armstrong Custer and that shitbird's last stand, they took to calling George "Custer," or sometimes "Custard." He had to fight them one by one to get them to go to another nickname, and he settled on Army. Army followed his nature where it led him, so he was Doc's favorite, the boss mascot until Ted replaced him. Doc seemed to like Army because he was a first-rate bullshitter.

His dad lived in Alaska, according to Army, where he was a trapper. Army told his friends that his dad sent him letters all the way from some igloo on the North Pole, and nothing he wrote was boring. Army's old man caught salmon with his bare hands—which were "swift as quicksilver," Army added—and "cut this polar bear a new asshole" with his hunting knife after the bear stalked him across an ice floe. His dad taught the Inuits how to trap and hunt and fish and build kayaks out of "a hundred percent natural materials." The reason Army's birth dad was so nice to the Inuits was to make amends to Native Americans. You see, he'd been a monster kickass in the last Indian war fought on the frontier. This would have been a little after World War II, and nobody knew about that war with the Sioux, Army explained, because "the government has to keep it hush-hush." His old man had suffered awesomely; he'd been scalped, for instance, and buried alive up to his chin, his face painted with honey so he'd be eaten alive by ants, or by bears, if they caught a whiff of him from afar. Nevertheless, his father—who'd escaped his bad fix "on his wits alone," who'd "crawled out of the badlands on his hands and knees, eating bugs and poisonous snakes and cactus to stay alive"—bore the red man no ill will.

Army's mom had bought a log cabin on the other side of the common-land meadow, beyond the Blackberry Mountain property line and back from the lake. She was a real estate agent, and Jinx said she put a high value on clear title to her land. So technically she wasn't part of the community, but she used to be a pothead, Army claimed, and she was still a weaver. Her wall hangings and little rugs were very pretty; Jinx and Ann had bought a throw rug and bath mat.

Army was acclaimed in Maisie and Ted's crowd for a question he'd asked during a sex-education lecture in Ms. Champion's class. She had warned the kids not to snicker or crack wise, then explained that the human body was a holy vessel. (To which Army said, under his breath, "I know which hole I like best.") Someday, she told them, they'd understand the beauty of holistic sex. ("You show me the hole," Army said, "I'll provide the sex.") Ms. Champion didn't tell them anything they didn't know already, according to Ted; seeming to realize this, she had wound up her lecture fast by asking, "Any questions?"—hoping they wouldn't dare to ask. Army spoke right up: "Yeah, why do my nuts shrivel up in the bathtub?" And this girl whose dad ran the Raven Kill ski area answered, "Because you bathe in cold water is why, because you have a woodburning, hippie hot-water heater."

Maisie's best friend was Helen, the Daimlers' daughter. Dr. Daimler and his wife had come up from New York City a few years before Ann and Jinx moved up. Leda Daimler had a lot of money, and she bought the Raven Kill Country Emporium and fancied it up with wine bins and a bakery and a gourmet-food section. The Emporium was set beside the Raven Kill; in the summer, Ted and Maisie's friends would take soda pop and twin-sticks out on the deck canti-levered over the falls and spy on swimmers and sunbathers stretched out on the rocks, exposing their good health. On the few days when the temperature got up in the nineties, the kids would hide out in the beer cooler until Mrs. Daimler caught on to them and came in and made a great show of shooing them outside with a broom. She was a good sport, even though—as Ann told her kids—a gang of smart-ass loiterers wasn't any store owner's dream. Mrs. Daimler put up with them because her daughter, Helen, was Maisie's classmate at the elementary school, and Helen knew who shoplifted gum and maple sugar candy, and Ted and Maisie didn't steal.

Dorothy interrupted. "Why do you call Leda 'Mrs. Daimler'?"

"Because everyone did," Maisie said.

"But why?"

"Because she was in business. No, because she lived in town."

"And that made sense to you?"

"Sure," Maisie said. "I guess." It was quiet now. No tapping. Maisie thought she noticed Dorothy sneak a look at her wristwatch. "Is my time up?"

"Not if you don't want it to be. Do you want it to be?"

"I don't know. No."

In winter a fire snapped and glowed in the big potbellied stove, and even as a kid Maisie realized that the Emporium was like a museum of countryness. Locals would hurry in from the cold and clap their hands in front of the fire and turn their backs to the stove and say how frozen they were. Maisie remembered reading somewhere that Eskimos had many, many words for cold, but up where she lived it was always the same thing: "Jesus, cold enough to freeze the balls off a brass monkey" or "This is what I call *cold!*" Then Ted showed Maisie in a nature magazine that Eskimos don't have a bunch of words for cold after all, which figured. After a while, what more could you say about it?

Dr. Daimler was a therapist, what Helen called "a licensed psychologist." Upstairs, during ski season, he'd shrink the heads of bored vacationers on afternoons when the runs were icy or the snow was falling so thickly that skiers couldn't find their way down. Dr. Daimler had a good practice, with lots of walk-in business.

Helen knew how to break into a storeroom next door to the Shrinkery, her name for her dad's office. There was a bonus, since that was where Mrs. Daimler stored cigars, and Helen and Maisie would light up a couple of stogies while they peeked through cracks in the wood-paneled wall. To put an eyeball right up against the storeroom wall and look straight into Dr. D's puss was freaky, to see him pull his beard and maybe sneak a glance at his wristwatch and stare out his window at the river. He had the office arranged so his patients couldn't see his face, but the spies could see both his face and the patient's; they seemed to be talking right at Helen or Maisie or Ted, as though some crazy skier was so depressed by the black ice and bare spots on Free Fall that she just had to tell Maisie and Helen and Ted how she was still cheating on her husband with his car dealer. The gang heard some great stories hunkered down in that storeroom.

You might say they learned the facts of life those winter afternoons. Helen's dad was an unconventional therapist, although Maisie didn't understand this at the time. For one thing, Dr. Daimler adjusted his style to the patient. Sometimes he'd sound like a Dutch uncle, scolding someone for feeling so much hate for her mother. Another time he'd be all sympathy and honey talk, especially if the person was really bumming. If it wasn't lost love that sang the blues, it was money. When Dr. Daimler heard a patient complain about being broke, Maisie noticed the analyst make a little hitch with his eyebrows; Maisie became aware that a broke patient made Dr. Daimler feel hinky.

In any case, love was topic number one. And what struck Maisie was how it always sounded the same. I love her, she doesn't love me; I love him, he doesn't love me. How unfair this was. Many an hour spent on how unfair.

Occasionally the spies heard really weird tales. Once they heard someone tell a story about behavior—incest—that could have landed the complainer in jail. Completely outrageous, and Helen's father tried without much success not to show how shocked he was. Maisie would remember that session even if it hadn't come during a special afternoon, the day that she almost burned down the store. She was showing off and had lit her White Owl with a piece of paper. She'd been doing that for a couple of weeks; she had seen on some la-di-da TV show that it wrecked a good cigar to light it with a match, which *infused* the tobacco with the *aroma* of sulphur. So she rolled up a piece of newspaper and made this torch to fire up her stogie, but it got away from her and fell on packing material that immediately began to smolder, though Ted managed to put it out with Helen's sweater, but the sweater was smoldering, too. The room was thick with smoke, but they knew if they ran away or opened the door, Dr. Daimler would be onto them.

His patient quit talking about the little girl he simply adored. "Do you smell something?"

"Why?" Helen's dad asked.

"I smell something."

"Let's talk about that," Dr. Daimler said. He blew his nose; he had a cold. "Let's talk about the smell rather than the memory that provoked it."

"Memory?"

"Your daughter. Let's not talk about the young lady just now. I prefer to hear you talk about what you think you smell."

"Smoke. Cheap cigar smoke."

"Ah!" said Dr. Daimler. "Let's talk about that next time." And then he reached under his Eames chair and pulled out his credit-card machine.

Even though Maisie was helping Helen smother the fire, she remembered to whisper, "Cash, Visa, MasterCard?"

Sometimes, when Maisie was alone in her dad's crow's nest, she'd open the French doors and look down forty feet to the ground, wondering how it would be to jump or to dive, with or without an audience. Once, when she was alone up there, she wrapped a rope around her waist, fastened the other end to a leg of her dad's oak desk, and leaned out, facing down, using her heels as pivots, and paying out line until she got scared. After all, she'd watched Doc screw and glue that desk together, and not everything he put together stayed together, so she hauled herself, with difficulty, back inside.

Standing there alone, thinking how it would feel just to take off, she imagined the audience, saw the people's faces turning up to meet her face, heard them go *oooooh* and then, when she came down, *aaaaaah!* She'd grow dizzy sometimes and feel so light-headed that she feared she'd fall despite herself, and then she'd look up, not at the sky but at Blackberry Mountain, and she'd think about climbing it, deliberately, one step at a time, leading someone. In her thoughts she was the only one who knew the way, and someone needed what she knew, was afraid to venture up there without her. Maisie remembered now feeling so desperately needed that she quit looking down, quit dreaming about falling or jumping or diving. She remembered being so needed that another's need saved her life, but now she wouldn't remind herself who needed her in such an awful, purposeful way. Whoever it was, when she finally climbed the mountain, she took Ted with her.

Maisie wanted her therapist to understand how big a deal it was to try to climb to the top. She and her brother had grown up looking at it, and it was the first thing called "mountain" that most of the kids thereabouts had seen. She and her brother checked it out every day, unless it was obscured by rain or fog or blizzard. Days on end it had to be taken on faith, which added to its mystery. It had a humped summit above two shoulders, like the upper torso of a gorilla. First-growth evergreens grew almost to the top, and in the winter it was beautiful, all green and white, and through the telescope Maisie could see icicles hanging off the spruce boughs.

For them, the name had magic. It was where they said they came from, their creation myth. Never Lake Discovery or Raven Kill. Blackberry Mountain. So Maisie was interested to discover that Ted—who'd been nursed by his mom as she looked out the window at that mountain—actually believed it was named for black bears. Maisie chanced to learn this a couple of years before the spring they made their climb, which was the spring before the summer of her dive. The afternoon of the first big snowfall in early November, they were coming home from school when the school bus skidded into a ditch; everybody up there ended up in the ditch that time of year, just as they had to relearn every year the trouble with snow on frozen dirt roads. Anyway, their bus driver, Bud Ormsby, hadn't put chains on, and the bus plowed into the ditch not far from the farmhouse where he holed up with his old man. He invited the kids to come into their house to warm up while they waited for the tow truck, the ten or so that were left on the route, mostly from Blackberry Mountain. Bud's dad was standing in front of the woodstove when they tramped in. The students took off their boots, as they'd been taught, but Mr. Ormsby called them a bunch of damned fools, said their toes would frost up and fall off, so to leave those boots on. The kids must have seemed bewildered. Mr. Ormsby seemed to want to put them at ease, so he invited them downstairs, where he promised they'd see something interesting. He wasn't kidding. For one thing they spotted a jumbo pile of empty bottles, pint flasks of whiskey on top and, a couple of layers down, colored bottles of cough medicines and elixirs. But Mr. Ormsby hadn't invited them down in the cellar to see his bottle collection. He gestured at a walk-in freezer, where he said he stored the pigs and sheep and cattle he slaughtered. Then he opened the freezer door—"Ormsby's Wild Animal Show Pre*sents*"—and there, standing up, facing the students, fur and all, was this monster black bear.

"I bagged him up the mountain," Mr. Ormsby said. "There's a bunch of 'em up there."

"Of course," Ted said.

Nobody else picked up on that, but later Maisie grilled her brother and got it out of him that he thought their mountain was named for all the black bears that lived on its slopes. She could have done a lot with that information. She might've invited Ted to expand on his theory in the school cafeteria the next afternoon or gotten him to spell the name of the mountain in front of their gang. But instead, she stored it away in the bank for later, for their climb together to the summit.

They planned the climb carefully. Trying to remember for her therapist, Maisie could see the inventory on the back of a paper napkin, in her handwriting and Ted's: tent, sleeping bags, foam mattresses, stove, potato chips, cigarettes, BB gun, slingshot, hunting knife, hot dogs and buns, mustard, relish, canned tamales, beer, Snickers, Red Hots. They would've needed pack animals to haul it all. Ted wanted to bring airtight jars to collect "specimens," as if going up there were like traveling beyond Pluto to Planet X.

They shoved off on April Fool's Day. Maisie remembered with regret and shame that she'd shaken her brother awake, giving him the business (Get out of bed, there's an earthquake; the sheriff arrested Dad, led him away in handcuffs; guess what, I'm not a virgin anymore) until he had to say, "Put a cork in it, okay? Can't you just wake up and say good morning? Just once?"

Maisie understood that her brother was right to be sick of her act. Why couldn't she just leave Ted be and spend some—what did they call it in homeroom?—quiet time with him?

Now they were awake. There'd been a hot spell and the snow had melted off the trees down at their altitude, but across the lake they could see the rocks at the summit shiny with ice; in her heart, Maisie suspected they'd never make it to the top. She wanted to try, though, and do something with Ted that they'd remember forever. She'd begun to feel herself drifting away from her brother. That had a corny ring in her memory now, but it was how she'd felt. She was almost fifteen, and most of her friends had driver's licenses, and maybe she was in a hurry to grow up. Whatever it was, Ted seemed like someone from a different life, and that sometimes made her feel as if she'd said good-bye to her brother a long time ago, even though it wasn't a long time. She was suffering her first ache of nostalgia, though she wouldn't have used the word. She envied her brother's power to show surprise, to look at a thing or an experience and wonder what the hell it meant. She needed a reunion with Ted, maybe even believed she could learn from him the whereabouts of something essential to her welfare that she had misplaced, or that had been misappropriated from her. Just at the time, though she couldn't say why, she didn't feel friendly to the girl she was, and she had a hunch Ted could help return her to herself.

What set them down the path with packs on their backs was an ugly brawl between their parents. Money again. Jinx had bought a kayak because Doc Halliday was into that now, and spring was of course the best time of year. Doc had told Jinx he'd teach him the Eskimo Roll, and they'd planned a guys-only trip down the Raven Kill, into the Muskrat, and then into the Hudson. Jinx had told Ann he was under a lot of pressure, as he always said when he decided to do something with Doc. Ann said she'd had it up to here with Doc jerking him around like a puppet on a string, which was what she always said when he spent money to follow his friend into some new hobby.

For some reason that fight really got to Maisie, and she told Ted that she, too, had had it up to here with Jinx and Ann's bitching at each other. Ted said, "Me, too." So they decided to run away from home.

Ted

He wrote a note the night before they did it:

Good-bye and good luck. Don't worry about us. We know what we're doing. Please water my lemon tree and don't let the sun burn it. You can set it out on the deck if it's a warm day, but don't forget to bring it in at night until summer.

He wanted their parents to believe they were gone for good, or at least for a couple of seasons, and that was okay by Maisie. She'd been at him since Christmas to run away with her. They agreed they had to, because they couldn't bear their parents' dream-versus-reality clashes, which were in reality about money. After Ann and Jinx had said their piece once, then twice, again, and then again, Maisie and Ted decided their mom and dad must enjoy these quarrels. Hopeless.

In truth, though, they didn't run from the war: they split because they wanted to, for the fun of it. Also, Maisie flat out declared she *had* to climb the mountain. Everyone who lived there resolved someday to get to the top, but Maisie meant it.

They lit out before sunup. They humped their gear down the path and walked along the lake. Mist was hanging like smoke over the still water. There was just light enough to see the circles of waves making for shore, where a beaver was swimming and diving near his dam. Ted stopped to watch. They could hear another beaver working on one of the few birches left standing near the dam, and Ted spotted him first. Those days, Ted seemed always to notice animals before Maisie saw them, maybe because he looked harder or because he was more interested.

"Son of a bitch!" Ted said. "Look at those teeth. That guy's a regular chain saw."

Maisie held up a hand to quiet him.

"It's just a loon," Ted said.

"It's not *just* a loon, butthead. Loons are dynamite."

Ted pointed, as though he hadn't really heard her. "It's taking off," he said, waving toward the edge of the lake. "Look."

Maisie stared toward the sound of the bird's wings beating the water's surface during its extravagantly difficult struggle to lift off. He saw it first, already finishing its landing approach, tottering up the pebbly beach of a little island in the lake on its stubby legs set so absurdly aft on its body. "What a stumblebum," Maisie said.

"What a diver," Ted said. "Those legs kick serious ass when it's in the water."

"It's not in the water," Maisie said.

"It's building a nest," Ted said. "But listen to that beaver chew!"

Maisie shrugged. "I can't hear a thing. Let's go," she said. "We've got a long climb before dark."

Ted liked the way that sounded. He thought of movies

he'd seen of difficult adventures, lonely ocean voyages, desert crossings, jungle treks; they always said that: "Let's go. We've got miles to make before sundown." Still, he dawdled to watch the beavers.

"So," Maisie said, "maybe you want Mom and Dad to wake up and find us missing? Maybe you don't even want to go with me."

"Okay, okay," Ted said. "Let's go, then."

An hour later they were higher than they'd ever been. They'd followed the footpath that corkscrewed up through the blackberry patches the community kids raided in summer; the path was choked with alder, petering out till it quit at a wall of brambles. By now they were beyond the meadow where Doc had organized toboggan races and they'd entered the second-growth woods that had grown back after the farmer who'd sold out to Doc had given up clearing brush. Along the difficult way they helped each other, tentatively at first, Maisie lending a hand for balance, Ted pulling his sister up a slippery boulder. It began to seem natural.

By ten, they were tired. They sat on a big rock, breathing hard, drinking water from a jug. Ted stared at the rock. "You know what this boulder is?"

"Oh, please, Dr. Wizard, do tell!"

Despite her words, Ted could tell she was interested. "It's granite, of course. But it's old, millions of years. It's called an erratic, and it might've been carried a hundred miles in a river of ice."

"Well," Maisie said, "I'll be dipped in shit."

"They found coral near the Raven Kill," Ted said. "They think whales used to swim around here."

"Who cares?" his sister said.

As soon as she said it, Ted could tell she wished she hadn't. He stared at her and blinked, as though he didn't recognize her. "I do," he said.

Snow crusted the scrubby ground, and Ted noticed paw prints in the snow. He said they looked like a big dog's prints, but Maisie said she could tell the animal was a wolf because one of the pads had made a deep indent.

Ted laughed. "Don't bullshit me, Maisie. There're no wolves up here."

"How do you know?"

"I'm Dr. Wizard. I know all."

"Seriously, how do you know what's up here? You know how this mountain got its name?"

"Sure."

"How?"

"I don't want to talk about it."

"Look, Ted, if there are bears up here, why are you so sure there aren't wolves?"

"Because," Ted said.

Even so, he felt jumpy after that, sneaking peeks over one shoulder and then the other, pretending he was just exercising his neck. Maisie was doing the same thing. She led the way, and Ted didn't mind. He trusted her and worked hard to hang close. His sister was in tip-top shape. Also, he figured that if they met anything on the trail, he'd sooner let her meet it first. A coyote, for example. They could hear them at night even down home. Jinx said they were making a comeback, and Ted knew there'd been a debate at town meeting about restoring the bounty on them. And despite Ted's "because" and the frequent claim that there were no wolves left in the county, one had been shot recently just outside the Adirondacks, in the Alder Brook Range. And there were bobcats, and Ted knew if they ran into one, it would be over before it started. Some said there were copperheads and timber rattlers up here, but Ted wasn't afraid of snakes. Neither was Maisie, who liked to find them in the grass and put them down the back of her brother's shirt.

The animal he most didn't want to meet, though, was a bear. A couple of weeks ago, some golfers rushing the season up at the Raven Kill public course had run into a bear shaking a juniper bush. They said that bear was six to seven feet tall, "as big as a refrigerator," with a "head the size of a basketball."

Maisie's face was ruddy from effort, but she breathed easily. They didn't talk while they were climbing; she'd told him they should shut up to save their breath for the work ahead, even though he knew she knew he didn't like the silence. Speechless, plodding uphill, breaking through the snow's crust, dislodging loose rocks, they sounded to Ted like just another couple of animals, and not the biggest animals, not the kings of the mountain. Ted was thinking he and his sister were in the food chain now; he was recalling nature shows on TV, how some big cat or hyena came hell-for-leather out of the tall grass or brush and singled out the youngest from a pack of vegetarian grazers and tore that lame sucker's throat open, then buried its muzzle in the victim's belly and gobbled its guts.

"You daydreaming about food?" Maisie said.

"Not really," he said.

"You ever consider we *are* food to some animals? We're prey, man."

"They eat fruit," Ted said.

Maisie for sure knew who "they" meant. "Bullshit," she said. "They eat anything that drifts into their range."

"I know what they eat, Maisie. Apples and beechnut and chokeberries." He added, "Blackberries, too."

"Because they're black bears?" Maisie said.

"What's that supposed to mean?" Ted said.

"Come on, Ted, I know what you think this place is named for."

"You don't *know* what I think. About *anything*."

"Hey, dude. Calm down."

"I'm sick of you telling me what I think. I'm your brother, not your fucking pet."

"You're adorable," Maisie said. She'd never said anything like that to him. He looked at her; she looked at him. To his surprise, he didn't feel himself blush. She might've been blushing, or maybe just flushed from the climb. He couldn't tell. "Speaking of pets," she said, "bears are weird motherfuckers. They don't even take a leak when they're sleeping. They just veg out in some cave with their eyes open. It's not like you can mess around with them, even if they look like they're sleeping."

"I know," Ted said, though in fact he didn't. Now he believed it.

Maisie said, "You remember that guy we saw on educational TV who lost half his face when he shoved a thermometer up the ass of a sleeping bear?"

"The word's *hibernating*. And that was a griz."

"Oh, pardon me, Mountain Man! I'd like you to meet my brother, Teddy, alias Griz to his friends Bambi and Flower. Gimme a break!"

"You're just wasting your breath, Maisie. Let's shut up and climb."

So she shut up. He knew he'd made her feel younger than she'd wanted to feel. They had that effect on each other, had even discussed it. Maybe it was just a thing that happened between brothers and sisters; maybe he was like a vacation from being old.

She must have heard him thinking. "Don't think you're so old, *Edward*. You're just a kid scared shitless you're about to get scarfed by a bear."

"Come on, Maisie. Lay off. I've got a blister." He was

hungry. He'd realized by midmorning that they wouldn't make it all the way. They had been climbing slowly, weaving through spruce and hemlock, the understory laminated with thick crusts of snow. Up here it wasn't melting, and icicles dangled from boughs.

Maisie swept away some snow with her mittens and they sat down. Beneath the snow was delicate moss, and for a minute he felt all gushy about how fragile and soft that moss was, growing up there without anybody to see it, and he wanted his friends—and not just Maisie—to see it; he wanted his mom and dad to see it, and he looked across the valley toward their house. He wondered if his dad was looking for them with his telescope. And then the weirdest thing: Maisie waved at their house, as though she'd been thinking the same thing, and suddenly he was glad to be with his sister, to have such a sister. He felt safe with her. He understood how alone they were up there together; even if his mom and dad were looking for them just then, and he doubted it, they could never see Ted and Maisie where they sat under the boughs of a black spruce, so far away.

"I wonder if Doc can see us up here," Maisie said.

"Doc?"

"It's just so beautiful," she said. "I bet he knows that."

People liked to believe that Maisie was a real tomboy, but Ted knew there was a more complicated version of her that only a few special people understood, and he wondered then if she realized he was one of them.

After a little while, sitting Indian-style on the ground, the cold drilled into him. They were sweating, and the sun was lower in the sky, and now his damp sweater steamed and Maisie's ski cap was stiffening in the cold. Ted figured they were three or four hundred vertical feet from the summit; it didn't sound like much, but it was a steep climb on ice-covered granite, then across a saddle of deep snow.

Ted had slipped out of his backpack and sat rubbing his shoulders, looking thoughtful.

"What's the matter?" Maisie said.

"Those damned twigs rubbed them raw," he said.

Putting hemlock boughs under the straps had been her bright idea. Doc claimed if you slipped a hemlock bough under the backpack straps, they'd smooth the load and, as they were crushed by the weight of the pack, give off a pleasing fragrance. Those had been Doc's words—"pleasing fragrance"; when she used them, Ted had been impressed. But he had noticed Maisie dump her own hemlock boughs way back down the mountain, while they were still below the toboggan slope. They did make a sweet smell, but they hurt like hell.

"Let me see those foot blisters," she said. Ted was taking off one of his sneakers, and Maisie warned him to be careful not to get snow in his socks. They'd both brought extras, but it would be a bummer to have wet feet up here. She peeled off his sock and said, as if she had to say it or he'd be disappointed, "Wow! What died in your sneaks?" His foot was already bigger than Maisie's; she took it gently in her hand, as a doctor might, and checked out the nasty blister on his heel. He guessed she was grossed out, but she wouldn't let on. She had a reputation for being impossible to gross out. Her specialty—before she got too mature (she pronounced it ma-*toor*) for that kind of thing—was grossing out the kids at school. She'd mix her boogers into a cup of chicken noodle soup at the cafeteria, for example, and swig it, going, *"mmmm-mmm, good!"* "Let me put a little whiskey on that wound," Maisie said.

"Why?" he said.

"To sterilize it."

"What is this—*Gunsmoke?*"

"Be serious, Teddy."

"*General Hospital?*"

"Trust me," his sister said.

Ted said okay, and she swabbed at it gently. Ted was quiet, lying back and looking up through the boughs at the clear blue sky above them, wondering if she thought he was some little kid who didn't know his ass from his elbow. The whiskey burned on that raw spot, but he didn't flinch or say anything. They lived by the local code and they'd all been banged up in rock fights and by falling off bikes and out of trees, and they'd all been stitched up at the clinic, so they knew how to act.

"Why's Mom so hard on Dad all the time?" he said.

"What do you mean?"

"Mom's such a bitch to him."

"How?" She'd quit tending his blistered foot. She was staring at him, alert, wary.

"Come on, Maisie." He sat up. "You were as pissed off as I was last night. She's always ragging on him."

"It's not Mom," she said, "and it's not Dad. It's marriage."

"What are you talking about?"

"Marriage," she said. "It's a doomed institution."

"How would you know?"

"You'd never guess what I know."

"Sure," he said.

"You want to put that sock back on, or a dry pair?"

"I'll hold my dry socks in reserve."

Maisie laughed. "Where'd you get that expression? I'll hold *you* in reserve." She pounced on him, tickling him, and he squirmed out of her arms and stood in the snow, one foot bare.

He was gasping for breath, laughing and mad all at once. "Can't you be serious about anything?"

Then, not for the first time that day, his sister took him by surprise. "Serious? If you only knew. I'm way past serious. You've got to wear dry socks," she said. "I squirreled away an extra pair."

"Yours are too small."

"They're your socks."

"What are you doing with my socks? Did you rip them off?"

"Sort of. I packed an extra pair for you, just in case."

"You're not my mother, you know."

"Yeah, I know." She rummaged around for his socks and also found moleskin pads for his sore heels. She fished out a Snickers bar, too, which she knew he liked. "Let's saddle up," Maisie said, and they began again to climb.

For Ted, their trip up the mountain was a big deal, an assault on Everest. He was breathing hard, and it wasn't only because he was tired; he was excited. But for Maisie, he guessed, what they were undertaking was just a hike: one foot and then the other, back and forth across the face of the mountain, angling up. Then Ted twisted his ankle, and that scared them, but after half an hour the pain dulled. It was the wrong time of year for what they were doing: Not only were coyotes and wolves and bears and animals of all kinds hunting for chow for their cubs and protecting them against dangers, both of which they might have thought Maisie and Ted were; it was also colder than a witch's tit.

By late afternoon, Maisie paused and wondered aloud whether they ought to set up a base camp and rest before making "the final assault" in the morning. Ted didn't argue. He was beat, and Maisie said the rocks above were "varnished with ice." He knew that the best time to take on the rocks was late morning, when the sun was hitting them hard. Also, Ted could see caves up near the top, and he figured caves equaled bears.

The cold was serious now and the shadows cast by over-hanging boughs had disappeared. Ted looked up at the gray sky. It looked like snow and the wind was testing its strength. Way off in the distance, the peak of Mount Marcy was disappearing in windswept clouds.

"Let's pitch the tent," Maisie said.

He looked at her, weighing whether or not this was an order and whether to obey it. "Okay," he said.

They worked together, Ted driving the tent pegs with a hatchet, Maisie drawing the tent loops taut. They knew how to do this and didn't have to talk. "Mom has her reasons, you know," Maisie said. "Dad can get pretty unrealistic."

He was testing the tent, rocking the center pole. He pretended to know what he was doing, and maybe he did. "He experiments," Ted said. "He's an innovator."

"You've got a pretty amazing vocabulary," Maisie said.

Ted blushed. "Well, I can read."

"Is that Dad's word, 'innovator'?"

"I guess. Maybe Doc's."

"Let's not talk any more about Doc. Just today." Maisie asked gently, almost a plea. "Okay, Ted? Let's not talk about Mom and Dad, either. Let's do just this, be up here."

Ted stared at her, wondering what she meant.

"Do you think Mom has a thing for him?" Ted asked. He was looking back toward home, along the brilliant midnight blue surface of Lake Discovery, beyond the lake, then beyond the horizon north. He shivered.

Now Maisie stared at him. She laughed, too loudly. Ted flushed with anger; his neck went red. "No," she said. "Mom doesn't have a thing for Doc. Besides, she's old enough to be his sister."

"What do you mean?" Ted said.

"What do *you* mean?" Maisie said. "What makes you think they have something going?"

"I mean *had.* I was just asking."

"Let's smoke a Camel," Maisie said.

"Okay."

"I'd walk a mile for a Camel," she said. "And after, we'll drink some of this whiskey."

"Dynamite," her brother said.

"And after we've wet our lips, we'll spark up a bone."

"Whatever you say," her baby brother said.

Maisie rummaged around in their supplies for what she called "contraband." Ted's worst habit, he figured, was chewing Red Man or Sköl, which he'd picked up playing Little League, but Maisie had made him promise to stop. She said it would stain his teeth and give him bad breath, and maybe she was right.

They'd pitched their tent beneath balsams alongside a deep, narrow gorge. This looked almost like a place where the earth's skin had been split by an earthquake, but Ted knew that Blackberry Mountain was part of a system formed by erosion, so that during the old days its summit had been level with the ground around it, and then that ground around it had been worn away, leaving the humped summit looming there above them. It comforted him that this process had taken so long, because he had been thinking lately about erosion. The ground was rumbling beneath Ted's family; it felt like tectonic plates rubbing against one another, making fault lines like this gorge.

Maisie and Ted sat dangling their legs over the edge of the gorge, looking across at a huge shaft of ice on the left shoulder. In summer this would be only a trickle, but now the thaw-freeze cycle had turned runoff into a humongous icicle. Blue-green and white, it was a serious piece of nature, and it reminded Ted where they were and that they were alone together. There was no one else he'd rather be with, not even Doc, although with Doc he knew he should feel safer.

Ted explained to Maisie that Blackberry Mountain was called a monadnock, an exposed piece of resistant granite. He'd studied that kind of thing in school and in the Raven Kill library, and now he was showing off for his sister. He told her about glaciation and pointed out the kames and kettles and eskers above and below them, even if they weren't—technically—kames and kettles and eskers. But he liked the sound of himself pronouncing the words.

"Look," he said. "See those boulders?"

"Where?" Maisie said.

Ted gestured to a snowfield above them. "I could see those through Dad's telescope. They look like some giant just scattered them around like marbles. They're erratics, like the boulder we sat on this morning."

"I like that," Maisie said. "It's a good name. Maybe we're erratics."

When dusk came and then night, they opened cans and heated spaghetti and meatballs on a one-burner kerosene stove. After they ate their dinner over a cookstove, they saw spooky lights up to the northeast. Ted tried to sucker punch Maisie into believing they were from World War III, that he could see the mushroom clouds. But his trick didn't work; she wasn't as scared as he was about World War III. He'd seen a TV movie that showed how it was after: Children saw their parents turn into toast, and then those children were left to figure out for themselves how to drive around and grow crops for food and fight off marauders. That was a movie Maisie hadn't seen.

She said, "They're probably just UFOs."

"Bullshit," Ted said.

"Well, believe what you want to, but I saw one hovering over Doc's roof a couple months ago."

Ted thought she probably believed she had, but he also

suspected that she'd been smoking grass, which she smoked too much of.

Maisie bit her lower lip and looked off toward the eerie light show way up at the edge of the world. "If I told you I'd been in a spaceship, maybe even kidnapped for a couple hours, would you believe me?"

"You want the truth?"

"Shoot."

"I don't see how I could believe such a thing. I'm not a hundred percent sure, but I think it would take more than I've got to believe my sister hitched a ride on a spaceship."

"You know," Maisie said, "that's the trouble with this world. People risk their all telling about close encounters and abductions, and all they get for their honesty is grief. Honesty just doesn't pay off, which is why people learn to be cautious and middle-class."

Ted said, "I don't know what you're talking about."

So Maisie changed the subject, got them going about what they'd do with the spoils if one of them won the lottery.

"You tell first," Ted said. "It's your topic."

"That gives me the right to go first or second, and I want to go second."

Ted stared at his fingernails. "Well, I sure wouldn't keep it all for myself. I'd give half to Mom and Dad and split the other half with you."

Maisie laughed. "I'll believe that when I see it. I'd keep it all, spend every penny."

"No way."

Maisie winked. "Right. I'd be *so* generous! I'd buy Mom her own newspaper to run. She could write editorials telling everybody what to do. I'd get Dad a research company, hire only the best inventors, and let him sit around brainstorming—"

"Yeah," Ted interrupted. "Even Doc couldn't compete with him."

Maisie smiled. "I'd buy you a science and nature library."

"What about new racing skis?"

Maisie snapped her fingers. "They're yours."

"What do you want?" her brother asked.

"Nothing. Not much. A pretty cotton dress. Let's not talk about it," Maisie said.

They sat outside the tent, watching the lights, smoking dope, and Ted was glad the snow they'd felt in the air that afternoon never came. It would have been a horror show up there in a blizzard. After a while, he explained that what they were seeing was the aurora borealis.

"It's an impressive show," she said.

Ted wasn't experienced at dope smoking and he coughed if he tried to inhale. When Maisie asked if she was a bad influence on him, he said she wasn't, and he meant it. He said he didn't respond to peer pressure, and that was such a load that he knew Maisie would laugh at him. But she didn't. Shivering now, they went inside the tent.

Ted and Maisie talked about sex, and she seemed shocked by how much he knew. But when they reached a certain point in their conversation—"Helen thinks you're cute," she'd said—Ted wanted to change the subject.

He could see the northern lights flashing through the thin membrane of the tent. "Look," he said. "Isn't that amazing?"

But Maisie didn't look at the wall of the tent. She looked at her brother, who figured she'd lost interest in the aurora borealis. She talked about sex again. Whenever Ted said he didn't want to talk about sex, Maisie asked what was wrong with him, was he queering up on her? Not that Ted hadn't gone along for the ride when she'd gotten her hands on dirty movies and a movie projector a couple of months ago. They'd told their parents they were going to the town rink to skate and maybe get a hockey game together, and then Maisie and Ted and Army and Ben and Sam and the rest of their gang humped all this gear, including a "portable" generator that weighed about a ton, into the woods. They hauled the generator and projector up to their tree house with ropes. Maisie was in charge of the "film festival" and got everything hooked up, although it was so damned cold she could hardly thread the film on the reel. She'd blow inside the cuffs of her mittens to warm her fingers and then quick pull off the mittens, throw them aside, try to get the film moving through the projector before her fingers seized up. Ted envied his sister her mittens that their mom had knitted for her, navy blue with pretty white snowflakes. The gang watched *Tillie Goes to the Dentist for a Drilling and a Filling*, an unbelievable story about a guy in a dentist's waiting room, reading a dirty magazine and wearing a mask, who got lucky with the dentist's receptionist and then with another patient—this must have been Tillie—who walked in on them. It was a silent movie, which was fortunate because the generator snarled like a chain saw. The other movies, whose titles Ted couldn't remember, were pretty much the same as *Tillie*: Events happened fast, and it was hard not to laugh. Maisie did most of the talking while her associates watched. Most of what she said sounded technical to Ted, and—he couldn't say why; maybe it was his sister's know-how, her easy way with the jargon—he never felt right about it that she'd put that plan together.

"We went to a lot of trouble," he said, "to see those crummy movies."

"Wasn't it worth it?"

"What I don't understand," he said, "is why you didn't arrange a simpler night. Why didn't we just pop an X-rated tape in our VCR when Mom and Dad were out to dinner?"

"You got any X-rated videos?"

"I guess not."

"Besides, it was an adventure, wasn't it? Didn't it make you hot, seeing those chicks get it from that masked guy?"

"Not really."

"Why not? Because they were dogs?"

"No. Because it was unbelievable. It wasn't happening."

"Of course it wasn't *happening*. It was a movie, Ted!"

"I mean, it was like they weren't people. They were just pretending to be, like those animals at the circus they dress up in skirts and tuxedos. It just didn't turn me on."

"Good, Ted. Good for you," Maisie said, her voice diving deep into the grown-up register: "You're okay, kiddo."

Then they heard unearthly noises—animal sounds, something eating, something different being eaten. "What's *that*?" Ted said, his voice catching.

"It sounds like an owl to me," Maisie said. "No question."

"What's it killing?"

"Nothing. Why do you think it's killing something?"

"Something's crying," he said. The low whimper grew louder, more urgent. Then the lament went up the register to a shriek and down again to a whimper, as if it had grown tired of crying.

Maisie shivered.

Then it was really cold, and Ted heard what he knew was a bear outside. If it wasn't a bear, it was a human being, and up there, that night, he would have chosen the bear, even though he shook like a baby smelling its awful stink, thinking about its bored eyes and matted fur, about its yellow teeth in its bloodred mouth.

"I'm cold," Ted said, and he started to crawl into his sleeping bag. He looked over at his sister, hugging her knees, rocking back and forth. He thought she was crying. "Maisie? You okay?"

She nodded, but she looked sad. Ted figured her sadness was for the animal crying above the owl's screech. He had a picture of his sister as that poor animal, caught, in pain.

She was watching Ted snuggle into his mummy bag; he was zipping it from inside, where his hands were. He was in there all the way to his eyes. Now it was silent outside, except for boughs sighing above them.

"Take your hand off it," Maisie said.

"What do you mean?" Ted said.

She laughed. "You're hanging on to your dick."

"I am not!" Ted said.

"How often do you beat off?" she said.

"Lay off, Maisie!"

"*What?* You're telling me you never beat off?"

"That's not funny." He drew his hands out of the bag into the cold, maybe to prove what a good boy he was.

"Well," she said. "Do you or don't you?"

"Not that it's any of your business, but maybe I don't need to."

"The only guy who says he doesn't," Maisie said, "is a liar if he does and an asshole if he doesn't."

"I don't care what you think," Ted snapped. He didn't want to talk about it anymore. "Where did they go?" he said softly. "You think they're gone?"

Maisie shrugged.

"It could've had us for dinner. It must not be interested in us. You scared?"

"Now?"

"No, then," he said.

Maisie lit a joint. Ted told her not to smoke inside the tent, it might catch on fire. Maisie said the tent was fire-retardant, like little kids' pajamas. Ted didn't laugh.

"You want some dope?" she said.

Just then a sapling cracked, loud, right outside. They'd hoisted their dirty plates and utensils and cans high up a tree, but Ted wondered if a bear had smelled the garbage. Something was out there. "We've got to do something," he said, "to scare it off." And then he began to shriek, loud piercing shrieks like the sounds in a zoo's monkey house, hysterical and shrill and crazy. And right away his shrieks were answered by all kinds of animal calls, rabbits and birds. The clomp outside the tent stopped, but Ted kept shrieking.

"Shush," Maisie said.

And he did. "I'm scared," he said.

Then Maisie started up about sex again, which pissed him off. He told her that he was losing respect for her. That shut her up, and Ted thought she was crying, and he said things to comfort her. She was sitting cross-legged, with her sleeping bag wrapped around her shoulders like a cape. She said she was freezing to death in her sleeping bag because it was summer-weight and Ted was in the goose-down bag. "I'm cold," Maisie said. "Can I come over there?"

"I guess," he said.

And she went to him, and unzipped his sleeping bag, and crawled in with him. For comfort, she said. She came over and Ted's mummy bag got unzipped. She unzipped it; he didn't unzip it. It was a one-person sleeping bag. She was shivering. To make room for her, Ted had to put his arms around her, and she had to put her arms around him. Ted let her figure out how they could fit together. He let her zip up the bag. He let her do everything they did. He wasn't sorry, either.

The kerosene lantern lit her dull orange with flashes of blue and pink. Her face was alert. The kerosene lamp smoked, its heavy fumes trapped in the tent, but he smelled only the perfume that mingled with the familiar soapy scent of her hair, baby shampoo. Her long sweet hair fell across his face and he inhaled her smell. He felt he'd suffocate if he didn't shift his face, but he lay there still, letting it all wash over him.

It was not yet too late to pretend they didn't recognize what was happening. It wasn't too late to crack a joke or wrestle or begin a ghost story, as though they'd huddled for warmth, from fear, like lost animals. Then Maisie took his hand and held it, and then she moved his hand, and now it was too late to pretend they didn't grasp what was happening.

"Maisie," he whispered into her hair.

"Shush," she said.

"Maisie," he said.

"Do you want to stop?" she said.

He shook his head, burying his face in her long hair, and his lips brushed her neck, her ears, her throat. She wore a flannel nightgown, and it smelled of soap, of cigarette smoke, of perfume. He breathed in; he smelled her. Her breasts pushed against his chest. She unbuttoned his shirt, and her breasts felt soft against him. His hand moved against her and he was astonished how soft that was, how soft her hair. He had never understood her as soft, and now she was soft wherever he touched. She pulled her face from his face and stared at him, her eyes wide open. He looked away.

"Look at me," she said.

He looked at her. They stared at each other, lying perfectly still. He was afraid to move. His hand moved, she closed her eyes, he closed his eyes.

"Easy," she said. "Yes," she said. "Good. That's nice."

Now her hand moved to him. He bit his lip, would not make a noise. They heard noises near the tent, something

moving out there. They paid no mind. He let her do everything. She kissed him. He opened his mouth when she opened
her mouth. He tasted her; she sucked his tongue. He wanted
this never to stop. His hands touched her soft back, moved
down her back. She was whispering in his ear, but he couldn't
make out her words. Please please please please pretty
please . . .

It was done. They rested in each other's arms.

"Sleep," she said.

He made himself be still, then moved his hand back between her soft wet legs. She shut her legs together, gently.

"Sleep," she said.

He pretended to sleep. His head was pounding. He was
hard against her soft leg, her legs locked, and he was not
ashamed. His life had changed now, and shame had no part
in it. He wanted to stay here. He had said nothing since he
said her name. He said her name now.

She moved. She was unzipping the bag. He was still. She
was on her hands and knees. He wanted her to come back.
She leaned over, kissed him on his cheek the way his mother
would when she tucked him in. She gently zipped up his bag.
He wanted to look at her, but he was afraid if he opened his
eyes, she'd be gone.

She was gone. Across the tent. Climbing into her sleeping
bag. He didn't know how much time had passed. He lay
awake, pretending to sleep, and heard her breathing, her measured, deep aspirations in time with his own. He wondered
if she was sleeping or pretending. He studied the back of her
head, her long hair. The lantern guttered, then died with a
sighing billow of smoke. He couldn't smell her perfume now.
He squinted into the dark. He said her name softly. Her
breathing was steady. He stared at her, could begin to see
her hair in the first violet light. She was facing him now, four
feet away. She seemed to be smiling.

Later, she stirred. He had not stopped staring at her. Her eyes fluttered awake and she saw his eyes. She smiled.

"Maisie," he said.

"Shush," she said, putting her finger across her lips.

"Maisie," he said.

"No," she said.

And Now Is Then

Edward

He knows a few things. He knows he didn't push her off that ledge. She didn't dive to free herself from his grip. He knows this. He never held her, really. He knows. When she rushed to discard herself a season after their climb together, way back then he knew nothing. He's learned a few things. He's learned that he's an unreliable judge of motive. When he hears himself telling himself why a person did this or that—is one way or another—he feels the ground give beneath his feet. But he can't make himself stop believing that his sister has been too unkind to herself, has let herself crab forward and back helter-skelter and by inches. She hasn't been true to herself; she should be, once was, headlong.

Years ago and seemingly yesterday, when Maisie stirred awake, when she spoke, when she gave them bits and pieces of her story, Ted's family didn't guess that she'd never come home. Not that he could imagine then what home would be or how they'd live together. Now what? Oh, how he misses her. Oh, does he miss her. Does she dream about him or drop his name into conversations? See a sight and say to herself, if only Teddy could see this? He doesn't know.

There are facts, a history: she has a life, friends who value her, a job. She pays her way, manages the complications of New York City, has interests. What Maisie lacks, he understands, is a reflex natural to others—a sense of home, a curiosity about how we come to be who we are. She seems unnaturally hostile to personal history, cannot abide recollection, especially the habit of recollection that views now through the lens of then. It is as though some fragile but fundamental sensing mechanism—call it nostalgia, call it memory, call it love—was undone together with those other nerves she severed that day at the falls.

From the hospital in Lake Placid, she had been flown by helicopter to New York City. The family had moved down to Westchester County, to Ann's mother's faux Tudor, to be near her. It was an oddly sweet time, or so Ted remembers it: Ann and Jinx had no leisure to fret about themselves, and they were guests of a woman accustomed to goodwill as it might be expressed in courtesy and affection. Recollecting those days, Ted recalls a haze of pleasure, drowsing poolside between hospital visits, drinking lemonade and reading Farley Mowat paperbacks. Ann was sunny and determined.

"I know this sounds crazy," she said, "but if we look at what's happened in just the right way, we can thank Maisie. Maybe she's showed us what's really important. Maybe we can start fresh. Does that sound crazy?"

To Ted, it did.

Jinx said, "I think Ann's onto something here. From now on it'll be smooth sailing."

"Well," Ann said, "maybe not smooth. But we can do better. We will."

This was made easier to believe by Maisie's remarkable recovery. In the bracing early days of her comeback, she was pliant and vulnerable, prone as anyone would expect to unexpected tears. Maisie had always been a tough cookie, and this showed itself during her resurrection in fixed purpose. She trained like an athlete; and by the time she was moved to the rehabilitation center on the Hudson, the Jenks believed that—despite partial paralysis of the left side, whatever the severity of her memory deficit—she would recover her fundamental nature. They understood that her recovery would be incremental. They were resigned.

A little more than a year after her fall, Maisie took up a normal life, whatever those words might have meant to any of them. She enrolled in a day school near Pound Ridge and lived with her grandmother, who paid her tuition. For Ted's part, he was in high school at Raven Kill Union High, with a life of his own. Much of that was taken up with ski racing, which required year-round training. That first autumn, with Maisie at another school in another town, had flown past before he took account of the reality of his family. They were discrete now, joined only by an abstraction of "family" that they continued to honor. By mid-November of her second year away, unable to discount the deepening fractures between his mom and dad, Ted recognized what was happening to them all, and he campaigned hard to seduce Maisie home for the Thanksgiving feast at the boathouse.

Before the boathouse had been built, everyone had joined for Thanksgiving with as many from the town of Raven Kill as wished to assemble in the woodloft of Doc's workshop, vacuumed clean of sawdust for the occasion. Those gatherings had been Maisie's favorites; she'd thrown herself into them with as much appetite as anyone, excepting Doc. In the spirit of the Independence Day floats, Doc had rallied his neighbors to build rough tables and benches for the loft, and they'd worked for days and days to build furniture that accommodated a hundred citizens and more. And in that spirit of community everyone gave what she could, ate what he wanted. No one stinted. There were no toasts or ceremonies, other than the annual pet show, in which all beasts took a prize: Most Interestingly Ugly One-eyed Cat, Fuzziest Bald Dog, Longest-Tailed Tailless Animal. At those Thanksgiving feasts, Maisie ran around making trouble, eating other people's food, squatting down behind some fat woman to make fart noises. And then she suddenly grew up and took an interest in cooking and baking and decorating, with the same pep she'd showed as a tomboy.

Ted shared with his sister the details of this year's banquet in long letters, thinking she'd be amused by the situation at home, hoping she'd come. He had explained that people needed her, promised that it would be the best homecoming ever, reported that everyone missed her, which they said they did, and they probably meant it. He certainly missed her.

But Maisie said thanks, no thanks, nope.

Their family seemed to come unraveled like a cheap quilt. Ann spent more and more time downstate with her mother and with Maisie. Jinx tried the windmill business just after it decided to go nowhere, and Ted was left alone in the house for weeks at a time. Not that he suffered in solitude; Doc was eager to shoot the breeze, to teach him to mark rafter angles on a shed, to build an oak desk using dovetail joints, then a walnut side table using through-pegged mortise and tenon joints, then a Honduras mahogany dining room table for his mom and dad using spline miter joints. Ted imagined that if he gave them a table, they'd sit at it, and if they sat at it, staring across food at each other, they'd forget to resent each other.

Doc taught by example, and his best examples were his own worst botches. It was as if he didn't want to mislead his novitiates into believing he was infallible, or maybe he guessed that they'd already figured that out. He'd always told tales on himself before anybody else could, and this brought him pleasure. One day, for example, having declared that no one should ever heed a general precept, he'd offer Ted as axiomatic a general precept: A cantilever shouldn't extend more than x percent of the baseline length of y joist. Ted asked why, and Doc reached for a pencil and a scrap of paper to doodle on while Ted tried to figure out which dimension was which. Doc noticed his apprentice's bewilderment.

"Let me tell you why," he said. "You know the ski palace? My first project up here?"

"Sure, of course, I know the Seraglio."

"That house had a radical cantilever. I mean *radical—x* percent plus a shitload. This cantilever was a deck built on three massive beams jutting out as floor joists. It was one hell of a deck, hung over the north meadow."

"That's weird," Ted said. "I can't place the deck."

"That deck's *gone*, man. *Histoire.* I'll tell you. Really and truly. One night, the April before your folks moved in, I was lying on my back in the bedroom, looking through the sky-light at the snow falling like milk. Huge flakes, big as silver dollars, and wet. Heavy, you might say. They piled up on the skylight and stuck, and they must've been piling up on the deck. Think of that deck, heaped with a load of wet snow, as the weighty end of a badly balanced seesaw. I heard this slow grinding noise and the lady beside me—let's call her Ms. Z, since we've used x and y—said, 'What the fuck is that?' She hadn't seen anything yet, because the next thing that happened"—he was doing a pantomime with his hands—"was this slow catapultic—is there such a word?—motion toward our *roof*! I mean the bed was lifting toward the ceiling, like some giant was bench-pressing us above his head. Can you guess what was happening?"

Ted said, "I think I'm getting the point."

"Right! Our bedroom floor was nailed to the light end of

a teeter-tottering fulcrum, and by the time *our* joists quit rising, we were pinned against the skylight."

"Did you get hurt?"

"What do you think? I could say the rescue squad had to come with the jaws of life to cut us free, but in fact the only bruise was to my pride. But then, you know, we were pressed together in this sandwich, and what are you going to do in a case like that? Carpe diem, you know? She was a good laugher, Ms. Z. Like your sister."

Doc kept Ted busy all right, teaching and telling stories. Not that Ted had time to waste. He had a crack at becoming a national-class junior slalom racer. Like all good racers, Ted was feral; coaches speak of attacking a course, attacking the mountain, and that's exactly what Ted did. When he rolled over on his edges in a turn, it was as though he was taking a straight razor to the slope's throat, grunting with fury as he hurled himself down the mountain. In those days, five and six years ago, conditioning had taken all the time left over after his studies. He was an ambitious student, determined to study at Middlebury or Dartmouth instead of settling for the University of Vermont or Norwich Academy, where most of his teammates hoped to race.

He'd promised Maisie he'd write every week, and at first he did, mostly gossip and weather reports and geography lessons—that's what she called them—about the seasons changing, the hills losing light in seven shades of purple, northern lights showing off, blah blah blah. She never said her brother's letters bored her, or never said it bluntly, but when he wrote her about another bear sighting, she answered that Blackberry Mountain, "for the little thing that it is, sure lights a fever in your imagination. It's just a pissant hill, Teddy. Let it be."

So he let it be. He let her be. He went to her high school

graduation, but she was unavailable, working a summer job in Manhattan, for his. He'd gone to her graduation from Barnard; she drove up from New York to his from Dartmouth, just last year. It wasn't that they encountered each other only on such occasions, but the spirit of their relationship was ceremonial, dutiful. Their intimacy had leaked away. Not out of bad will, he knew. Not out of carelessness, he hoped.

His sister now works for a travel magazine in New York. She's a copy editor and fact checker, and she's been promoted a couple of times. Ted understands that she's demanding on writers. She doesn't travel herself, says she's not interested. He sort of understands. When he began at Dartmouth, he'd expected to develop a taste for the wider world, but it never happened. He was a good racer, but he grew too tall and then blew out a knee. Surgery fixed that, but something didn't come back—the demented will that racing above his level demanded. So he never skied in Europe and never worked up an appetite to see the great world his Dartmouth friends explored so casually. He is anchored, like his sister. This doesn't sadden him, but neither does he confuse his steadfastness with a virtue. It's a fact, period. He lives where he grew up, not merely because he happened to grow up there but because he grew into this place. Every other lake seems too big or too small, too blue or too green. Other sunsets seem garish or pallid. The Alps and Rockies are too theatrical, the Green Mountains too tame. But he can't tell how much longer he'll stay put; for one thing, the house is for sale, but he knows there is more to it than that.

Nowadays, Ted and Maisie talk on the telephone every couple of weeks. His mother keeps him up to date, and he keeps his father up to date. Love you, they always sign off, miss you. All of them. They say these words as if they mean them, and he believes they do. But my God he's alone.

For the past four summers, beginning after Ted's freshman year, he's worked for Doc—*with* Doc, as Doc prefers to say—building improvements to the Lake Discovery School, a boarding school for would-be ski racers, where the tuition fees of out-of-towners pay the way for local students. The school began as a business venture with a narrow focus: to prepare rich kids for success on the slalom course, or, worst case, as ski bums in Telluride or Jackson Hole.

Doc engineered the purchase—a sweet deal, he admits—of the school's property. He's taught Ted the history and sociology of Lake Discovery and the school set beside it. It's a story complicated by manners and assumptions as foreign to Ted as the customs of the Sun King, but he knows how to listen. The building and grounds—as comforting to easterners with oldish trust funds and athletic offspring as it is inspiring to new-made moneybags with athletic offspring—had belonged to, indeed *was*, the Lake Discovery Inn, which had gone tits-up rather than tolerate a mixed clientele. Doc does a pretty fair burlesque of the sad-sack board of managers pulling their woebegone chins—alas, we must surrender to the realities, boo-hoo—when they negotiated their sellout to Doc, who took over at a fire-sale price by promising to translate the inn into an "exclusive" school.

In fact, Doc had bigger fish to fry. After brokering the purchase, Doc was commissioned by the school board (which was in his debt) to build an art and dance building, and he'd been in the school's business up to his eyeballs ever since—raising new buildings, raising money to raise new buildings, reshaping the curriculum, seducing guest gurus to lecture.

Doc has no official title at the school, and didn't want one. But he's everywhere, tossing off aphorisms, popping like a bead of water on a hot griddle. He and all those rich kids make a funny match, but Ted noticed recently that Doc's never uncomfortable around people who can do any damned thing they please.

He's never gone on staff because he wants to come and go as he pleases, but he teaches the students to throw clay, to weld sculpture from discarded farm and logging implements, to aim a video camera, whittle wood, carve soapstone, shape pots, and, Ted suspects, grow pot. He invites them up to Blackberry Mountain for picnics and sled races. He tousles the kids' hair and gives them nicknames like Champ and Ace, Legs and Slick, Honeybee and Scooter. They show up at his studio at school and call in the window, "Hey, come out and play!" He'll enlist them during the school year to whack out a piece of school furniture better suited to fun than academic utility—a table shuffleboard game, for example, of the sort you see in roadhouses. He'll show them how to put an addition on an existing building, sketching plans on his brown paper lunch bag. "See," he says. "Can't you see it?" And before the first kid can shake her head, he'll bang congratulations on her back. "I knew you had a good eye. Now let's get it made!"

They love him, and why not? If this makes Ted feel sour, understanding this, it's because he's maybe a little jealous. Maybe more than a little. He's had his day in Doc's sun, and the sun beamed down warmly. But like Army, Maisie, and all the others, Ted felt he'd been the special favorite, the only one who really understood Doc, the one whose star was best aligned with his, better aligned than Doc's wife's or daughter's.

Doc had married the daughter of a client from Seattle. This client, the older brother of the lawyer who'd represented the inn during early negotiations, had commissioned Doc to build a house on an island he owned in Puget Sound. Doc had designed the lodge around a totem pole a money-mad branch of the Suquamish tribe had sold with the island; he'd built it using timber he felled from the house site, finishing the boards at a Port Angeles sawmill. Doc had taken a crew from Blackberry Mountain out west for that job. This was the summer after Maisie's dive, and despite Ted's pleas, Doc had left him behind. He came back with a young woman—either eighteen or twenty, as Doc claimed—named Juliet. Six months later they had a daughter, Becky; a couple of months before she was born, Doc and Juliet put on a winter wedding ceremony at the top of the toboggan run.

That day was sunny but wicked cold. Doc and Juliet arrived at the wedding site in dogsleds driven by sisters who bred Samoyeds. A few of these dogs had made it to the Iditarod, despite having been raised as house pets. Doc was tricked out in a raccoon coat and huge fur mittens and a white silk scarf and a top hat. Juliet wore a pale fur coat, and there was some muttering: it looked alarmingly like the laboring Samoyeds' creamy coats. Doc had built a little chapel out of ice, with a free-form ice altar, above which sat an icy heart. Jinx was best man, and he was beaming. Ted couldn't remember when he'd seen him so happy recently, so proud and relieved, as if he were brother of the groom and father of the bride. A little girl from Blackberry Mountain was the ring bearer. The guy who married them was a computer-graphics whiz moonlighting as a justice of the peace.

Jesus, it was cold! The guests had to remove their mittens to drink the champagne Doc had bought by the case. He also had oysters up there, and smoked salmon. Jinx sighed and said it was just like the old days, before the high had been rubbed off by a terminal plague of common sense. After the ceremony and the toasts, the songs and the drinks, Doc and Juliet, wrapped in sealskin lap robes, took off on sleds.

Juliet's parents didn't attend, but their house in Puget Sound made it to the cover of *House Beautiful.* Ted remembered Doc holding up the magazine soon after the wedding and saying, "Why's it house beautiful? Doesn't the modifier usually precede the noun?" Inside the magazine the owners were quoted saying hurtful things about Doc's casual working habits, his scruffy work crew, his charmingly primitive finish work. Juliet's mother said, "He's not an architect, of course. He's just a builder."

Juliet was said to come complete with trust fund, or maybe that was petty malice on the part of locals who'd married people independently unwealthy and more or less their own age. Doc's neighbors seemed surprised that he had married at all: He was priestly, almost community property. Juliet was quiet. Some said she was shy; some said deep, some callow; a few said a moron. Whatever, in the conversations Ted had with her, her responses were limited to surly *uh-huh*s and *far out*s, *beats me*, and *I pass.* Since she took pictures, Doc built her a darkroom, and she spent so much time in there that her skin bleached out paler and paler, in high contrast to her black hair. There was a TV character called Vampira, and some of the little kids knew her by that name.

If Ted has become resentful about his displacement in Doc's attentions by new acolytes, this isn't Doc's fault. Ted's simply outgrown his apprenticeship. Nevertheless, Ted had hoped as recently as his junior year at Dartmouth, when it became obvious that he wouldn't be racing for the gold in this lifetime, that he'd follow in Doc's wake, become a builder like Doc.

Ted's father had supported him in this ambition, if only by rooting for him. It didn't escape Ted's notice that Jinx, too, had wanted to be a builder, instead making his mark—

or at least some money—selling empty air above office buildings. To Ted, his dad seemed uncomplicated in his response to Ted's relationship with Doc: "I'm glad you have someone to admire, and work to aspire to."

Ann was unimpressed by designers and builders; she seemed to her son to believe that every bad thing that had befallen her and Jinx, and maybe even Maisie, had been blueprinted. The family's money woes were real enough, which is why Jinx and Ann put the house on the market. At first, Jinx had offered it to others up on Blackberry Mountain, folks who were renting or house-sitting, at a moderate price. He'd said he was determined to "keep the place in the family." He'd sought advice from Doc about turning it over to someone else who could appreciate it, but whatever went down in their discussions had left Ted's father red-faced and blue. He wouldn't say anything about it, but Ted had a sense Jinx might've asked to borrow money—more money—from his old college roommate, or asked him to accept the house as collateral.

Anyway, the Jenks house was vacant. Jinx had located his failing windmill business in Hartford. So Doc drove Ted over to Dartmouth after Thanksgiving of his senior year, which was surprising. It wasn't like Doc to play the fatherly role; he was more of a jovial uncle. East of Lake Champlain, in the Green Mountains, Doc pulled over. Even though snow was still coming down at the end of a three-day storm, Doc suggested they hike into the woods on the snowshoes he had in the back of the Range Rover. Ted had never used snowshoes, and he for sure didn't need exercise; but Doc insisted, so he went along. They slogged into a Russian forest of paper birches, and in the flat light Ted was soon disoriented. Doc, like Maisie guiding him up Blackberry Mountain way back when, was in control, leading with a steady gait, instructing him how to step, clearing the tail of one shoe before picking up the other, telling him how to breathe. At first it irritated Ted that he—number three on a goddammed ski-racing team—was being taught a winter sport by Doc, but pretty soon he surrendered to Doc's confidence and remembered how to enjoy learning from him.

Ted guessed that was the point. Doc was passionately lecturing him to be a teacher. Nothing in this world was more satisfying than teaching. Frankly, as a woodworker, as a potential builder, he was so-so, B-minus, precise but uninspired. Less daring than his old man, no offense. But as a teacher . . . Ted could be a *great* teacher. Doc had watched his disciple share lore with the little kids at home, and he was *good*.

As they shuffled through the snow two abreast, Ted opened up a little. Doc had the power to open him up. Ted's worry was that he wasn't in love, hadn't ever been. He knew how to go through the motions, even if he lacked the moves that were considered slick at Dartmouth. Small talk, he could deliver; his trouble was big talk. He had difficulty not wanting to leave the side of any young woman who believed she understood him, who seemed to want to understand him.

"I put in too many solo hours. I'm sleepwalking through my life." Ted surprised himself saying this, felt shame for his recklessness just as he realized that too little recklessness was the problem he had just described.

"Have you had a lover?" Doc had paused and was looking up at the sky, letting the snow fall on his face, breathing hard.

"What do you mean?"

"Have you been fucked?" Doc had bent over to fiddle with straps on his snowshoes.

"Whoa, Doc. That isn't how I'd put it."

"Okay." He laughed, straightening, squinting at Ted. "Take the high road on me, will you? So how about: Have you ever balled a chick?"

"Come on, Doc."

"Just ribbing you, old boy. Just putting the realities in perspective for you."

By then it was going dark in the woods and they'd been moving deeper and deeper, away from the road, and their trail was already covered by the snow falling wet and heavy upon them.

"Let's get out of here, Doc."

"Where's here?"

"Are you kidding?" Ted said.

"I never kid," he said. "Hey, even when I kid, I'm not kidding."

"So what now?"

"Trust me," he said. "Follow me."

And Ted did.

So now Ted has packed up his life and taken it off Blackberry Mountain a little way up the lake to the Lake Discovery School, as a first-year teacher and dorm supervisor. Doc has made much of letting Ted know he'd had no hand in his hiring, and Ted believes him, sort of. Ted did well as a history major in college, and he's qualified and then some to coach ski racing, and anyone with a tolerance for mayhem and folly and anguish is capable of supervising a dormitory.

Now his name is Edward. His parents called him Teddy until he asked for Ted; even now they slip back to Teddy, but he takes this as a sign of affection. He's not a stiff, though he worries about becoming one. Now Eddie *would* bother him, but hardly anyone has ever called him that—except Maisie, of course, to put the needle in him when they were little. Back then she'd also call him Edward. She'd stick her nose in the air, emphasize the syllable breaks, and put on a phony chauffeur's accent: "Ed-WAHD, would you like me to bring the LEE-mo-zine around?" Recently she started calling him Edward without the wiseass edge; she says she likes the name, so that's what he goes by now: Edward.

He teaches high school history. Next year will be his second year of it, if he renews his contract. He doesn't know. He figures the principal will probably ask him back, but he just can't figure out how he feels. It's not the school. Lake Discovery is excellent. He likes it that local children train and study here for free. The academic standards are high. In fact, quite a few of the local parents complain that their kids have to work too hard, that the teachers aren't flexible enough, that they're old-fashioned.

But Ted's uncertainty about his future here is really an uneasiness with the whole world hereabouts, side-by-side communities and cultures alien to one another, neighbors glowering suspiciously at one another across invisible frontiers. There's what's left of the Lake Discovery Inn's fellowship of exclusion and unexamined self-approval. There's Raven Kill, with its sullen descendants of Dutch settlers— now farmers and contractors and plumbers and mechanics. There's Blackberry Mountain, and he isn't sure how he feels about its peculiar attitudes about itself. Is it him? Is this why people leave home? Has he left before he's left?

Something has happened to him. Laura has happened to him. It's not what you'd think. Laura: She's a local girl, sort of a neighbor, from Blackberry Mountain. He'd seen her around, but he didn't recognize her when she showed up in his American history class. She's a tenth grader, fifteen, and he's seven years older. Edward mixed her up with her twin sister, Marcia. When they were babies, Maisie sometimes baby-sat them; he remembers that one of the girls was bratty and the other wasn't, but he never got a handle on which was which. At some point he realized that she'd been the ring bearer at Doc Halliday's wedding.

He first really noticed Laura this past September. She'd been at Lake Discovery for a year, so she knew the ropes. It was his first day as a teacher and he was anxious as hell. Fifteen students, and she sat in the front row, directly in front of the teacher's desk. The room smelled of paint; it was converted from a seminar room back to a traditional classroom design after a faculty vote last year to teach their students rather than rap with them. That was a controversial decision; a few teachers quit, and one of them was the history teacher, which was why Edward got his job. Some of the students, along with Doc and the Blackberry Mountain contingent, were sore about this retreat to a hierarchical classroom layout. The resentful students sat in the back and groused and passed notes ragging on the new teacher. Edward was always an easy blusher, and he could guess that his face was red that first hour because a few girls giggled. He had been giggled at before, and it didn't bother him, not much.

Laura didn't giggle. She sat in the front row with her head cocked, studying her teacher. He felt encouraged by her; she seemed to be listening attentively to his description of what he hoped to accomplish in the course, even though she wasn't taking notes. Not a hanging offense that, not on the first day. Edward noticed only because she was sitting directly in front of him.

She had become a striking young lady, with bright red hair and pale, pale skin. Gorgeous eyes. She wore a sleeveless blouse and a short white skirt, too short. She jiggled her leg aggressively. Before he started, Edward worried how he'd do teaching pretty girls. In fact, he had too much else on his mind—getting through the hour without stuttering or throwing up from anxiety—to think about who was foxy and who wasn't. The only reason Edward thought about Laura's legs (he told himself) was to acknowledge, as an attentive observer of his new environment, that the way she sat wasn't the way the other girls were sitting that day, or in other classes that day, or in many classes on many days.

Edward aspires to teach American history from primary documents. This was the method of history he was taught in college, and he believes in it. He began the year with diaries and journals from Colonial times, and then his class moved on to slave narratives and southern pulpit and stump oratory and Native American speeches lamenting their persecution. An entire course at Dartmouth was devoted to the study of tribal chiefs, and for all the horror of their destruction, Edward envied them. He found himself longing to have experienced the spiritual complexity of their social rites and taboos regarding blood relatives. They knew what they meant by kinship, whereas here every kid he'd teach would have a screwed-up family life. Really, is there any other kind?

Wanting to be relevant, he chose "bygone families" as his organizing motif. He assembled a collection of photocopied texts to distribute to his students. He understood he was violating copyright laws and soberly acknowledged this transgression to himself and his class. (Like many an apprentice teacher, Edward apes the manners of his college professors, and it's not lost on him how slavishly he sometimes mimics their gestures, making a steeple of his forefingers when listening attentively or lowering his eyes modestly to confess a small failing.) He isn't a zealot, and Edward will do what seems right to him even if it's technically against the law. The property law Edward honors absolutely is the principle protecting clear title to ideas. He told his students, probably too often and stridently, that he wouldn't countenance plagiarism. Plagiarism makes him angry. Wherever this repugnance originated—in the high-minded atmosphere of New Hampshire lecture halls or at his own dining room table, listening to his dad tell, as though they were his own, stories already told (and told better) by Doc—Edward feels this revulsion through and through.

Which is why he is so provoked when Laura cheats on a writing assignment. He had assigned a fall term paper that was due before the Christmas break. His students have been reading frontier journals, especially diaries kept by farmers and their wives, and he has asked them to imagine themselves into the skins of those who came north rather than went west. What motivated them? What drew them to such a cold, thin-soiled, bony, fruitless place? There, for the plucking, was the Ohio River Valley; what tempted the English and French and others to journey upriver, against current and logic and self-regard? Raven Kill's hard corner of the Colonial world was first settled by Dutch folk, for whom even the Catskills weren't cold and mean enough. Edward's assignment to his class was to write imaginary journals of this migration, recording the perils and conquests and incentives and misgivings of a Dutch father, son, daughter, wife, servant, whatever.

This project began in late October, giving his students plenty of time to mull it over, choose a point of view, and start writing. The following day, Laura had approached Edward on the mountain. It was a gray afternoon, drizzling and cold; she was drenched. Edward and the team were on the seventy-meter jump the school uses for climbing exercises. Before Raven Kill has snow to train on, the ski team is obliged to run up one set of the ski tower's stairs and down the other set, single file, the equivalent of four or five stories. Edward stands at the top to keep the kids moving, though they don't need much motivation: These are mostly serious alpine racers.

Laura had already done six or seven circuits; and each time she reached the top she cocked her head at him, as if she expected him to say something to her other than *come on come on come on keep it up move move come on that's the ticket*. Finally, red-faced and bright-eyed from exertion, her sweaty hair stuck to her cheeks, she paused at the summit and began to talk to him all in a rush. Edward wasn't listening carefully; he was irritated because she'd jammed the system, blocking the students below her, breaking the rhythm of the exercise. He asked was she sick or hurt, and when she shook her head, he told her to *move, go go go*. But she just stood there, talking, and Edward realized she was telling him she wanted to write about someone other than a dumb Dutch farmer or his wife. Behind her a student hollered, "Hey, enjoying the view up there?" In fact, it is a remarkable sight, looking down the sheer headwall and then below the run-out to spruce and pines and across the lake's gray shoreline to Blackberry Mountain. But Laura wasn't looking. She was saying she wanted to write about a young girl going west instead of coming way up here. Edward might have sounded out her reasons, but the students were shouting, cold in their sweaty clothes, and he just wanted her to keep moving, so he said okay, okay, then forgot all about it.

Every week he asked the class how the imaginary journals were coming along. Some would ask him to look over their journal entries or to help them develop a topic paragraph. He tried to explain that journals, written on the fly, don't trade in paragraphs, don't express theses. This made the students nervous. They didn't know what he expected from them; would he mark down for faulty grammar, written on the fly? He said, "Surprise me." And he was surprised by their anxiety. They pretended to be tough, indifferent to authority. But they were forever asking him, "What do you want, Mr. Jenks?"

If his other students fretted about the assignment, Laura seemed to have it under control. She was casual when he asked her how it was coming along, though Edward did sometimes wonder whether he was observing calm or apathy. Most other students showed him drafts in progress, but when Edward asked to see what Laura was writing, so he could help her with the process of revision, she smiled.

"Don't you trust me?"

"Of course," he said. "That's not the point. I want to help you."

"You've already helped me, tons."

"Well," Edward said, "I'm pleased to hear that."

In fact, he wasn't pleased. He couldn't put his finger on why this was, but Laura talked to him in a way that gave him the willies. And once he had the willies, he was ashamed of them.

"Be patient, Edward. I'll give you exactly what you want."

He let the casual "Edward" pass. Many of the younger teachers allow it, but he knew she was playing with him, and he didn't like it. But students practice their moves. Boys posture; girls flirt. So he chose to ignore her come-on and say nothing more than he meant: "It's not important that you imagine what I want. What's important is that you imagine what it would be like to be a young woman living on a frontier."

"Frontier?" she said. "You bet!"

Fifteen papers and two cases of plagiarism! A lout from the back rows, a sullen dolt from Shaker Heights who can ski like a demon, hastens his inevitable expulsion by a word-perfect theft of an excerpt from Governor William Bradford's account of Plymouth Plantation; the lifted pages have been roughly torn from the school library's copy of *Famous Colonial Diaries*. It's almost impossible not to laugh at this pathetic larceny.

But it is not possible to laugh at Laura's submission. Her paper tells of a holiday trip west, visiting gift shops and diners and theme parks and caverns and lakeside log cabins and all-you-can-eat buffets. This journey is undertaken by two people. They overnight at mountain resorts with antlers jumbled in heaps in the circular drive. The names of the motels are familiar, promising Kozy Kabins situated in shady groves. And there on page five of her paper, without sign of shame, appears legendary Room 342, Humbert Humbert's temporary abode within the fabled Enchanted Hunters. Laura has changed the point of view of the narrative, causing Dolores Haze to tell in tumescent prose of her climactic night with her stepfather, disguised in Laura's first-person account as "the Man."

Edward reads her submission the afternoon he receives it. He has arranged the papers alphabetically, and Laura's last name begins with *S*; nevertheless, he reads her account first.

That night he approaches her at dinner. Although she's local, her mother pays full boarder's tuition to lodge Laura at the school. She's seated at the principal's table, and Edward feels self-conscious leaning down between her and another girl, whispering in her ear that he wants to see her immediately after dinner. She smiles and reaches out to squeeze his arm, which is a gesture, Edward has noticed, that she lavishes on other teachers. He pulls back from the girl's touch as though from a copperhead and blushes. His employer, sitting at the head of the table, gives Edward a puzzled glance, and why not? It's unusual to intrude on dinner with school business.

Edward's two-room apartment is on the second floor of the Boathouse, the dorm where he is housemaster to the male boarders. Committed as it is to co-education, the school makes a policy of giving female teachers a number of male advisees, and vice versa. Advisees come by at all hours of the day and evening, right up to bed check, and it isn't out of the ordinary when Edward answers his door just before ten that night and finds Laura in the hallway. Since she rooms on the ground floor, it's only marginally odd that she's dressed in a flannel nightgown and wearing pink slippers with fur bunny ears. He motions her in. "It's kind of late," he says. "Only a few minutes before lights-out."

Laura shrugs and smiles. "Well," she says, "here I am." Then she shuts the door behind her.

Edward reaches behind her and opens the door. "I need to talk with you."

She reaches behind her to shut the door and says, "What can I do for you?"

"Open the door, for a start."

"But I'm cold, Edward."

"Open the door, please."

She pushes it open with her foot and follows Edward into his study. When she sits beside him on the sofa, he moves to his desk chair. He feels heat like windburn on his face, like furious sunburn on his shoulders and back and belly and behind his quivering knees. "Why did you plagiarize?"

"What makes you ask such a question?"

"Don't play around with me, Laura. I've read Nabokov."

"Edward! Don't you think I take you seriously?" She licks the end of her finger, pretending to remove a speck of something—cigarette paper?—from her tongue.

"Why did you steal from *Lolita*?"

"Don't you think someone else stole from her before I came along?"

Where did she learn to talk this way? "Laura, this is serious. I take this seriously."

"Of course you do." She reaches out to take her teacher's hand. "Isn't there anything we can do about this?" she asks, leaning toward him. Her robe is falling loose.

"I want to hear your explanation," Edward says, covering her hand with his. When she takes his hand and squeezes, he remembers where they are, and who. He pulls his hand away.

"Isn't there anything I can do to make you feel better about this?" she asks.

"I want you to tell me what you thought you were doing with that paper."

"I think that's obvious," she says. "I found a little love story and I improved on it. I hoped it would please you. I don't see why you should have a cow about some make-believe diary. Why not enjoy it?"

"Because it's not your idea!"

"It's never the girl's idea. It's always the man's. That doesn't make it a bad idea." She sits up straight, yawns, fiddles with her hair, turns to the end table and picks up a framed photo of Edward's sister, smiling, fourteen. "I've seen *lots* of pictures of Maisie. She was beautiful, don't you think?"

"What? What are you saying?"

"You know." She yawns again. "So, what are you going to do?"

"What do you think I should do?"

"Close your door," she says.

"Here's what you're going to do. You'll submit another make-believe journal. The journal will conform exactly to the assigned paper. It will be about a young Dutch lady's experience on the northern frontier."

"Okay," she says. "if that's all you want. But I'm not a young lady."

"You are young."

"I don't buy into your definition of young, and I don't want to be a lady. Age is an arbitrary fiction."

"Says who?" her teacher asks. "That sounds like another stolen notion."

She shrugs, and Edward sends her away, doesn't watch her leave. He stands at his window overlooking the dark water, as though watching something out there; he stands there a long time, trembling.

Because he doesn't bust Laura, because he gives her a chance to redeem herself, Edward is stuck with letting the Shaker Heights simpleton get away with his plagiarism. When his teacher confronts him with the excerpt of Governor Bradford's account of Plymouth Plantation, in every particular identical to his imaginary account of Raven Kill Plantation, the boy's vacant eyes narrow.

"Son of a gun!" he says. "The guy ripped me off!"

"That doesn't quite account for it," Edward says. "Bradford died more than three hundred years ago."

"Well, there you are," the boy says. "It's just a coincidence. He lived the same life I dreamed up."

Edward sighs, then says he's thinking of having him expelled. The boy says he aspires only to be a credit to his school and Edward's, that he longs to be a great ski racer. Besides, if he gets the ax, his father will be royally pissed off, and his father's a lawyer. His father's *really* smart, but he has no sense of proportion.

So because of Laura, Edward instructs the nitwit to submit another paper; and when the smirking boy says this would be a major hassle just when race practice is beginning on snow, Edward tells him he should definitely submit the paper, then warns him if it isn't manifestly stupid, he'll know for a fact that it has been stolen. Maybe Edward piles it on a little heavy, but he doesn't like this kid.

Edward gets Laura's resubmission the day after Christmas vacation. What she has written is a diary set in the back of a four-wheel-drive automobile, in motel rooms, and in her mother's bed. It is explicit. It tells of exploits Edward would not admit he's dreamed of. It is tarted up with a thesis about "new frontiers" and pretends to mount a revolution against repressive orthodoxies and bloodless proprieties. Edward doesn't know whether this half-baked philosophy has been cobbled up to satisfy her teacher's assignment that the term paper present a version of life at the edge of a frontier or whether the speculation about the "tyranny of mere chronology" is something Laura had been taught. And on the topic of schooling: much of the pawing and moaning and licking and sucking and humping in her diaries happens on and near this campus.

The second day of the new year, Edward mails her paper and his report of its making to the county's Office for Abused Children, in the person of Helen's dad, Dr. Daimler. The teacher adds a postscript: "I believe this girl has been sexually misused by someone closely connected with Lake Discovery School, and I know I'm not that someone. Now what?"

Fools' Rules

Edward approaches home on foot, skirting the lake, picking his way scrupulously among the icy rocks along the water's edge. At the beach he turns uphill toward his house. The January night is clear, and the air tastes like cold metal. It isn't the cold that takes his breath away. It's Blackberry Mountain, silver-blue under the moon reflecting off the ice; blue spruces glow, creamy with new snow. Across the treeline he sees Doc's house, extravagantly lit, spilling stray light. Edward rubs his hands together, blows into the cuffs of his gloves.

He remembers cross-country skiing with his mom and dad and sister and friends on nights like this. Someone would see the moon and call a neighbor, who would call a pal, who would call a pal . . . . The kids always joined those adventures; they'd wax the skis while their parents fixed hot food. His mom would load a battered stainless-steel thermos with beef broth or thick pea soup. Some of these expeditions began as late as midnight, and they'd all move out in columns, skis hissing through the dry powder, across the meadows, babies riding backward, strapped like papooses to their mother's or father's backs, older kids showing off their flamboyant energy on the uphill leg along an old logging road to the lower slope of the mountain. It has been a couple of years now since Edward has skied with his neighbors; they don't do that anymore, or rig lights for an ad hoc hockey game. Maisie was the skating nut, and after she left no one seemed to get it together to arrange games or figure-skating exhibitions.

He catches himself dreaming in reverse and realizes he's too young for nostalgia. He enters the path to his front door, breathing steadily after his climb up the path, and sees red-rimmed yellow eyes staring at him. It's the raccoon, too hungry to submit to experience and recognize there's no more garbage to be plundered from this house. Edward knows this fellow: He's the grandson or granddaughter of a raccoon he and Maisie used to chase away from the compost heap years ago; until one day, after they'd sent him lumbering into the woods, he suddenly decided what the hell, turned, stood his ground, and spat a warning at the kids. They'd put out a Havahart trap and found him at sunup. He'd dragged the heavy trap thirty yards, to the deck outside their bedroom. The peanut-butter crackers they'd put in there for bait were gone, and he was curled up fast asleep with his bandit's mask across his eyes. He was plump and healthy, and Maisie took his picture. Then Teddy contrived a way to spring him loose, and after that they all lived in peace and harmony one with another, on the coon's terms, happily ever after.

Thinking *happily ever after* makes Edward shake his head. He's becoming comfortable with irony. He opens the front door, switching on the antique lantern in the front hall. It's cold in here. Not freezing, because he hasn't drained the pipes. A Raven Kill real estate agent told him that an unheated house chills prospective buyers, so Edward's kept the thermostat at fifty. A few people have seen the house—bottom-fishing for a steal in this depressed market. Now Edward turns up the heat, recoiling from the flamboyant *whoosh* as the furnace fires up. He thinks about his father. What happened to them all? Once upon a time they thought they were lucky, that they'd made good luck by being good people. Maybe most people think such things—for a while—about their parents, their kids, themselves. Edward doesn't care now what most people think or thought; he wants to know what happened to his family. He wants to understand.

On the second floor he sets about making tea, after he lights the crumpled paper and kindling beneath the birch logs ready in the Franklin stove. The stove reminds him of better days, when he and Maisie, sitting near the fire, read and bullshitted and played Battleships and Monopoly and Scrabble and then—in her mature phase—chess. He remembers that Maisie meddled too much with his fires, moving the logs, even though he knew better than to mess with hers.

Edward sighs. He wants to control his memories tonight, not let them wash him away willy-nilly. He has a purpose. He stoops to open a cabinet door beneath the red-oak bookcase and removes a slide projector, carousels, a Super 8 movie projector, a shoe box filled with fifty-foot reels of home movies. He begins with the slides, gathering a couple of trays labeled "Raven Kill Independence Days" in his father's fussy calligraphy. The kettle whistles, and he pours boiling water over his mom's leaf strainer, filled with her favorite Ceylon tea, into his father's favorite cup, something Doc had made and given him as a birthday gift. Edward blows steam from the tea, sips, takes a deep breath. He projects the first slides against a wall beside the stove. The projector's light mixes on the wall with firelight; the effect is soft, confused.

What he sees is ancient: laddies in kilts blowing bagpipes, marching together with hippies in tie-dye and long hair who are sucking on bongs and giving the peace sign, brothers and sisters all. Then, a couple men near his age now, parading with a banner: MAKE LOVE NOT WAR. Despite himself, Edward laughs. He's laughed at this before; it's Doc and his father. But his laughter tonight sounds forlorn in the empty house, and it calls back memories of his dad telling stories he himself found so amusing that Jinx'd break up before the punch line, gasping incoherently and weeping from pleasure while the family tried to figure out what he was trying to convey.

The slides have been arranged chronologically; Edward moves through the early years, pauses for a moment to examine a baby—held by her mother—wearing American flag diapers. Maisie. He can hear his parents arguing about exactly when that picture was taken, but they could argue about pretty much anything.

Here's a slide of the lakeshore, Doc's Fool's Rules Regatta: a blue ribbon to the first vessel to reach the little island and return, whatever could float, moved by oar or paddlewheel or sail. The trick was, contestants couldn't begin building their boats till an hour before the starting gun. Ann and Jinx had won the first two years. Now here's Maisie watching her mom and dad raising sail, a Blue Seal Feed croker sack on a broomstick mast. Maisie's four or five, skinny and gawky. Her fine hair falls below her shoulders, but she looks like a boy: it's how she carries herself, swaggering, leading with her chin. Later pictures show them together: There Teddy's holding hands with his sister, who must be eleven or twelve; here she's standing on her head, grinning. Maisie just can't be serious. She sticks her thumbs in her ears and wags her fingers like rabbit ears, sticks out her tongue, plays grab-ass with whoever's around. Maisie's all grin and fuck you; Teddy is composed, solemn in front of the camera, aware that he's being put into the record. Watching this now, he is discouraged with himself, realizes he's always been too old for his own good. He feels fatally conventional, the very type of middle-aged, middle-class oldster this place stood in opposition to.

He sighs, focuses on an image projected against the wall. The Independence Day parade is grand in these photos, with out-of-town sightseers clotting the route past the bandstand, down past the Emporium and covered bridge. The floats have become elaborate, and Edward remembers staying up all night to build them. Here's a slide of the construction site in Doc's huge workshop, another showing Maisie in a carpenter's apron and bandanna, tenpenny nails between her lips, hammering a cross-member to the frame. This float was to represent "The Great Flood." Doc had designed a motif showing hail falling (mothballs time-released from buckets— painted to look like thunderheads—suspended on invisible wires), cresting waves, mermaids; Maisie and half a dozen other young girls from Blackberry Mountain were the mermaids. Doc was Triton, carrying a three-pronged farm tool that made him look from certain angles like Noah and from others like Lucifer brandishing his pitchfork.

That was the only Blackberry Mountain parade float for twenty summers that didn't win the grand prize. The flood of that spring hadn't been the stuff of magic or parody to local farmers, some of whom were wiped out when the Raven Kill overran its banks and devastated their crops. There were no foreclosures, but a few farmers working close to the edge in the best of seasons had been forced to sell out to ski developers, whom the environmentalists of Blackberry Mountain routinely opposed.

Now, as the slides show Maisie in her mermaid outfit, Edward notices her breasts. She wears lipstick and rouge on her cheeks. She is willowy. She strikes poses. Edward rubs his eyebrows, sips cautiously at his tea, but it is cold. The room is warm, and as he leans forward to shut the damper, he thinks he hears a noise somewhere in the house. He couldn't say what causes him to call out, "Maisie!" He is

surprised how loud his voice sounds. Most of the furniture
has been removed by his mother, the curtains likewise, and
the hardwood floors are bare of rugs.

In his memory he hears her name called out again, but now
it's his mother's voice: "Maisie? Teddy, Teddy, answer me,
Ed-ward! Where's Maisie? Let's get a wiggle on. Maisie?
Where are you? We'll be late."

This was the Independence Day following the spring of the
flood, and Maisie was in his room, asking him to help arrange
her costume. Her muttered response to their mother's urgency: "Put a sock in it, for Christ's sweet sake!" She was—
what, fourteen? "They sound like Ozzie and Harriet, can you
believe it?" He and his sister had heard some antique radio
show on a nostalgia station broadcast from Troy, and now
Maisie did an accurate takeoff of Henry Aldrich's refrain:
"Co-ming, Co-ming, Mother!" Now their father chimed in.
"If you're late, young lady, it'll be your funeral!" Maisie said,
louder than Teddy would've, "Oh, stuff it!"

Watching these slides, Edward smiles as he recalls his sister's brassy nerve. She had raced from the house that year,
running headlong to Doc's to board the parade float. Teddy,
in costume, had been right behind her. They sat beside each
other up top while the tractor pulled them down to Raven
Kill, where the parade always began south of the bandstand.
"Birds of a Feather" was the float's motif; its theme was
diversity, the fabled melting pot. The float was designed as
a huge cage, with all its doors and windows wide open so that
birds in different-colored costumes—blue, yellow, green—
could come and go, gather and part as they pleased. A black
crow walked weeping beside a white dove wearing eyepatches
and a sign around his neck: BLINDED BY RACISM. Maisie
perched inside the cage on a crossbar; she had a gorgeous
coat of white feathers, and attached to her face was a long

predator's beak, yellow, with a red spot at the corners of the hinge, like a seagull's: BILL OF RIGHTS, it was labeled. Edward soon tires of this juggernaut of goodwill, so patiently recorded. Advancing the carousel, he sees Maisie in several other slides, proud in her startling costume, secretive maybe, with her eyes diverted from the camera, pictured usually beside Doc, tricked up as a cardinal, in bloodred silk. A final slide shows her whispering in his ear.

That series is the last in the slide tray, and Edward has yet to find what he's searching for. Now he sets up the movie projector and watches grainy, jumpy pictures of him and Maisie playing as kids, of the raccoon caught by floodlights as it looted the compost heap, of his parents hugging and laughing.

Edward watches parade after parade. At seven or eight he's scrambling up a foam and papier-mâché Blackberry Mountain—snowcapped, with a little sign marked EL. 23,500 FT—wearing glacier goggles and a backpack, with Maisie climbing behind to goose him. Even the dogs wear flags and bunting. Another year: Here comes the float "My Busy Honey Bee," inspired by the state insect; Teddy and Maisie, wearing long cardboard stingers and squash-racket wings, buzz dangerously and dart in and out of the cheering crowd.

Edward feels a pounding ache behind his eyes, rattling his nerves. This cuteness, this pep, this zip and enterprise, this irreverence, this novelty and invention, this *playfulness*—it was all so exhausting, one bright idea coming right after another with the same relentless high spirits. It was a drag, Edward thinks, and at once he tries to hide the thought even from himself. He wonders what it would've been like to grow up in a regular town, in Albany or even Syracuse.

His hands feel heavy, fingers numb. He threads into the projector a fifty-foot reel of Maisie turning cartwheels. She's nine or ten, he suspects, and dressed in a peasant skirt. She goes through her routine with deliberation and self-conscious grace, over and over. As she kicks her legs into the air, her skirt tumbles down her skinny tanned legs, and Edward can see her underpants, cotton, with little teddy bears stamped on the cloth. The machine feeds out the end of the spool, and he sits there, listening to the raucous slap of the film's tongue as the take-up spool spins; the projector's dusty lens throws mottled white light against the white wall, and the stove sputters in the background, casting an orange pall through the room. Next he watches a reel taken by his sister, the movie devoted to a pair of black-capped chickadees feeding on suet she'd put on the snow-covered deck outside her bedroom window. The chickadee was Maisie's special bird, a kind of mascot or spirit fellow, plucky and persistent, impossible to frighten or dissuade.

By now it's almost dawn, and Edward doubts he'll find what he wants: scenes from the day when she went in. He rummages again in the storage cabinet, sees the dusty video camera. Their father had bought the camera for Maisie a month before that final parade. He slips a cassette labeled "4 July" in the VCR. His father had taken this tape. The slides, the movies—those were mostly his mother's work, since Jinx had been busy building floats, parading, joining in the action. But this time, Maisie's year, he hadn't joined the parade. He had held himself at a distance; at the time, Edward had been bewildered by his unaccountable standoffishness. Now his heart goes out to his father. He father must have seen enough, had it—as he used to say—up to here. Edward remembers that back then, in the weeks and months before Maisie's last parade, his father's spirits had sagged. He'd seemed distracted, and Teddy had put this down to business losses. But those, of course, were nothing new.

The first sequence shows the float being built. The motif was the Olympic Games, and the challenge was to invent games unlikely to provoke the competitive spirit. It was a foggy notion even then; now Edward knows it's bullshit. Turning up the volume, he watches and listens to the float being put together from scratch: hurdles, rowing oars, a diving board. Doc runs around, giving orders—"Come on, man, get that thing framed up; hey, baby, bring me a joist hanger"—pulling his crew together. It seems never-ending. Edward's mouth is dry; his eyes burn. About to switch it off, he suddenly sits up straight as, off-camera, Maisie's voice says plainly, "I told you, don't call me baby."

Her father must've been as surprised as Edward by the anger in her voice. The video camera wheels around, seeking her out. But she remains out of sight. Then, off-camera, Doc says, barely a whisper, "Getting pissed off won't change anything. Grow up."

The voice that replies is edgy, unfamiliar. It might or might not be his sister's. "I *did* grow up. That's my sin, isn't it?"

The tape sweeps to Doc. Shrugging, he's standing beside a girl of about fourteen from down in Raven Kill. Somebody's baby-sitter. Edward tries to remember her name. Didn't she live that summer on Blackberry Mountain? He doesn't recall seeing her since. She helped Doc around the shop in return for woodworking lessons, claiming she wanted to become a cabinetmaker. On tape, Doc's helping her align two framing members in a crude joint. She drives a couple of nails, and Doc applauds her rough work extravagantly. The scene, sustained as it is, concentrating on the girl's uninteresting achievement and Doc's excessive enthusiasm, makes Edward uneasy. And he wonders why his father held the shot so long. Then he guesses why. This *is* Doc Halliday, teaching by reward, blarney, naked charm. Doc hugs the girl, and she blushes; she looks him full in the face. He brushes a strand of hair from her eyes. He notices the camera then and stares at it, squinting. He's mock-angry, or truly angry. Just then Maisie enters the frame, approaching her father and filling the frame. Her face is red and distorted by—what, shame? Anger or grief? The shot breaks off.

On the tape, Edward can hear the rock band warming up on the balcony of the Emporium: the Fandango Groovemasters, the leader proclaiming, "Dudes laid down their lives so we can lay down our licks and groove for you, DO YOU DIG!" There are several dutiful shots of antique cars; the VFW marches past carrying rifles with flowers stuck down their barrels. A flyover of jets from the Air National Guard provokes baleful looks skyward from Edward's friends and neighbors, handsome young men wearing suspenders and straw boater hats, bearded, their faces gaunt with good health from strenuous exercise, the women freckled and tanned and exuding competence. A community to excite pride. So why is Edward cast down? He shifts in his chair. The collar of his crewneck sweater chokes him; his back aches dully. But he continues to sit there. It's coming now, he can feel it.

Now the *tableau vivant* of the Blackberry Mountain float: Maisie stands on a springboard cantilevered from the rear of the truck bed. Her role is to make diver's motions, and she does this listlessly, grimly. Below her, marching in matching athletic uniforms, a half dozen or so communards affect a victory march. They variously hold hands or drape their arms over one another's shoulders in a show of concord. Once again his father holds the shot uncomfortably long. The camera is unsteady, but not unsteady enough: from a vantage abreast of the float, moving with it, the lens shows Maisie looking down at the marchers beneath her, and in the front row, holding hands, Doc and his apprentice woodworker. So there it was—lovebirds, that's the story. Part of the story. Enough of it. A band plays a Sousa march, but Edward can hear the wheels of the float turning, the axles wanting grease. Maisie wears a black one-piece bathing suit. Doc walks close to the pretty young apprentice; she takes a hit off a balloon filled with helium and the sound track picks up her inhumanly squeaky giggle. Doc laughs heartily. Edward believes they're squeezing hands, but maybe he's imagining this. Maisie looks straight down at Doc; he looks up at her, then looks away. He rests his arm on the bare shoulder of the young girl— what *was* her name?—and she leans into him. The penny rattles around, rolls into position, drops. Now Edward knows, if ever he didn't, where Maisie learned what she learned, and who taught her. Back on the float, Maisie springs on the diving board, higher and higher and higher; she will surely dive into the marchers below. From behind the camera, their father shouts, "Maisie! What are you doing?" And Edward, too, shouts into the empty room: "No!" The shot is broken.

Now Maisie is on the road, standing stiffly between the police barrier and the floats, poised for an act. Then she turns a sudden, awkward cartwheel. The crowd stares at her, bewildered. She turns another, and another. Where is Doc? People have begun to applaud. Maybe this is part of the show. She is into it now, cartwheeling past the bandstand, inward and private, going against the flow of the parade. The crowd is raucous in its approval. She keeps going, crests the little hill beyond the church, and disappears from the frame.

There is a final sequence, truncated, at the swimming hole. His sister stands on a lichen-coated rock, wearing that black one-piece bathing suit. The falls trickle fitfully down a mossy ravine behind her. She looks down, full into the lens. She makes a quick move, lowering the shoulder straps of her suit. The camera draws the curtain across this scene, but in the confusion it had been left running. It shows nothing of the event, but Edward hears the clamor of amazement and fury and pain; he hears his own voice, shouting helpless nonsense. He hears Doc telling everyone to make way for him. He hears gossip, the awful things people can say when they think they can't be heard. He hears the siren. And that's the end of the picture show.

Now he knows. And his father? Who can say what Jinx understood? Now Edward understands that it wasn't because of him that his sister dove into a rock a few months after their climb together, their exploration.

The sun has crossed the horizon now at Edward's back. He feels light-headed, as though he's been drinking all night, all week, all his life. He's shaky; his eyes are red; he can't swallow. The video makes snowy static on the television screen.

He doesn't hear him, but he sees his outline shadowed against the wall behind the television set. Edward doesn't turn around. He knows who's at his back. Let's see.

"Hey," Doc says. "Shouldn't you be in the dorm? What are you doing here?"

"It's my house. What are *you* doing here?"

"What do you mean? I have an interest. We're way beyond titles and deeds in this community. Anyway, your father asked me to look in on the place when you weren't here."

"I'm here."

"I can see that." Doc comes around the chair, faces Edward, stands above him. "So what have you been looking at all night?"

"You don't know?"

Doc shakes his head.

"Should I believe that? Should I believe you're looking after my family's best interests?"

"Why not?"

"I was looking at pictures my mom and dad took—Thanks-givings, fall cleanup, brush clearing, house-raisings, Indepen-dence Days."

"You should've called. I would've loved to see all that with you."

"Really?" Edward says. "You think so?"

He waits for Doc to say something that will start this thing moving to its end. But when he doesn't speak, Edward's frus-trated and relieved. This is more difficult than he'd imagined. He can't connect the man standing above him—cautious in his speech and anxious in his eyes, stinking of sweat—to the figure that he'd just discovered caught on tape.

"Those were sure the days," Doc says. He waits for Edward to answer, and when Edward says nothing, staring at the television screen white with static, Doc turns around and shuts off the set. "Weren't they?"

"What?" Edward says.

"Those days. All you kids growing up. I'm glad I was able to give it to you."

"You? Give us what?"

"Why, *this*," Doc says. "The mountaineers, Blackberry-style. All of us bound together. Playing together. Learning. Teaching. You know, to each according to his ability, from each according to his—"

"Or *her*," Edward says.

"Pardon?"

"His or her ability, his or her need."

"Yeah," Doc says, "that's right."

Edward knows he isn't going to start this now. Perhaps he's afraid. Perhaps the habits of affection are slow to die. Edward hasn't yet learned to hate this man he hasn't even learned not to love. He doesn't know what to say.

"You miss her," Doc says.

"Who?"

"Your sister."

When Edward begins to rise from his chair, Doc puts a hand on his shoulder.

"Take it easy," Doc says. "You're tired. Go to bed. I'll leave you alone now."

"Yes," Edward says. "That would be good."

"We all miss her," Doc says. "I do."

Brother and Sister Act

This morning, Edward asked for a couple of days' personal leave, which the principal hesitantly granted. He's been guarded with Edward, who can understand the human instinct to shy away from someone who gets the black spot. But the principal has visibly recoiled from him and seems disgusted by the sight of Laura's teacher—as if Edward had traduced that child.

No sooner did he request personal leave than the rumors began to fly. Edward assumes that the principal is the author of this gossip. As soon as he'd reported Laura's situation to him, the principal warned Edward that he was climbing way out on a limb, that the girl hadn't officially complained, that repeating allegations was a reckless act.

"You've put us all in a hard place, Edward. We're looking at a lot of potential damage here."

"How about actual damage?" Edward came back.

"I beg your pardon?"

"I'm talking about the girl," Edward said.

"I'm not," said the principal.

In any case, by lunchtime today Edward hears conversations switch off whenever he comes near. He's certain they're whispering, his colleagues and the students, that Edward Jenks is about to be charged with sexual harassment, contributing to the delinquency of a minor, statutory rape, violation of the Mann Act, whatever. He's been put on indefinite unpaid leave. It's a smoke-and-fire deal, case closed. It doesn't help that the principal approaches Edward at his table and tells him, in a grave voice, that he'd appreciate seeing him "in a formal setting"—that's how they say "lawyer" these days—as soon as he returns from leave.

Now he's in the air above the Mohawk River, flying to New York City. He hasn't seen his sister since last summer. When Edward was about to graduate, he talked with her briefly about the possibility of going to graduate school in New York, or finding a job there. Maisie hadn't told him in so many words that she'd rather he kept away, but her tone—taciturn and wary—told Edward more than he wanted to hear about how she felt.

It isn't that his sister doesn't seem to care about him. The idea of him seems to suit her fine. Every now and then a friend of a friend, cousin of a cousin, brings him reports of Maisie. He knows that she praises him behind his back, sweetly, with pride, overselling his achievements, his reliability, his loyalty. He himself exaggerates the goodwill of his mom and dad when he describes them to strangers; to cohere, he believes, is natural. He is ashamed of what has happened to them all—what they've let happen, the carelessness of it—even as he understands that their history is a common story, letting one day slide into the next without noticing, without taking care.

These past few years, when they talk on the phone, her voice flattens as she asks about his plans and dreams, but he can hear in her persistence a restive urgency. And when he phoned to share what seemed at the time a calamity—their parents' mutual distrust, or another of his failed romances— her response had always been fiercely possessive: *Remember, Teddy, we have each other. No one can know us as well as we know each other. Don't let anyone take us away from each other.* When he recently pointed out that they seldom see each other, that they know each other chiefly through occasional letters and telephone calls, she accused Edward of being "literal," whatever that meant. No: he knows what she means.

The plane banks as they turn down the Hudson, and before long he sees the city, lit at dusk, and he's dizzy from imaginative overload. He doesn't know what he'll say, or ask, or learn, or do. He wishes he could stay up here, circling like a falcon on an updraft, looking down at a grand illusion of beauty, disengaged from the mess that human beings make of their earth, their neighborhoods, their families, themselves.

Maisie insists on cooking him dinner. Edward would prefer to treat her to Chinese food or—what the hell—Cuban or Portuguese or Thai, a meal of shared dishes, food a travel magazine editor should enjoy. But Maisie says she doesn't need the hassle of taxis and overheated restaurants, but that's exactly what he longs for, the novelty, noise, and motion. He sits at the card table in the dining nook of Maisie's efficiency apartment while she cooks vegetarian spaghetti sauce. At first it's all small talk: "How's Mom doing? Is Dad paying his bills? Is teaching still intimidating you?" Edward glances around his sister's apartment. It's on the Upper East Side, Sixty-ninth between Second and Third, in a nondescript cream concrete high rise thrown up during the late fifties, early sixties, one the same as the next, with their plastic-paneled elevators, linoleum-floored hallways, Sheetrock walls, gray metal doors. Maisie had moved here from another apartment not unlike it, and Edward's surprised. He had expected his sister to choose something funky for herself; reading about New York, imagining her here, he's forever putting her in a loft in TriBeCa or a brownstone in Brooklyn Heights or at least a big shabby flat on the West Side. She has explained the economic and logistic realities, but still.

Except for the cat fur, the interior is antiseptic, generically homey. A fine Turkish prayer rug hangs on the wall behind a convertible sofa bed, and several throw pillows are covered with remnants of other Oriental rugs. There are framed photographs on the end tables: Ann and Jinx, their house, the raccoon poised at the compost heap, the vegetable garden her mom had helped Maisie plant when she was fifteen. The photo of that midsummer garden strikes a blow to Edward's heart, because he realizes it must have been taken while Maisie was in the hospital in Albany. Maisie didn't have a green thumb. She was impatient, which was why Teddy hated to fish with her. She must have burned the plants with too much organic fertilizer, because they poked up stunted, an unwholesome Day-Glo orange.

While Maisie stirs the sauce and tells about the "ruinous price of tomatoes, imported from goddamn Holland," Edward pours himself a Genesee ale and notices an elephant's foot umbrella stand bristling with a collection of his sister's canes. She walks with a limp: one leg is shorter than the other, and visibly withered. She punctuates her steps with a slight grimace, more from habit, he suspects, than from pain, but in this, as in much else touching his sister, he understands he might be mistaken. He's relieved at least that she doesn't wear slacks to hide her trouble. Tonight she's wearing a short denim skirt, and her legs are vividly pale, luminously white. He wants to stare at them, but he looks away; he's afraid she'll misunderstand his interest.

The canes are gifts from friends and colleagues, brought back from far-off lands. Silver-headed, brightly painted, blackthorn—the variety is impressive, and a testament to the number of her friends, to their affection, and to her unblinking view of what she calls her "glitch." What can Edward say? He has no sense of humor about the canes. The canes make him sad. That Maisie's such a good sport about what she's done to herself and to the rest of them, it's unfathomable.

The phone rings a couple of times while she cooks. She's switched her answering machine on, but still it broadcasts the caller's message. "Maisie, where are you? I need to confer. Can you *believe* what that pill Madora said about my edit of the Yucatán piece . . ." and, "Pick up. I know you're in. Susie has gum disease. Help!" Each time, she turns the heat down to simmer, motions Edward to stir—"Be a sweetie"— and picks up. The guy complaining about the managing editor gets an empathetic ear from Edward's sister, though the piece itself can't possibly be as lengthy as their conversation. Maisie is diplomatic and attentive, explaining that "Madora's under a lot of pressure now that the book goes to bed a month earlier; I'm sure she didn't mean to be hurtful," et cetera, et cetera—a conversation Edward wishes he couldn't hear. His beautiful sister—brushing the bangs out of her eyes, fiddling with the appliqué on her Mexican blouse, doodling on a Post-it pad, expertly cradling the receiver in the crook of her neck, turning away from her brother's line of vision—is wholly engrossed by who said what at the office, and in what tone of voice. The second call absorbs her, too, somebody's bleeding gums. After five minutes, into his third Genny, Edward realizes that the ailing one is a cat. His sister lavishes medical advice, home remedies, a vet's emergency phone number, all of it with a mannered reassurance. He crosses his fingers in hopes that when she finally hangs up, she won't tell him more about either call than he already knows.

She doesn't. She smiles, pats his hand, asks him to open a jug of Chilean red she's put on the harvest table. He feels jittery, sour, and angry at himself for his selfishness. All this time he's nourished a version of his sister as she was, and these phone chats and cute canes violate the soft boyishness of that vision. He wonders if the emotion so bewildering him now is jealousy. They sit across from each other, spooning out portions of spaghetti and salad. Maisie's cats rub aggressively against Edward's ankles.

"We have a case of unrequited love here," he says. "These cats are making a heavy pass at me."

Maisie stares at him and cocks her head, seeming almost ready to smile. She does not smile: "Hero and Leander."

"Better than Cupid and Psyche," he says.

"Or Pyramus and Thisbe," she says.

"Better than Maisie and—"

"They've been fixed," she says.

"Pardon?"

"Spayed. Neutered. They're not in love with you; they're only hungry."

"You just fed them."

"They're always hungry."

Edward hates that Maisie has cats. He hates that their litter box occupies so much space in this pinched dwelling. He hates that the stuff in that box is called Kitty Litter. He hates that her cats have cute names. He hates that she's a member of a cat sorority, that whoever has a cat named Susie with bleeding gums thought first to phone his sister for authoritative advice and sympathy. He hates that they're sitting across from each other in a brightly lit room, divided by colored candles flickering cutely in cute little painted Dutch candleholders showing cute farm kids in clogs standing beneath cute windmills. He hates that they're eating skimpy portions of predictable food. He hates that Maisie sleeps in a convertible bed whose spread is covered with cat hair, and most of all Edward hates what makes him hate all these things. He wants to be different, wants not to have led the life that has brought him here tonight for the reason he has come. He wants to go back—to the tent, to before the tent. He wants them to have reached a fork in the road way back home and to have taken the other way. He thinks this in confused sequences while he watches his sister wipe burgundy from the corner of her mouth. She is beautiful, and he wants to tell her so.

She stares at him, then sticks out her tongue. "More wine?"

He nods. "It's good." The excellence of the wine isn't why he's drinking so much tonight. He's drinking to transfer command to his instincts. As soon as he tells himself this, he realizes that he's not drinking for that reason either, or for any reason that needs words.

She brings grapes to the table and a wedge of Brie softened in her toaster oven. Then the phone rings again. In a room so small, the sound makes Edward jump. "Please don't answer," he says.

Maisie blows her brother a kiss as a woman's voice comes over the answering machine, hysterical, weeping, complaining about "Derek" and his need for space, fouled weekend plans, every unhappy cliché that Edward has ever heard about people who live lives like those. He catches himself: Lives like *whose*? Then the woeful one seems to bore herself with her litany, signs off: "What should I do? Call me back right away. Are you walking the kitties? Ciao."

Maisie makes no move to answer. He walks behind her

chair, rubs her shoulders. She feels tense, hunched, cramped. "Why are you here?" she says, arching back her neck, letting her hair sweep over his hands.

"I want to know what happened."

She turns in her chair to look up at him. "What *happened*? What?"

"Don't be that way," he says. "With him."

"With who?"

"Please," he says.

"You're a fine one to pry," she says. "You have secrets, too."

"One secret. And it's our secret, not mine."

"Whatever," she says.

He's still standing behind her, but he can see that she can see his face in an oval mirror that distorts his features. He doesn't like the picture he makes, and he removes his glasses. "Did you ever think, when we ran away that time, when we hid out smoking dope in a tent with wild animals out there, did you ever dream you'd end up hiding in this shithole, married to a couple of fucking cats?"

Looking into his face, Maisie doesn't seem angry. "Don't be a drip," she says. "We didn't *run away* and there weren't any *wild animals* and I haven't ended up anywhere."

"I love you, Maisie."

"Do you really? That's nice."

"Don't be so hard. What did he do to you?"

"Who sent you? Mom?"

"I came for myself. We've got to understand this."

"You sound like some social worker. What's the routine? Are you going to *empower* me? Am I supposed to go to victims' group sessions, sit on a folding metal chair in the gym and say, 'Hi, my name's Maisie and I'm a survivor'? Doughnuts and decaf at intermission? Hugs all around afterward? From-the-heart sympathy, 'Thanks for sharing that with us; I love you, Maisie'?"

He laughs, despite himself. "Tell me a joke," he says. "You used to tell great jokes."

Maisie stares at Edward. She stands facing him. He wonders what she'll do now. Flush with anger? Slap him? Anything's possible. She raises her arms, circles them around her brother's neck, and says, "You're sweet."

He leans toward her. Her face's a blur.

She draws away, cocks her head again, blinks once, and limps into the kitchen. "We need another bottle of wine. This could be a long night."

After the wine has been opened and poured, they sit beside each other on her sofa bed. "Maisie," he says, and says nothing more.

"What do you want?" she says.

"An account of what happened."

"Put your head in my lap," she says.

He does this, staring up past her face at the ceiling.

His sister leans back against a pillow. "I think I'll let you begin this," she says.

And Edward begins. He tells his sister at tedious length about the assignment he set his class, his devotion to primary historical documents. He detours back to college, his favorite history courses, professors who made an impression on him. What he's doing here . . . what he's trying to get told . . . in a war movie a soldier called this "walking the rounds in." It's so easy to make a fatal mistake. Maisie doesn't interrupt, but he feels her legs stiffen when he names Laura, explains about the *Lolita* paper. Finally, he just says it, "She came on to me."

"And what did you do?"

"Come on, Maisie! What do you think?"

"I don't know! That's why I asked." His face is against her; he can feel her words in a rumbling purr.

"I did the right thing!" His voice comes out tinny, false.

"Which was?"

Now he sits up, looks at her, shakes his head. "Are you kidding?"

"Oh no, I'm not kidding." She pours more wine into both glasses.

"I tried to help; I pretended to ignore it."

"Is she pretty?"

"What's that got to do with anything?"

"Plenty," Maisie says. "It has plenty to do with everything. Don't be a dope."

"I guess she's pretty."

"You guess?"

"What's the matter with you?" he says.

"What's the matter with *you*? You used to be a red-blooded boy." She pats his forehead as if she were his mom and he were a boy with a fever.

"I'm a teacher!"

"Yeah?"

"She's wicked pretty." Trying to drink from his wineglass, he spills on his shirt and her bedspread. "Shit! I'm sorry, Maisie."

"Calm down. Don't be so supersensitive." When he dabs at his shirt, she stills his hand, squeezes it.

"How can you be too sensitive?" he asks. Something is happening to him, and he wants to listen carefully; maybe she knows things he doesn't know. That's why he's here, isn't it?

"Sometimes," she says, "you have to let your body tell your head what's what. Your head debates with your body, not with the outside world."

"Say what?"

Maisie laughs, running her fingers through her brother's hair. "The homilies, I guess. Wisdom of the tribe."

"You were his lover, weren't you?"

Maisie's fingers stop what they've been doing, and her body freezes. She laughs again, differently, a sharp intake, a nasty, mirthless bark. "Oh," she says, "what an old-fashioned boy. Aren't you darling!" The way she says "darling" couldn't be less affectionate.

"Why are you like this?" her brother asks. "You're playing with me."

"Am I?" she asks. "I can't imagine why." Maisie stands and limps to the kitchenette; the cats stumble after her, rubbing gracelessly against her ankles, wanting to be fed again. Edward thinks then of something Doc told him: that people are like animals, creatures of habit, that what feels good once, they'll do over and over until they can't do it anymore, or can't afford to do it, or until they find something that feels better. Edward's sister busies herself rinsing dishes, turns to her brother and smiles. "You can't expect this to be easy, Teddy."

"You're right. I'm sorry. I don't have any rights here. This"—he makes a sweeping motion, taking in her apartment, her new life—"doesn't belong to me."

"Don't say that," she says. "That's theatrical."

"Do you remember what happened?" Edward asks.

"Remember what?" she says.

"Do you remember what you did? What he did to you?"

She shrugs and, pouring another glass of wine, asks if he'll join her. He nods. "I can't remember," she says, "what I can't remember."

"Can you feel holes in your memory? Subtractions?"

"What they call deficits?" she says, staring at him as though this is a test and he's failing.

He tries to see this from her point of view: She has spun a fine web for herself, workable but fragile. Edward imagines her as coiled, alert to predators. He sees how he must seem to her, reckless and naïve in his appetite for answers and justice. "Maisie, this has got to stop. It can't go on. We've got to put a stop to this."

"To *this*?" she says, doing a pretty good imitation of someone simply confused.

"What did Doc Halliday do to you? When did it start?"

"Let's listen to some music," Maisie says. "I've got something I want you to hear."

"I'm not here to listen to music, goddamn it! I can hear music anywhere. I didn't come this far to listen to fucking records!"

"Come this far? You've got a country boy's sense of distance. You're still a Blackberry Mountain kid—stuck in the mud. Learn from me," Maisie says.

She sits on the floor with her ankles crossed and pats the floor beside her for him to join her.

He thinks he's being patronized but can't be certain. As bewildering as these hours have been, he's hungry for her company and somehow feels himself connecting with her after all these years. "I learned a lot from you," he says, in a voice harder than he intends.

Maisie laughs. "Oh, that! Forget about it. That was nothing. That was just to calm you down when you got all freaked out about grizzly bears or Bigfoot or ghosts or wind in the branches. That didn't mean"—and she snaps her fingers viciously—"squat."

Edward feels his face flush with anger and shame. "You don't mean that," he says. "I think of it all the time. How could you say such a thing?"

"Maybe to teach you to be a little careful with me. Do you dream about me?" She flicks hair from her eyes, licks her finger, and brushes away a nonexistent piece of cigarette paper from her lower lip. Laura did this, in just this way, in Edward's dorm room.

"Sometimes," he says.

"Well I don't dream about you. Telling a girl you dream about her . . . Teddy, that's a tired pickup line. You want to retire that line, learn some smoother moves." She puts a record on the turntable. He's heard it before, during that evil summer. Muddy Waters singing the blues. His sister smiles at him and sits beside him and takes his hand in hers. It's a gentle gesture, familiar and unstudied.

"It doesn't do you any good to make me feel like a kid," he says. "I'm going to find out what he did to you, and when, and what he did to others."

"On behalf of little Laura?" Maisie says.

"In part."

"What a good citizen. Does that make you proud of yourself?"

"No," he says.

"Good." Then she leans forward awkwardly and kisses him lightly on the lips.

"What do you remember?"

"Everything," she says. "I've always remembered everything."

Maisie talked quietly, haltingly, as though finding her way through thickets:

"It all began with Dad's Jeep Cherokee. I shouldn't say it *all* began, because I can't say what *all* is, but the turn in the road came when I was thirteen, almost fourteen, and Dad let me drive the Cherokee along some logging trails, with him riding shotgun, and then up and down our driveway, solo. Remember how you pestered me to bring you along? Dad wouldn't allow that. If Mom had had her way, I wouldn't have driven any car anywhere, which made me sore at Mom, but I've got to admit, thirteen was a little young for driving—"

"Don't horse around, Maisie. Talk to me, just tell me."

"It's not like that. It's not like that. It's different. Where was I? Okay, after school let out, Mom and Dad took you in the Subaru to see Grams and visit New York; you were going for a weekend, and I had to stay home for a gymnastics competition, and I was supposed to get a ride to Lake Placid with Army's mom, but when I went to her place Saturday morning, Army said that she'd taken the truck to a fiddler's contest over in Vermont. So there I was with my gym bag and no ride.

"I could say I got this bright idea to steal Dad's Cherokee because I wanted to go to the gym competition. But you'd know better than that. I was glad to be off the hook, hated being judged against other girls. Just because I liked to turn handsprings and wasn't bad at it, that was no reason I had to be what Dad called 'competitive.' That was his trip, admit it. So was your ski racing. And even if I'd wanted to compete, I could've cadged a ride from somebody, so what I really felt was relieved. I had an excuse to blow it off. I also had an excuse, I figured, to drive the Cherokee, although I hadn't worked that out a hundred percent. The important thing was I'd sniffed out where Dad hid the keys, which he hid because he knew I wanted to drive so bad. He trusted me, but not that much."

Edward thinks about this. "He trusted you. He trusted both of us, all the way."

"No, he didn't," Maisie says. "And he was right not to—me, at least. Unqualified trust's foolish. They expected me to lie sometimes. You can't live a life without lies."

Edward blushes, shakes his head. "I don't know where this

is coming from. Lies? You don't know what you're saying."
But he knows she's right. He stands to stretch his cramped
legs, then slouches on the sofa bed. His sister smiles, holding
out her empty glass. He leans forward with the bottle.

"Don't look like your pup died, Teddy. Get with the program, kid. Lies make it possible to live in the same house
with somebody else. You wouldn't want to know the truth
of what I thought of you sometimes. Don't stick out your
lower lip that way—I hate it when you pout. Hey, just kidding! No lie."

Maisie has always been able to throw him off balance. She
was like that on skates, or had been: treacherously deceptive,
taking too much joy from faking him out. Now, trying to
sort out Maisie's story, Edward feels dizzy. Maybe she sees
this, because she slows the narrative.

"So anyway, Army and I swiped the Cherokee and decided
to drive it down to Raven Kill to show off in front of the
Emporium. This was early summer, and the kids would be
hanging around out in their bathing suits, right? And the idea
was, we'd slide up there, and I'd say to Army, like it was our
regular shopping drill—Be an angel, Arm, and grab us some
provisions. And hey, while you're at it, pick me up a root
beer twin-stick. And if one of the kids asked for a ride, I'd
say, Sorry, me and Arm are overdue down in New York City.
And if somebody asked if my 'rents knew I had the Cherokee,
I'd go, Sure I let *them* use it just last night.

"It was a stupid plan, right? Not that it mattered. We never
even made it down the hill. I was dicking around with the
seat, trying to figure out how I could reach the pedals, and
I drove the goddamn thing into that culvert near old man
Brinker's house. Amazingly, I didn't do any damage you could
see, except for a few scratches from saplings. It didn't roll
over, either, though Army was screaming the whole time,

'She's going over, Jesus Maze, she's going over, Jesus, we're going to die.' Good old Army, grace under pressure.

"I don't have to explain why I couldn't use Mr. Brinker's phone to call for help. Anyway, who would I call? You couldn't see the car from the road, so Army and I tried to figure out what to do, and we decided we'd walk back home and see if any of the gang had a good idea. We'd sure helped some of them out of the shit before—"

"What shit?" Edward says suddenly. "How do you mean?"

"Huh? Never mind what shit. Anyway, like I was saying . . . Do you mind if I smoke?"

"Smoke?" he says. "I didn't know you smoked."

"Sometimes I don't. There're lots of things, tons of things, you don't know about me."

"Do tell," Edward says.

"Of course." Maisie touches her fingertips to her brother's fingertips, then takes a cigarette and lighter from her skirt pocket.

"Let me," Edward says. He lights her up, and then himself.

She sits crosswise, facing him, Indian-style. The skirt rides up her thighs, and he knows she notices him glance down. She smiles. "I didn't know you smoked," she says, tugging at her skirt.

"I don't," he says, dragging deeply on his cigarette.

"Where was I—heading home? We hadn't walked more than a mile when here comes Doc in the Range Rover, and of course he pulled over. Army got scared, and I thought he was going to run, so I told him under my breath to let me do all the talking. He said that was cool with him, and before I had a chance to say anything, he looked at his watch, except he wasn't wearing a watch, and he whacked his palm against his forehead and muttered something about being late for supper. So he took off like a sprinter, and Doc laughed and said, 'Which cat swallowed the canary?' So I said, 'What's that supposed to mean?' Doc told me to hop in, that he'd give me a lift. As I climbed in, I noticed the winch bolted to the Range Rover's front bumper. What was that called?"

"A come-along," Edward says.

Maisie snaps her fingers, blows a smoke ring. "Yeah, a come-along. How did I forget? You know a lot, Teddy. You should be proud of yourself."

"Don't be such a wiseass."

"I'm not. I mean it! I admire you," Maisie says. "Do you admire me?"

"Of course," he says unsurely. "What do you want me to say?"

"Gee, thanks for the vote of confidence."

"Maisie, please. Don't be difficult."

"I'm not. I'm being sweet. Don't you think I'm being sweet?" She lies on her back and rests her head in his lap. "Where was I? Okay, so I told Doc I'd run into a little trouble in Dad's car. He looked at me hard, then he shook his head and laughed. 'You have a license?' he said. 'Not exactly,' I said. 'Well,' he said, 'it doesn't matter. If you know how to drive, you shouldn't need one. Don't you think?' I said that sounded right to me. He asked where the Cherokee was, and I told him, and we drove there. When he saw what had happened, he whistled and said this was going to be messy, and I said why didn't we just winch it out with the come-along, and he said we really ought to call the wrecker from the Gulf station, and I said I hoped we could do it without calling anyone. So he said, 'You want to keep this between us, do you?' I said that made sense to me. He looked at me funny again, the way he'd looked when I first said I'd had some trouble in Dad's car. I looked straight at him, too—it wasn't a moment to act like a child. He said he could probably keep a secret, but could I count on Army to button his lip? I said I'd whip his butt if he didn't, and that Army knew as much. So Doc said, 'Let's winch this baby out of the culvert and get her back home.' I slid behind the wheel of the Cherokee and Doc hooked up the cable and started to drag me up. He was up on the road, where I couldn't see him, and I opened my door to look behind and see how we were doing. That was what you might call my biggest mistake yet: When I opened the door, we were just moving past a sugar maple. The door caught on the trunk, and I hollered at Doc to stop, but it was too late or he couldn't hear me. The door made this bending noise, and then a shriek, and there was the door, dragging on the ground alongside the Cherokee, attached by one bent hinge."

Edward is deep in the dream of Maisie's story now, as though Teddy is listening in their darkened bedroom to his big sister bring home from middle school some tragic-comic epic. "I didn't know any of this," is all he can say. "What did you do about the door?"

"Doc thought the whole thing was a hoot. Especially how I lost my temper. I was wearing my Little League cap and I climbed out of the car while he was still hauling it up the embankment, and I took off my cap and jumped up and down on it, yelling—I don't know—'Shit,' I guess. He said, like it was some gem of wisdom from the oracle, 'You can put another door on a car, you can even buy another car. But the cap—that's a treasure, a keepsake.' Then, can you believe it, with the Cherokee dangling from the end of his cable and the Range Rover's ass blocking the road, he goes into this oral history of the Padres-Dodgers league championship the summer I hit four triples and won the game for us—"

"A triple and two doubles," Edward says.

"What? Okay, who cares, a frozen-rope double and two triples. I don't remember any extra-baggers from our right fielder, do I, right fielder?"

"A double," Edward says. "And like I said, for you two slapped doubles and a triple."

"Whatever. So Doc's explaining to me—Jesus, didn't you get sick of the explaining?—why none of the teams were named Yankees or Red Sox or Mets and why they always put siblings on the same teams. Blah, blah, blah. I told him I knew all that. What I didn't know was what I was going to tell Dad. 'How about the plain truth?' Doc said. Something about the way he put it—something *amused*, maybe—suggested he didn't expect me to answer, Oh great, there's a good idea. Why don't I just tell Dad I stole his car, put it in a ditch, ripped the door off. No prob. So I said, 'What's another option?'

"Doc said to get in the Cherokee and follow him home. *'Carefully,'* he said. He said he had an idea, and when we got back to the house, I went along with it. Why not? It got me out of the soup. Doc agreed to tell Dad he'd needed the Cherokee to pick up some plywood because his fuel line was clogged. He'd hot-wired it because he didn't know where the keys were kept. He'd say I'd told him I wasn't sure he should use it, because Dad would have a cow if he knew someone was driving his car. Doc would tell Dad he took it anyway, despite my gripe, and when he was backing out of the lumberyard, he'd opened the door at the wrong time and—bingo, bye-bye door. Doc would offer to have the door repaired. Okay, I didn't see the downside for me. I explained I couldn't pay him back, and Doc made that gesture he makes, dismissing, like money wasn't what friends talk about. I said 'Thanks thanks thanks.' I was so psyched to be off the hook, and I said, 'How can I ever pay you back?' And Doc acted annoyed when I asked that, said friends didn't owe friends for favors.

We were friends, weren't we? Of course we were friends, I said."

"Wait a minute," Edward says. "He was friends with Dad, wasn't he? Why didn't it bother him to lie to that friend?"

"Don't be so literal," Maisie says. "Of course he was friends with Dad, but our friendship was different."

"How so?" Edward asks. Whenever he interrupts her account, Maisie chews on her lower lip, and he notices now that her lipstick is smeared.

"We were soul mates, Doc said. He'd always admired my nerve, and stealing the car was a display of that nerve. Dad was a different kind of person, and he wouldn't understand. I admit I didn't like the sound of that, Doc putting Dad down like that, but I was flattered when Doc said he wouldn't bullshit for just any old friend. Only for special friends, and I was a special friend. Doc was in our driveway, reeling up his cable, and he said, 'Let's shake hands on our alliance, comrade.' That sounded weird, not the way I'd heard Doc talk before. But I shook his hand, and he looked me straight in the eyes and said, 'I think this is the start of a beautiful friendship,' like in *Casablanca*. Now it was hot, and the wind was down and mosquitoes and deerflies were biting. I wanted to get inside the house. So I said, without thinking anything special about it, just like Mom or Dad would've said, 'You want to come in and have a pop?' I guess I blushed, because I remember my face feeling really hot. Doc stared at me again. Those looks didn't make me uncomfortable. They flattered me, as though I was interesting—*surprising* would be the best word. He shook his head and said, 'I don't think that would be a good idea. Not today. We've got all the time in the world.' He said it so seriously that I giggled, and he smiled and put his finger across my lips and said, 'Don't giggle, Maisie. Act your age. You're not a little kid.' And so much had happened, so many things were suddenly different, that

I didn't know what to think. So I said the words you always say I never say: 'I'm sorry.' "

"I'm sorry, too," her brother says, so quietly she can almost pretend not to understand.

"For what?" she says. "What's this got to do with you? This is my story. You listen, I'll tell. But you try to tell me how to feel about my story and I'll shut up right now." Maisie grinds out a half-smoked cigarette, draws a deep breath and holds it as though she was smoking dope. "There isn't going to be any reasoned debate here about the interpretation of events. Get it?"

Edward shrugs. Maisie narrows her eyes and fixes him with her hard stare. He nods. "I just don't understand why you pretended to forget."

"Jesus, Teddy. What a dope." She stands abruptly, walks to her desk, and rummages in the bottom drawer. She pulls out her battered baseball cap and puts it on. "*P* as in Padres," she says, "as I don't have to remind you."

Edward pours more wine. "I'm with you. Go on."

"After that, nothing much happened for a couple of weeks. Just before the Fourth, I found myself over at Doc's work-shop, helping build a bed out of black walnut. I was running planks for the headboard through the planer when he said we should knock off and smoke a number. You know, Doc didn't have strong feelings against dope, like some moms and dads I could name."

"Wait a minute," Edward says. "This was different. Don't pretend you don't understand how it was different."

Maisie lights another cigarette. She studies its glowing end, draws in on it, and blows smoke above Edward's head as if she meant to be considerate. "Why, because I was fourteen? So what if I was fourteen? What, I'm just a little girl and Doc's a grown-up, and this isn't appropriate? It doesn't work that way."

Edward removes the cigarette from Maisie's fingers and inhales deeply. There's something about this gesture that makes him realize he's acting a part, though no one has showed him the rest of the script. He's winging it. He hands back the cigarette. "It should've worked that way," he says.

"I know that's what you think, but it didn't. It worked like this. In my mind, Doc was wasn't like anyone else. He was always erasing the lines that other people drew to keep us apart from one another, to keep us in bounds. For example: You remember that there was this state law against being buried on your own property? It had to do with the purity of the groundwater or something, but Doc said that when he croaked he wanted to be buried right on his place, with a Norway maple planted on top of him, so he could give shade, remind people in spring that he was still alive, and have birds nest in him and whatnot, and in fall, when his leaves turned purple and yellow, they'd remember he was dead, but also that he'd be back the next spring. I'm not saying it the way he said it. You know what his voice was like. He sounded so hot when he talked. It was sexy. And that afternoon, after we'd smoked a couple of joints, Doc and I were looking out the picture window of that room right at the lake's edge, where he kept his drafting table, where he had strung that hammock. We were alone there, listening to Van Morrison. This nuthatch flew into the window, came right at our faces. It hit hard, and Doc was on his feet in a jiffy. He ran outside, and there it was. There wasn't a mark on it, and I held it in my hands. It was as light as air, like an idea of a bird and not even a real bird. But it was real, all right, and the bird shivered when I stroked it, and I hoped it would come to, but Doc said, 'She's a goner; that's it for her in this cycle.' This was so corny, but it blew me away that he decided it was a 'her,' for starters, and I liked that he believed that each lifetime is one ring of a series, like a spiral or something, which

was why a moment in time—a person's legal age, let's say—
was an arbitrary convention, without spiritual weight—"

His sister's voice is in a monotone now, and the words
tumble out too fast, piling up, bumping into one another.
"Time out," Edward says. "What the fuck are you talking
about?"

Maisie laughs, shaking her head like a fighter coming off
the ropes. "Search me. I don't get it anymore. Let's just say
that what my memory erased when I did my swan dive was
Doc Halliday's theological position. Anyway, Doc said, 'I
want you to bury it for us.' That 'us' was another thing that
got me. So I did it, of course—dug a shallow grave, and fuck
the aquifer. After we finished our little rite, Doc folded me
in his arms and said that now, finally, he knew he could trust
me. So sappy! It was—what can I say?—seductive."

"Come here," Edward says. A plea.

She stands over her brother and brings her face close to
his face. He takes the baseball cap off her head. They move
toward each other by unmeasurable degrees, each waiting for
the other but both moving together. He kisses her. The kiss
is unhurried, deliberate, soft, wet.

"What's this about?" Maisie asks, her face against his face,
her eyelash blinking against his cheek.

Edward motions toward the bathroom, unfolds himself
from the sofa bed, and shuffles in there. Running cold water
in the sink, he notices that Maisie has decorated the walls
with posters: the Matterhorn, a pink sand beach rimmed
with palm trees, a cathedral. Freebies she picked up at the
magazine, places she's never been. Does she ever dream of
going? All Edward knows is that his sister once had a life
connected to his life, and that their lives were connected to
a place, to a house and community, to family history, to some
future grander than this mean waste. He bathes his face in
cold water, then buries it in a bath towel, and smells soap,

his sister's soap, his sister. He runs his fingers through his hair, blinks, and takes a deep breath as if he's about to dive off a cliff.

Now he returns, settling himself beside her, and says, "So that's when it started."

"Is that a question, Teddy? When it started? Is that what you want to know? It started *before* it started. You see? It started the first time I saw him and heard him, which was before I knew what the words meant. But I know what you mean, when did it start? We became lovers the night of that Independence Day, when I was—technically—young. You want to know, I'll tell you. It was the night after we made that mermaid float. You remember how we looked? I mean the girls: We had pearl necklaces in our hair, and rouged cheeks, and we'd made old-fashioned bow mouths with ruby lipstick; we wore platform heels and long skirts Mom dyed to look like fish scales. It was a dynamite look, and Doc and I designed the costumes together. The morning before the parade, he came over to my bedroom when I was getting ready. He'd never been in there before. He stood in the doorway, smiling, looking at me. I could see him in the mirror. He told me not to wear underpants. 'They'll show a visible line in your tight skirt, wreck the illusion.' I asked him if he'd told the other girls, and he said no, he didn't care about them, he cared about me. 'I want you to be perfect,' he said."

Edward has moved his eyes from his sister's face. Chewing at her nails, she's smeared her lipstick so luridly that she looks entirely out of control. He angles his eyes up, studying the ceiling above and beyond her head, and then down at the floor.

"Look at me!" she shouts. "Don't you dare look away! You came down here; you wanted it! I haven't made you listen. You want to know how it happened? Well, I'm telling you. . . ." Maisie abruptly stands, puts her hand to her mouth, limps to the bathroom, leaves the door open. Edward can see her at the sink, leaning into the mirror. When she returns, her lips are freshly and fastidiously painted, a new flamboyant ruby. She smiles brilliantly. "Am I pretty now?"

"Where did you do it?" he says.

"You want to know *where* we did it? Are you getting off on this, sweetie? Don't climb on your high horse now. Your curiosity might give me the creeps. It should give you the creeps, too. We did it everywhere. That first night, above the river, on the flat rock beside the—"

"The rock where—"

"Yes, Teddy, *that* rock. Those falls. Do you want to know if it hurt?"

He shakes his head.

"Well," Maisie says, "you want to know everything else. It didn't hurt much, not in a way that made me want to quit. We were stoned. I was. The truth was, I think Doc didn't like dope. Dope undid him, made him what he called Mister Softee. He was more into having control than losing it, and—"

"Where else did you do it?"

"Where *else*? Okay, we did it in his car, his bedroom, his workshop, standing under a tree. We did it in the parking lot of the school during my lunch-hour recess, and we did it in my bed, with stuffed animals on the pillow beside us, and we did it in Mom and Dad's bed. We did it—"

"In my bed?"

"Teddy! Why would we do that? I mean, what was the draw? Maybe Mom and Dad's bed made sense . . ."

"Made sense?" Edward snaps. "What did sense have to do with any of this?"

"Whatever. Mom and Dad's bed was useful—is that the word?—because it was queen-sized, and because of the view.

Why are you crying? This is so stupid, Teddy! This is *not* your business. This was something I wanted to do, and I did it. Don't you get it? Can't you try? Why did I walk up that mountain with you, spend that night with you, if you can't figure that much out?"

He leans forward on the sofa bed and squeezes his temples between his palms. Maisie calls to one of her cats; Edward can see it at her feet, coiled to spring. His sister makes a low purring noise, nothing he's ever heard come from a human, and he looks up at her just as the cat leaps. She holds the animal to her chest, rubs her face in the cat's face, and cradles it in her lap. Edward says, "What did they know?"

"Mom and Dad? She was really weird about Doc. I mean she hated him. I figured jealousy. I overheard them arguing about him, saying my name with Doc's, but it wasn't a conversation I wanted to hear. That's why it was such a good time to run away, Teddy."

"Edward." He hopes he smiles. "I'm Edward now."

"Don't pull that on me, Ed-wahd. We know each other."

"Do we? Anyway, I was kidding."

"Well, sometimes you're Edward, sometimes Teddy. Tonight you're Teddy. This is my place. I get to choose the names. What I think is that Dad saw everything. He came into the house, I know, and he came up the stairs to his room. He stopped at the head of the stairs. We froze. It was a bad moment, and—"

"A *what* moment?"

"Do I have to spell it out?"

"Yes. I think you do," Edward says.

Maisie ignores him. "So there was Dad; there was Doc; there was yours truly. None of us spoke, but I always wondered what Doc would've said. I wasn't interested in what I would've said, just Doc. I wondered if he'd lie, if he'd deny what Dad saw. He could—I don't know—say we were telling ghost stories to each other, got scared, and decided to hide under the covers."

"Like our night on the mountain," Edward says. "Same bullshit excuse."

"Huh? How's the thing in Mom and Dad's bedroom hooked up to our night on the mountain? Sorry, Teddy, you've lost me. Anyway, the topic was Doc."

"The topic is you."

"Sure, sure. Anyway, *about* Doc: Somehow—and this bothered me—I didn't believe he'd push it all the way through if Dad called him on what he'd seen. I couldn't hear him explaining in his explainer's voice how provincial and white-bread Mom and Dad were to object. But in my imagination I could hear Doc bullshitting Dad, and I knew that hearing this for real would break my heart."

"On the subject of heartbreak, what about Mom and Dad?" His face is flushed with anger. He wishes violently to change the subject, to talk about their chances as a brother and sister, what they can do together. Not now, exactly, but down the road from here, and now, too, as matter of fact.

"Oh, Teddy, you're so predictable. I knew *how could you do it to them* was coming! No, I didn't want to punish Mom and Dad. For what? I wasn't even thinking about them. I wasn't dreaming about them, either. I was dreaming of Doc. I was dreaming of me. Awake. Oh was I ever awake! That's what I loved about what we had. After it went away, I walked around in a daze, half-asleep. I still do. I know how my life looks to you, and that's why I don't show it to you. But it's my life, and it always has been. I own myself, clear title. Got it?"

Edward stares at her, trying to see into her, to pass through her unblinking eyes and understand how she can sit here with that cat on her lap, rubbing it rhythmically behind its ears.

He wants to figure this out. He knows he began this Q & A, but he's heavy-lidded from the ordeal of listening to this trite love comic. He's beat. Maybe the wine got to him. He remembers a time at college when he tried to tell his roommate about a disappointment in what had seemed almost like love. He'd begun his story in the dark dorm room, a tale of anxiety and injustice. Before long, his roommate, an even-tempered boy from New Hampshire, said in a low voice, "Shut up." When Ted asked him what he meant, the roommate said again, "Shut up. I've been hearing this story since fourth grade."

Maisie has asked, "Got it?" He gets it. Edward reaches out to the cat on her lap, lifts it gently to the floor, and holds out his arms to his sister. "Come here to me," he says.

"You really don't understand," she says, turning sideways to him, shaking her head. "I'm not surprised. I didn't understand either, back then. I thought I owned Doc because I'd let him own me. I tricked myself into believing when someone said a word like *forever*, that was how it would be. I believed that not because I was fourteen but because no one had taught me it wasn't true. You know that woman who called up tonight? Not the one with the cat, the one with the guy and the broken heart. She's fifteen years older than I am—almost forty—and she still doesn't know that *forever* doesn't mean a loving thing. And *next weekend* doesn't mean much more. . . ."

"Spare me the tough street wisdom. You're too young to be a cynic, whatever lessons you learned from Doc. Let me tell you something about yourself—"

"No, no you don't! Nobody can explain me, feel what my body feels, dream my nightmares. This isn't tragic. It isn't even pathetic, although you seem to think it is."

"Don't you tell me what I think," Edward snaps.

Smiling, Maisie takes his hand, then runs her fingers

through his hair. "Listen to us. What did we go to, squabbling school? We're so prickly."

"I just hate to hear you so bitter," he says. "It's like you're dubbing the sound track in some awful German movie, all black turtlenecks and dirty hair." Maisie holds up the wine bottle, but Edward puts a hand over his glass. He's had enough now.

"I am *not* bitter," Maisie says. "I wish you'd listen to me. Why won't you just listen? What do you think happened between Mom and Dad? Don't you think there was a time when they couldn't keep their hands off each other? When Mom thought of herself as a character in an opera, and that was fine by her? When Dad's dreamy promises sounded like visions instead of self-promoting rip-offs of Doc's schemes? What do you think *happened*? Where do you think all that yearning went? Away is where. Time is why. Just before the end of everything, Doc began to tell me a story about Dad and Mom. Maybe something really bad happened between them, but mostly it was time that wore away at them. Doc told me this thing about a jar of pennies. During the first year people are together, every time they fuck they put a penny in the jar—"

"I heard that in sixth grade, Maisie. For Christ's sake!"

"And after that first year, they take a penny out every time they fuck—and the jar will never be empty. It's true!"

"So what?" he says.

"Well, they never had the other thing. They never settled for quiet friendship. Mom and Dad didn't want to be a brother-and-sister act, like us—"

"Like *us*? Whoa," he says. "Which 'us' are you talking about? I remember—"

"Be serious, Teddy. You've got to let that night go. If I'd had any idea, I never would've—"

"And if you'd known how it would come out with Doc?"

"Doc was different. Doc was my *lover*!"

Edward laughs out loud. "Listen to yourself, Maisie."

"I mean it. Even if I'd known how it would be a year later, I still would've jumped in." She sees Edward's stricken face. "Figure of speech, sweetie, don't be so heavy. I mean that I would've taken him as my lover."

"Lover?" Edward says. "Is that—how should I put this?—is that the best word?"

"It's a soap-opera word, but it means something to me. Do I need to tell you it was more than sex? Sex was gravy. It was being initiated, catching a glimpse of him anxious, afraid, exposed. He was such a big deal to us, but finally, in bed, lit by a kerosene lamp, he was a naked boy with bony shoulders, a chipped tooth, a scar on his chin where he fell out of what he said was the only tree in Oklahoma. I touched that livid scar on his calf, you know, where the skin seemed scooped out and seared? We used to wonder about that, remember? It was from a motorcycle accident when he was my age—"

"Which age?" Edward says. He doesn't like the sound of his voice.

"My age *then*, dumbbell!"

"A little young to ride motorcycles, even in Oklahoma, don't you think?"

"Oh, Teddy. Teddy! You sound like a small-print artist. Dad says you're getting too exact for your own good. I figured he was sore because you're onto him, but now I'm not so sure."

"I don't want to be onto him. I don't want to be like this."

"Don't cry, sweetie. What's the matter?" Maisie holds her brother's head against her chest.

"You know," he says.

"I don't. Tell me."

"You should know," he says.

"Tell me."

"I can't." Edward blushes. "I mean, how could he have a motorcycle license at fourteen?"

"Are you jealous?" she says.

"What do you think?"

"Don't play games, Teddy."

"You think I'm playing?"

"Don't be such a sad sack. He laughed at you, Teddy. Don't pout. It amused him how you followed him around, walked like him, lowered your eyelids like he did. Tried to play with words, just like your hero. Everything was a game for Doc. How can you think of him as old? He was younger than we were. He just knew more." Maisie waits. She seems to want her brother to say something, to show anger, to agree, to challenge her, to tell her to shut up. Something. She waits a long time in silence. "In bed," she finally says, "he was shy. I had to dream up new things for him. He liked that. He'd shake his head, say I was a real piece of work, did I know what a piece of work I was? He said I smelled like pine sap. He smelled like sawdust, sweat, dirt. He wasn't hung up on hygiene like I was. He lectured me not to care, but I did. I knew he liked me clean and smooth. He wasn't all one thing—not *just* hip. He was also a fuddy-duddy. His first girlfriend had been a baby-sitter; he told me all about her, when he was eleven and she was sixteen. He said she was the sexiest girl he ever knew, and once he told me he'd dreamed of finding her, wherever she was, and taking her away with him, no matter whom she was with. Her dad had been in the air force in Oklahoma, and Doc had gone to a lot of trouble trying to track her down. No luck. He said she was probably an old hag by now, but I was always waiting for him to call me by her name—Gloria—even though he never did. I guess I'd seen too much television, even though we only got that one channel. . . . Don't laugh. I watched sometimes. You don't know what I did when you weren't around."

"I guess I'm learning," Edward says.

"Don't be a smart-ass. I mean what I did with my day-to-day life. And don't smirk at me. It makes me want to lie down and go to sleep when I see you smirk. Fucking Doc wasn't my entire day-to-day life—"

"Could we maybe tonight, just to indulge young Teddy, just so you don't have to worry about being a bad influence on your baby brother—could we maybe do without *fuck, fucks, fucked, fucking?*"

Maisie flinches. For the first time all night, she blushes. "It lasted a year. A year to the day, if you want to count from the moment I know you want to count from—"

"We're past this now, knowing what the other one wants."

"You're right," she said. "I'm sorry, I shouldn't speak for you. So when do you think I should start counting? From the afternoon I put Dad's wheels in the ditch? Or before, the first time I thought about Doc when I rubbed myself between my legs?"

Edward says, "Maisie."

"If you don't want to hear this, why are you here? You said you wanted me to tell you. I'm telling you—"

"There's got to be a limit," he says.

"A *limit*. I'll take you past the fucking limit, because that's what you came here for. I sucked his darling cock during the Christmas pageant at his house, when he was dressed up like jolly old Saint Nick. When he was reading 'The Night Before Christmas,' with all the lights off, so you little kids could imagine you were hearing reindeer on his copper roof. Please, Teddy, don't look at me that way. It's not that I can't bear it; it's that I'll get used to having you look at me that way, and you don't want that."

"Don't threaten me," he says. "Be careful now. Don't say something you can't unsay." He means his warning to come out growly, menacing. It comes out tinny, whiny.

"I'm *not* threatening you. Lie down, sweetie, and I'll give you a back rub. You're so tense. Baby, your shoulders are all in knots! What do you want? You want to hear how it ended?"

"No," he says.

"Another girl. *Toujours, amour,* another girl. I figured it out the night before the last Independence Day. He couldn't keep his eyes off her. You know who I mean. She was on the mountain that summer, blond hair almost white, my age. She went to boarding school in Massachusetts, so she wasn't around much. Remember? Her parents had rented the Boulder House?"

"I had a crush on her," Edward says.

"*You* had a crush on her? Teddy, Teddy, Teddy! Jeez Louise, she was a moron!"

"Nice bod, though," he says, relaxing his shoulders beneath the pressure of her hands.

" 'Nice bod'? Come on, baby, you're talking to your sister. I know what turns you on, and it isn't locker room hokum like a *nice bod.* Why did you have a crush on her?"

"Her voice was musical."

"How sweet! 'Musical voice.' You're so poetic. You're *nuts*! She had a snotty voice, high-pitched and affected. She sounded like a penny whistle."

"In your opinion."

"No, that's a fact. Anyway, Doc was making goo-goo eyes at her when we were building the float. She was modeling costumes for him, swirling around like a flamenco dancer, saying shit like, 'Isn't this super?' He was paying attention, and then I found myself paying attention to him paying attention, and then it dawned on me. Even so, I couldn't believe

I was thinking what I was thinking, even if I knew it was true. Does that make any sense?"

He's lying on his stomach, spread out on the sofa bed. She has quit rubbing his shoulders from above and behind him, where she kneels. "Let's do something together," he says into the cushion.

She turns his head to one side and brings her face down to his. "What?" she says.

He sighs. "I don't know. Open a bookstore together, or a bar or a school . . . I don't know. Be law partners. A figure-skating team. I don't know, live together."

"You're too young for me, cutie."

"I'm serious," he says.

"Don't be," she says. "It doesn't make any sense."

"None of it makes sense," he says.

"What part doesn't, Teddy?"

"You were wonderful."

"Why 'were,' Teddy?"

"I mean he didn't deserve you. You were special."

"Oh, that's darling of you to say. Special is all over the place. Special is thick on the ground. Special was the least of it. I can see the truth of it now, and it became one thing and nothing else between us. We couldn't keep our hands off each other. It wasn't good. I don't mean it was bad morally. I don't care about wrong morally, and maybe I don't even know what that kind of wrong means. I mean we had a fever. I mean it was all we did. Tricking people so we could steal off together and touch each other. I was in love, you understand. I don't know what he was. I guess I noticed at some point he didn't look at me when he touched me. Sometimes he looked over my shoulder, and a few times I could tell he was looking at his watch. We'd stopped talking about anything except what we were doing, and we talked too much about that. We were like those doctors who talk into a microphone while

they're operating so that the audience in the balcony amphi-
theater can learn what's going down. 'I'm installing a shunt
in the ascending aorta. You want it now? How's that? That
good? You want me to move this way? That better? Umm,
that's nice.' Like that. You know."

"I don't know."

"Well, you should know. What you can't know, because
I can't explain it, was how it wasn't like an old marriage
winding down, when the sex tapers off, and then the husband
and wife zombie along on automatic pilot. Sometimes they're
pals, like roommates, like brother and sister. At least in the
movies, in some books."

"You're repeating yourself. We've been here. What are we
going to do now?"

"I'm going to finish telling you what you came to hear.
You have to understand that we didn't even pretend to be
pals. It was like we'd cut through to the heart of us, like we
were want and need, feel and taste, rut. I don't know how
Doc felt about it, but my nerves were on fire. About sex, I
was a prodigy. Age had nothing to do with it. Wisdom was
in my fingers, my mouth, the rest. I was wise, you know? I
know I say 'you know' too much. It's a bad habit. My friends
at work have commented on it. I don't presume anything. I
just mean it as a plea. You know?"

"I don't know," he says, "how much more of this I can
take."

"I know, I know. Hush. Lie still now. Wait, before you
say another word, I'm going to play us a good song."

She climbs off, and he can hear her limp across the room.
A cat whimpers. He buries his face in the cushion.

"Muddy Waters," she says. "Listen, 'Good mornin' little
schoolgirl, good mornin' little schoolgirl . . .'"

When she comes back to him, he doesn't move, speak, or
even look. He knows anything can happen now, and he

knows that whatever he says will be the wrong thing, that however he moves he'll spook one or the other of them. If he looks at her, thinks, comes to life, what will he do? He's like Maisie in the hospital, after her dive. Frozen. "Why did you do it?" he asks.

"Which it? I've done lots of things. Doc?"

"The rock. Why did you throw yourself away?"

"I can't remember. I dove into a shallow pool. I can't remember anything. Refresh my memory, Teddy."

"Please, Maisie. I've got to know. Why did you dive into that rock? Did you want to die?"

"Oh, baby! It wasn't the rock. I wasn't thinking about the rock. It was the dive I wanted. *Flying.* I didn't think about landing, about what came after."

And then, finally, he sees her: as she is now, facing him, looking at him, scared like him, bewildered like him, full of hope. Like Ted. Maybe like everyone. But he also sees her then, alone up there, water glistening on her bare shoulders, black hair glistening, water falling, Maisie falling. She was beautiful. She chose to take off, fly, ignore the bottom. They were different. He always knew he'd land someday. She is beautiful.

"I love you," he says.

"I know."

"Don't say something sweet," he says. "Don't break my heart."

"Why are you shaking, Teddy? Have I upset you?"

He takes her hand, brings her fingers to his lips. He doesn't kiss her fingers. Ted and Maisie don't move. Then they lean toward each other. The music stops. They sit facing each other, still. They don't move. The world doesn't budge.

Chilling Out

Days pass and the scandal becomes knotty with speculations and subplots, but without specifics it's difficult to keep the fire fed. Edward's reputation has been explored; the rumor that he's the man who did what was done to Laura got a halting tryout, but it had no legs. The principal makes no move to fire him, and he quits calling meetings with the school's lawyer. Where are the accusations? Edward's grim-faced, tight-lipped, but there's been a late February thaw, and the community's attention is turned sunward. Skiing's great this year, and the price of heating oil and gasoline is down, bringing tourists. The town meeting next week looks to be a boosters' convention.

Then, the Friday before that rally, a notice is posted on the bulletin board hanging on the front door of the Raven Kill Country Emporium. No one sees the messenger tack it in all four corners, secure against an ill wind, but the message, meticulously hand-lettered in red waterproof ink, can't be missed:

J'ACCUSE!

Did I fight for our flag in the Iron Triangle so that some hippie sex pervert could do my little girl up on Blackberry Mountain? Moms and Dads of Raven Kill: that prick must be stopped! Come to Town Meeting Tuesday and

PROTEST!

Vietnam vets with daughters at or near puberty are not a dime a dozen in the Raven Kill Valley, and it is soon guessed who posted this notice. "Hippie" doesn't narrow the range of suspects much, but in the way that people comprehend truths before evidence has been marshaled, the citizens of this community, shopping for milk and homemade soup and *The New York Times*, stopping to examine the lurid accusation, fathom to whom "sex pervert" applies. Aaaah! That guru has been a clock striking thirteen for a long time now, hanging around with the youngsters, who won't shut up about what a good time he shows them. Of course!

Dr. Daimler, amicably estranged from the owner of the Emporium, and a frequent customer, happens along hungry for a loaf of fresh-baked sourdough bread. Entering the store this unseasonably temperate Friday, he pauses to read what many have already read. He looks, and he looks again. He rubs his chin, then looks behind him to see if he has been observed. He turns his back on the store, opens the door of his new Saab, slides into the glove-leather seat, hears the tape deck blast a pugnacious ballad of betrayed honor as interpreted by the Eagles, punches the eject button, and sits in silence, still rubbing his chin.

Dr. Daimler is accountable to young victims of physical and sexual abuse in this county. It is his responsibility to receive reports from mental health professionals and from officers of the law and to report to the county district attorney those offenses he considers severe. This is a humane system of safeguards, meant to balance protection of the helpless against competing interests of personal liberty, meant to protect a girl aged sixteen years and one month from a felony conviction for consorting with a boy of fifteen years and eleven months. This is not such a case. This is another kind of case altogether. This is not the case, Dr. Daimler understands, to drive away from.

There is another thing: Dr. Daimler has a daughter. He thinks of himself as a scientist, a trained student of the mind, for whom nothing human is aberrant, or astonishing . . . but still, he has a daughter, and perhaps because Helen lived during her adolescence with his ex-wife, while the doctor lived with his new young wife and their baby son, the doctor was extravagantly—irrationally, Helen says— protective of his daughter. Helen seemed to Dr. Daimler to grow in spurts, with the effect of time-lapse photographs, and he sometimes found himself wondering to himself what she might be like beneath her clothes. Because he thought these thoughts, he wonders now who else has thought them. Dr. Daimler has been trained to believe that it is natural for a father in his circumstances to speculate as he did, but he has thought thoughts he would not wish to share with another person, not even—not at all—with a person practicing the line of inquiry he himself professes. He realizes that thoughts are not deeds, but the poster on the door has stirred in the father uncomfortable notions. These anxieties had first surfaced when Dr. Daimler received a letter from Ted Jenks about that young student of his, but Dr. Daimler had till now let his apprehensions settle beneath his consciousness. Now he thinks of Helen, and he thinks of her together with the man described by the poster fixed to his ex-wife's door.

Dr. Daimler has come to a decision—an unexceptional

decision, even if it is unethical. He leaves his car, strides purposefully into his ex-wife's store, greets her, takes her aside, and whispers in her ear an abridged and generalized narrative he has constructed from several years of complicated complaints shared with him in the sanctuary of his office by local girls and young women, and most recently in a letter from the young history teacher at the Lake Discovery School. He commits this breach of confidence, then picks up his loaf of bread, wondering to himself whether his next move can wait for Monday morning or if he should call the DA at home, tonight, before dinner.

A few minutes later, Doc Halliday stops by the store to buy a pound of Blue Jamaica coffee beans. It's past dusk now, and Doc doesn't notice the hand-lettered red-inked sign. "Hi, honey," he says to Dorothy, behind the cash register. "How's tricks?"

Dorothy says nothing. She turns to Leda Daimler, who says, "Get out."

"Pardon me?"

"I said beat it. I don't want you in here. Don't ever come in my store again."

Doc looks around. She must be speaking to someone directly behind him. But there's no one behind him. "I don't . . . You can't . . ."

"Get lost!" She doesn't shout this. She doesn't have to.

On Tuesday, a blizzard. April's a bitch up here, and they're still in March. As Jinx never tired of saying, eleven months of winter and thirty days of hard sledding. Last night the snow funneled down the valley from Canada, sweeping through heavy and wet, sticking like flour paste to trees, power lines, windshields; it's falling now, or driven sideways by wind into the faces of the citizens trudging up the steps to the town hall. These neighbors are joyless, uniformly anonymous, weighed down by hooded goose-down parkas of melancholy colors, mittened, booted in felt-insulated Sorels. They're sick of this shit, even the newcomers, flatlanders who sold out their careers and worldly goods in cities and suburbs to the south, determined to find the decent verities in the farmhouse they dream of translating into a bed-and-breakfast—someday, next year maybe. Back home they'd read the statistics on climate up here, splitting the difference between Montreal and Albany, but nothing could have prepared them for the accumulated effect of snowfall, sunlessness, and shrewd wind stealing into the kitchen, parlor, and bedroom.

The folks carry casseroles to be shared at a potluck lunch in the town hall basement. They select seats in folding chairs solemnly, without the greetings and jocularity that could have sweetened such events in more compassionate weather. Their mood is not improved by the close stink of wet wool and wet hair. There's no place to stow scarves and mittens and damp parkas, and the meeting room is overheated by the roaring woodstove set below the dais, from which selectmen and one selectwoman preside. The room is quiet except for the cries and gurgles of babies oblivious to the civic gravity of the occasion.

First on the agenda: the roads. Today they're a sour provocation, frozen unpaved washboard; come the first thaw of mud season the dirt will bog up, sucking at the wheels, clipping off mufflers and tailpipes. The access road to the ski slope is another story, of course: gorgeously graded, responsibly plowed, with wide shoulders and state-of-the-art guardrails, with cat's-eyes down the center line. In ski country the haves cruise, the have-nots slog. Feelings about this run hard today.

A flatlander is on his feet, ex-CPA from Philadelphia who found this place three years ago after his firm got merged by a bigger firm. He wears a green chamois shirt and canvas trousers cinched by a brass-buckled web belt. He's clean-shaven, and his cheeks are ruddy, which shouldn't be mistaken for anger. He has lost weight up here, and you can see the good health glowing from him. All winter long he's sought advice and assistance: What's a fair price for a stacked cord of hardwood, and how can he light his stove without smoking his family out of the A-frame chalet? He's never learned to put chains on his studded snow tires, and so he's had to beg the farmer from whom he bought his lot and his firewood to pull him out of the driveway ditch after he said, "Fuck the chains; I can make it," despite his wife's contrary opinion. Now he's been studying the town budget, and he'd like to put a question to the road commissioner:

"Mr. Brinker, I note here that you've itemized quite a number of specific expenses, including the cost of gravel taken from your nephew's gravel pit. I note also that in this total budget of six hundred twenty-seven thousand dollars and change, you itemize more than half that amount as 'miscellaneous.' I'm pretty sure I speak for others here when I confess I'm bewildered. On what miscellanies, precisely, was that not insignificant sum of money spent?"

Clyde Brinker stands, holding the back of the chair in front of him. He's frail, dressed in a red-and-black-checked buffalo shirt. He addresses the selectmen and the selectwoman rather than his interlocutor. "That's for me to know and you to find out," says the road commissioner.

There is a murmur of approval from the citizens. Every year this question is asked by a newcomer, usually a former CPA or former business manager or former account executive who is compelled to utter the phrase "standard business practices."

During the meeting the blizzard turns furious and electric power is lost, so speakers must amplify their own voices to be heard in the gloomy room, and the din of shouting rubs

nerves raw. Babies fret and wood crackles and spits dangerously in the old woodstove, which belches smoke when the
chimney cap is rattled by a brutal gust.

Now a baby, swaddled in a quilt displaying astrological
signs, is inconsolable with hunger, and her mother, a recent
immigrant to Blackberry Mountain, unbuttons her blouse to
give suck to the child. The mother is seated beside a native
Raven Kill grandmother, who suddenly cries out:

"Shame on you! Who do you people think you are coming
down here and swimming naked and showing off your bodies
and seducing our daughters and granddaughters and nieces
and nephews? You should be ashamed of yourselves! Shame
on you!"

This lets loose an ugliness in the hall, and her cry is
multiplied many times over.

And now Doc Halliday is on his feet, to do what he's done
so often before, to cobble together a plan of harmony that
he can sell to all the good people of the valley and mountain.
"Folks," he shouts, "listen up!"

The silence is profound. No human sound is heard. Only
the wind is heard—battering the facade of this building, lifting and slapping down a loose roof shingle—and the stove,
hissing and popping an angry warning. Finally, Doc Halliday
sits down, and then the citizens of this place murmur and
whisper, and their voices rise, but the noise they make is
wordless, and then a prematurely bald man—his face florid
from hypertension or alcohol or fury—stands, points a
trembling finger at Doc Halliday, and shouts, "You! Him!
Get him!"

Nobody moves. Now the citizens add words to the noise
they make: *guilty, his fault, he's the one.*

Doc Halliday stands and deliberately begins to dress himself in scarf and parka. The flushed man pushes past his
neighbors in the row in front of Doc Halliday, and other men

rise tentatively, then more rise, and "Get him" swells to a chorus. Doc Halliday is walking fast down the aisle now, one arm jammed in his parka, the other sleeve still loose. Men and women follow at his pace, unsure of what exactly they mean to do, and Doc Halliday opens the door and at the bottom of the steps, blinded by blizzard, he breaks into a jog, and now he's sprinting toward the Emporium, with the crowd at his heels. He makes it inside, knows where to go—the walk-in beer cooler, where Dr. Daimler once upon a time stole away on especially hot afternoons to chill out after debriefing especially sordid patients. Inside the cooler there's a latch that can't be opened from outside, installed by Dr. Daimler to assure his privacy. Doc Halliday was taught about the uses of cooler and latch by a little girl named Maisie. It was one of many things she taught him, although to be fair to himself, Doc would probably have to admit she learned more from him than she could ever give back.

The crowd outside the cooler feels cheated and enraged.

"He's got a parka," the glow-faced veteran says.

"And mittens, for Christ's sake," shouts another father.

"Let's smoke him out," says a selectman.

"Let's cool it," says State Trooper Gamble, who has arrived in the company of Dr. Daimler and the doctor's ex-wife. "This party's over," he says.

A Ceremony of Love

Charles Halliday, managing partner of Halliday & Halliday (the second Halliday is self-parodying letterhead fiction conjured to suggest stability and consequence), is arrested and ordered to appear in the county district court to answer charges of first-degree sexual assault, statutory rape, aggravated sodomy, contributing to the delinquency of a minor. Interested parties are present at the arraignment, and these include Edward. Maisie declined to come home for this, explaining to her brother that the magazine is frantically putting to bed its annual "Resorts of the Caribbean" issue. Edward's mother and father also stay away, using remarkably similar excuses for two so estranged; Ann "closed the books" on Blackberry Mountain long ago, and Jinx has finally "put paid to that particular account."

This late-winter day, Edward sits in the last row of the airy courtroom. Other citizens of Blackberry Mountain are scattered among the witnesses, but as a community they are at odds. As individuals they know what they know, and each knows a different truth. To one neighbor, her former hero is a diseased man. To another, he's a victim of the youth culture into which all of them, if they will only be honest, have bought. To a third, Doc's just a kid himself and has no inkling he's fifty now, nor a practical sense of society's bounds. To Doc's wife, Laura is a husband-stealing slut. To the Vietnam vet who nudged this snowball downhill, Halliday's a criminal, a sick prick who should fry, if only this soft-bellied state had a death penalty.

But the vet is, the community now learns, no vet at all, at least of Vietnam. Having served his country in a community college that shared a roadhouse with Fort Bragg, he earned his camouflage pants and jump boots at wholesale prices. And in fact, he has no legitimate beef with Doc Halliday. Facts are raining down hard on the Raven Kill Valley. The bloodthirsty nonveteran's teen daughter—eager in the second trimester to fix the cause of her pregnancy on the local notable rather than on a would-be stock-car racer she met under the bleachers at Thunder Road Speedway, over in the next county—has never ever been alone with the guru of Blackberry Mountain. Doc protested that he didn't know the child even slightly; and after a night at the state police barracks established his story as fact, the young mother-to-be finally admitted she had no tort.

The plagiarist Laura does have a tort, though, and now it's being read in open court to Doc, without the use of the juvenile's name. Distanced from the girl's two pretty syllables, Edward—listening to the law's idiomatic representation of the encounters between Doc and the child—for a while can't imagine the specific acts described by "first-degree sexual assault" and "aggravated sodomy." Then, with Laura swimming into focus in his mind's eye, with fugitive flashes of her likeness standing before a shut door in his school apartment, he can't unimagine what the law's vernacular means.

To the state's charge, Doc Halliday pleads not guilty. After standing before the judge, saying those words with stern assurance, after turning to stare at Edward, his case is bound over for trial. Justice is to be swift. The judge, acknowledging the cloud shadowing this respected citizen's good name, sets a date for April. Then this husband and father (whose wife and daughter, with urgent legal business elsewhere, are not in attendance at today's ceremony), the court having considered his strong ties to the community, is released on his own recognizance.

In mid-April the state outlines its case to the presiding judge, a jury trial having been abjured by the accused on advice of downstate counsel. Edward, again seated in the back row, hears the plot outline: Beginning on the evening of Laura's fourteenth birthday, while the defendant was driving the victim a short distance home from a celebration on Blackberry Mountain during a thunderstorm, explicit sexual overtures were tendered. These took the form of extravagant flattery, an assurance that the child was singular and wise far beyond her years. Marijuana was offered by the accused and accepted by the victim. The accused then kissed the victim, sequentially on her hand, on her cheek, her throat, her lips. A few weeks later sexual intercourse was enacted; a date is specified, and Edward rakes his memory to recall where he was that July night. Sexual congress was repeated on many occasions, until a trusted teacher at the child's school—alarmed by certain pieces of writing the student had submitted in fulfillment of course assignments—alerted the appropriate authorities, who in turn alerted the state of the high probability of a crime against society and nature. The state prosecutor, turning from the bench to nod at Edward, alludes to "the trusted teacher's commendable sense of civic and moral and legal responsibility." Doc, turning his own head to look, winks at Edward, who—responding to a reflex of loyalty or fraternity or he knows not what—finds himself winking back. Immediately he wonders if his gesture has been noticed and, if it has been, whether anyone could mistake it for an expression of complicity.

The state explains that its preliminary presentation of the case is an abridged version; the details of criminal conduct will be specified during the course of the trial.

The defense moves to dismiss. Counsel is a young woman, evidently impatient with the casual dispensation of justice in this backwater. She is dressed in a blue suit and red paisley power necktie. Edward recalls reading that red ties look good on television. She has too much hair, he believes, and it's too complicated: curly and oddly piled on top of her head. She speaks almost too quickly to follow, punching her syllables like ice-pick thrusts: "I ob-*ject!*" Edward decides that whatever else Doc might have said to his lawyer, he hasn't tried to persuade her that she's "special" or "different" or that "kismet brought us together."

There are various prongs to the attorney's motion. First: The accused didn't know how young "the woman" was. Mr. Halliday recalls believing that the birthday was her sixteenth rather than fourteenth. His ignorance of the woman's age is for starters. Age isn't interesting to the defendant. He has long been respected in the avant-garde community, where he and the woman shared values and standards of conduct, for his aversion to middle-class proprieties and protocols, to small-print legalisms. In his view, chronological age is as irrelevant to love as is legal orthodoxy. Okay? Second: There can be no punishment in common law without *mens rea*, the guilty mind. Clearly the defendant, by his very demeanor in this courtroom today, does not believe he has acted inappropriately. Okay? Third: The woman is old far beyond her years. Would the state object, say, to a tender relationship between the defendant and a seventeen-year-old? A twenty-year-old? The court must have noted that the so-called victim seems and seemed to the defendant at least twenty herself. Moreover, the accused should not be required to submit his personal values, and the consenting affection of his chosen partner, to the sliding and arbitrary regulations of a community whose beliefs the couple does not share. Until the close of the previous century, after all, the age of consent in this state was fourteen, and thirty years before that date it was ten, and it wasn't until the thirteenth century that English common law (see Blackstone) made it unlawful "to ravish damsels," with or without consent. Maturity, after all, is an elastic concept. Okay? Finally, and most crucially, for the state to dictate with whom and at what age consenting lovers may enter into a loving relationship is a violation of their basic freedoms, depriving this client of due process and the right to privacy. Today the age of consent is fixed at sixteen, despite what Kinsey and others have reported of female sexual appetites. The court should remind itself that once upon a time society burned witches, and trials were by fire and water. Let us hope that we live now in more civilized and enlightened times.

The motion to dismiss is denied. Edward knows this should bring him pleasure, or at least the satisfaction of having been vindicated. So why does he dread the outcome of what he has set in motion?

The defense approaches the bench with the prosecuting attorney and tells of the accused's willingness—in the interests of the alleged victim's good name—to plead nolo contendere, were His Honor to entertain such a plea in good will. Edward recognizes at once that this is a done deal. Of course. There are, however, quite a few howevers. The judge makes it understood that he understands the state to be inclined toward leniency in the matter of incarceration. He understands that the victim's mother also inclines toward a sentence suspended in the interests of justice, inasmuch as jail time would throttle the accused's income and put in jeopardy the civil settlement—to pay for the victim's psychological therapy and other whatnots—to be agreed upon before sentencing. Understanding the utility of these accommodations between justice and mercy, and understanding that the defendant in pleading nolo contendere in effect disavows his rights to appeal, and understanding that sentencing will be conditional on a satisfactory testimonial from the county Office for Abused Children that this was an isolated incident, or was at a minimum the only official and verifiable report of Mr. Halliday's criminal trespass on the honor of a child, and understanding that restrictions will be imposed on the defendant's freedom of movement, pattern of behavior, and contact with juveniles—understanding all this, does the defendant wish to reconsider his plea of nolo?

The defense counsel says, making her words sound more like an accusation than a question, "May I confer with my client, Your Honor?"

The judge nods, then recalls the needs of the court stenographer and says, "You may confer with your client."

The defense counsel whispers in Doc's ear; Doc whispers in her ear. The defense counsel says, "My client pleads nolo."

"Very well," says the judge. "This is a complicated offense. You have, nevertheless, violated this state's consent law. The purpose of that consent law is to prohibit a girl from voluntarily becoming the author of her own shame and—in the language of the statute—'to set her apart from the lusts of man.' Prior to conditional sentencing, have you, Mr. Halliday, a wish to address the court?"

Doc stands. He runs his hand through his hair, looks to his right and to his left as though remembering rules of delivery he'd been taught in a high school public-speaking course. Edward can see his face in profile, and he's smiling. It's not a smirk, but a warm smile, designed to charm. "I would like to say something, Your Honor."

"Say it," says the judge.

"I loved her was all."

"Uh-huh. Sentencing is set for a week from Tuesday," says the judge. "You are excused."

Edward and Dr. Daimler rise when the judge stands to leave. The bailiffs wave their hands to urge the spectators to stand, but some from Blackberry Mountain remain seated, defiant of courtroom decorums and seditious in the face of authority. Edward notices that Doc, the founding father of liberty and insubordination, not only continues to stand but also dips his head, as though making a show of respect while a congregation not his own is at prayer. And like a visitor to a church for a wedding or funeral, Edward holds back while the front rows of the courtroom empty; he watches his friends and neighbors shuffle down the aisle and tries to read their faces, finding that he can't. These are the people in all the world he should understand as he understands himself, but now he knows he does not know them. He looks at Doc's back as Doc watches the judge vanish into his chambers, and then Doc turns to Edward and smiles a dazzling smile. Edward had expected to watch Doc melt in this courtroom, to shrink inside his ridiculous three-piece suit. Instead, Doc stands ramrod straight. For the first time, Edward notes the lines etched in his bygone idol's face. There's no question, age becomes the old goat—giving him the dignity of suffering, or the appearance of dignity.

Edward files with the others into a breezy hallway outside the courtroom. His neighbors seem occupied with examining their feet, like people leaving an X-rated movie. It comes to Edward then that for many of the people who raised him— played with him, rooted for him—he is a turncoat.

"Teddy!"

The voice comes from a chubby pink face with a fuzzy mustache. Edward doesn't recognize the face, and then he does: his old pal Army, who moved south after high school to work construction at Lake George, building condos. Army doesn't look good; after this dark winter, his skin is flushed with the burn you get from too many cases of Genny cream ale. "Good to see you," Edward lies.

"Man, what a freak show!" Army says. "Now I know why I could never get any nooky up on the mountain. The Doc cornered all our babes! Hey, where's Maisie hiding herself?"

Maisie and Laura

Maisie spends the weekend before sentencing cleaning out her old bedroom, poking around the house. Her brother sleeps in Ann and Jinx's room. Ted is tender, and it's a sunny and warm couple of days. They talk about the good old times when they were learning to swim, ride bikes, skate, clear a campsite, move a canoe up the lake. They walk together along the lake and recollect the first time Teddy ran away from home. Ann had told him he was too young to be such a sober fussbudget. He was maybe nine, and his mother's words made him cry. It was early summer, he remembers, and he took a canoe up the lake to a rocky beach where the family had camped before. He made his camp in the late afternoon and prepared to spend his first night ever alone. Here came another canoe, approaching the shore. Of course it was Maisie. She beached her canoe beside his and walked fifty yards down from him and laid out a tarp and sleeping bag on a bed of moss and clover. She sat on the sleeping bag, eating a sandwich while Teddy ate his. They never said a word to each other that night. That's how Maisie remembers it, and that's how her brother remembers it. He seems grateful to her for being with him now. He's considerate, doesn't push her to testify, though she knows he'd like her to. And he doesn't pressure her to stay with him after the sentencing, though she knows he wants that, too.

She has come home not—she tells herself—to see Doc judged, or to see him sprint free like a broken-field runner, or to see him period. She's come to see the girl.

Dr. Daimler, on behalf of the prosecutor, has begged her to give a statement, file a complaint. Is he nuts? What would she say? She knows what she is supposed to say: that Doc stole her innocence, defiled her body, victimized her. Oh, Maisie knows what Dr. Daimler wants from her, and what her brother maybe wants from her. No thanks. If Doc did it all, Maisie did nothing.

She sits beside Edward and directly behind the man to be sentenced. Dr. Daimler is sitting at the prosecutor's table, a thick file set before him. Just as the judge enters the courtroom, Dr. Daimler catches Maisie's eye and raises his eyebrow quizzically. Irritated, Maisie blows him a kiss, which brings a blush to the face of Helen's dad.

Maisie knows she should show respect, understands she's thought to be a hard case. It helps that Edward knows the truth of her; she squeezes his wrist now. And she smiles at Dr. Daimler. He's a guy with more answers than there are questions, but Maisie knows this isn't a reason to hurt him. He's okay. That she's here at all is thanks to him. Because of the alleged victim's tender age, the sentencing is closed to the public. Dr. Daimler, longing to draw Maisie into a tightening knot of accusations, has listed her and her brother on his interested-parties roster. All present have come to hear Laura, whose full name will not be disclosed, as she is led through a deposition conducted by the prosecutor and defense counsel, stipulated by title a "Victim Impact Statement." This Q & A is meant to specify the acts provoked by those emotions to which Doc Halliday referred in his declaration: "I loved her was all."

After it has been determined to the judge's satisfaction that Dr. Daimler cannot submit formal reports of other felonious violations of the state's sexual-abuse statutes by the convict, Dr. Daimler petitions the judge to be allowed to read for the court a document the doctor describes as "an informal narrative that might, in its sum and exposed to the analysis of common sense, reflect further discredit on the guilty party." He taps this document with his fingers. Maisie figures he must be proud of its hard-won disclosures; he has probably read it aloud, maybe disguising the names, to his wife, maybe even to Leda and Helen. Maisie, an editor, knows writers. She also knows men.

His Honor, annoyed, refuses to hear or consider "speculation, gossip, inference, and evasive third-party hunches." Dr. Daimler's shoulders sag and he looks down at his file.

Laura is summoned from an adjoining room to be this session's sole witness. Maisie is shocked. She's wearing a white blouse and navy wool skirt and loafers. No lipstick. Her scrubbed hair is fastened to the side by a tortoiseshell barrette. She has freckles. She is, Maisie sees, a child.

The prosecutor, clearing his throat, evidently unhappy with the task before him, wastes no time. "What is your sexual history with the defendant?"

"You want me to tell you the first time we did it? You mean petting?" Laura says.

"I mean *it*," says the prosecutor.

"Well, here's what happened. Mrs. Halliday, Juliet—that's what she says to call her . . . at least that's what she told me to call her before she put me down as some slut who hit on

Mr. Halliday—anyway, Mr. Halliday's wife has this little girl named Becky. She's really cute. Mr. Halliday was always nice to me. He was nice to everyone, never ragged on people. He had this way of making you feel special, and he made me feel especially special. He was always telling me how valuable I was, how 'dignified' was his word. He asked me wasn't it a drag hanging out with children when I was obviously beyond them in my interests and outlook. What he called my 'style.' And when I asked if Mr. Halliday meant 'lifestyle,' he said, 'Laura, honey, don't use that word,' and I never used it again."

The defense counsel is on her feet, poking a finger in the air. "I ob-*ject*, Your Honor!"

"I won't have this testimony interrupted," says the judge. "What's your complaint?"

"This woman never called my client 'Mr. Halliday' until today. He was Doc to her and to everyone else. This is a transparent stratagem to create an illusion of distance between the age of my client and the immaturity of the plaintiff."

"Illusion?" says the judge. "Sit down, and no more grandstanding." With a hand gesture, he instructs Laura to continue.

"We got to be friends, and I hung out in his shop a lot. Sometimes, when Juliet called Mr. Halliday into the house to eat or to help with Becky, he'd make a face and roll his eyes and sort of shrug at me, like we had this secret, like I was supposed to understand that Juliet was sort of a witch because she didn't even smile, and when she got pissed off, which she did a lot, her neck got red all the way up to her ears, like a stain. She didn't look all that sexy. She was too pale for one thing, and her knees were knobby and calloused, and she always had these gross insect bites on her legs."

Was this the same Laura, Maisie wondered, whom Edward had described, all come-hither moves, slick and subtle? This child on the stand, telling about her summer vacation?

"The thing happened the first time out west, at Juliet's parents' place that Mr. Halliday had built near Seattle, on an island in Puget Sound. It was late summer, a couple of weeks before school was going to begin."

"And how old were you at this time?" the state inquires.

"I guess I was at least almost fifteen."

"So that would be fourteen?" His Honor asks from the bench.

"Well, yeah, I guess. Mr. Halliday had said to Juliet, who was in a really bad mood that summer, 'Look, why don't you take Becky and visit your mom and dad out west, and you can bring Laura to take care of Becky, and you can veg out and go for walks and catch up with your old pals out there and charge your batteries.' Juliet said that would be too expensive, and Mr. Halliday said no sweat, he had more building commissions than he could handle and it would give him a chance to get a head start on a couple of them. I was cranked to go, because I'd never been out west before, and Becky was a sweet kid and independent and didn't whine like her mom did, and she liked me. Besides, I wanted a new stereo because I was going to be boarding at the Lake Discovery School." Laura seems to remember something, and she turns toward Maisie and Edward and points in their direction. "That's the school where Mr. Jenks teaches. He turned me in for my paper." Laura turns back to the judge. "But I guess you know that. Anyway, Mr. Halliday offered to pay me a lot more than anyone else paid. Would you believe eight bucks an hour, but that was supposed to be a secret between Mr. Halliday and me, and if my mom or Juliet asked, I was supposed to say four dollars, and even that was more than the other baby-sitters got."

Maisie is aware of her brother beside her, looking away from his student to face her. Maisie stares at the back of Doc's neck. She sees where the bushy hair high on his back has crept above the top of his starched white collar. The collar is far too tight, and she wonders where he bought the shirt, and when. She notices tufts of hair sprouting from his ears and a fresh scar just below his razored hairline. Maisie guesses he'd picked up this little nick getting a haircut for the trial. There was a time when such a small hurt would've melted her.

"So I said yes," Laura says. "I drove with Juliet and Becky to La Guardia Airport, where you have to fly from if you want cheap tickets. We drove down in Juliet's Beetle, and we were just checking in when here came Mr. Halliday, with this wacky grin on his face, out of nowhere. He said he'd gotten lonely when Juliet left and he couldn't take it, so he'd driven like a madman down to Albany and jumped on the first flight and he was coming along. It was weird, I thought, because I'd never thought of Mr. Halliday as lonely before, but he got Juliet all excited and kootchy-coo, and as long as I got paid it was cool with me, and besides, Mr. Halliday was more fun than Juliet, so I didn't see how any of it had a downside for me. Juliet asked wasn't the last-minute ticket really steep, and Mr. Halliday said so what, and that made Juliet pretend to be critical of Mr. Halliday's extravagance, but you could tell she was flattered.

"On the plane he sat with Juliet and I sat with Becky and it was just a regular airplane trip—boring. I liked Seattle, especially along the waterfront, and going over to Juliet's folks' place on the ferry. I thought that maybe Seattle would be a good place to live when I grew up. I mean, grew up in other people's opinions, because to me I was grown up. I mean, you don't exactly walk around saying, 'I'm just a kid.' Do you?"

Maisie is pretty sure that she once said these same words, and now, watching Doc's back move with his easy inhalations and exhalations, she remembers where she learned them. Or maybe learning is beside the point, whether you always know some things, or know them when you need to know them. Now, remembering what she knew, she wonders if what she knew is true. Any of it.

"So it happened the first night we were there. We ate dinner out on this screened porch overlooking the water, and I could tell Mr. Halliday was sort of pissed off because he'd designed the house, which was so cool, all logs and big stone chimneys, and I guess he hadn't wanted screens for the porch. But Juliet's mom and dad said they didn't care what *he* wanted, *they* hadn't gone into the poorhouse just to feed themselves to mosquitoes. Mr. Halliday pretended to laugh, but like I said, he was in a bad mood. After dinner it was nine o'clock, which was midnight by my time, and after I put Becky to bed in this bunkhouse that was for kids, and after I read to her and told her what we could do the next day to have some fun together, I was sleepy. We'd gotten up before dawn to drive to New York City, and I couldn't keep my eyes open, so I went back up to the main house to say good night to everybody. Then I went back down to the bunkhouse, where Becky was asleep with her thumb in her mouth, and I was too tired even to brush my teeth or change into my pajamas, so I just got into bed in my underpants, which is how I sleep at home."

Maisie wonders if her brother is picturing this child in her panties. He's looking away from Laura, out the courtroom window. The sun is bright out there, and the wind is moving the needles of a white pine framed by the glass. Maisie decides her brother is thinking about what's on the other side of the window: light, sun, air, an evergreen. Maisie leans forward until her mouth is within a couple inches of Doc's repulsive, pathetic neck. She blows gently on him, so he will feel her.

She expects him to lean forward, away from her, but instead he adjusts himself by imperceptible degrees closer to Maisie's lips. Maisie pulls back just as Doc's defense counsel turns toward her and seems about to speak. Doc turns in his seat and smiles. Now Maisie knows she's in over her head.

Laura has been telling a story. To Maisie, the little girl's voice is flat, undiscriminating, as though everything always equals everything, an airplane ride and her first fuck.

"I don't know what time it was. There had been a moon up when I went to bed, but now it was black outside when I opened my eyes. I could hear a foghorn, and at first I thought maybe the moaning woke up Becky and she'd climbed in bed with me, but it wasn't Becky. It was Mr. Halliday. I didn't know what to say, but I was scared, and I guess my body got real stiff. Mr. Halliday whispered, told me to relax, and he had his arms around me. He wasn't hugging me hard. It was more like he was trying to make me feel good. I still hadn't said anything, because I didn't want to wake Becky up. I mean, I wasn't a moron—I knew she'd be upset to see her dad in bed with the baby-sitter, even if she was a little kid. Mr. Halliday said, 'Oh Laura, I'm so sad!' He was holding my hand then, and I was looking at Becky, with my back to him, and I didn't know what to do, so I squeezed his hand to make him feel better, because I liked him a lot and I didn't want him to feel sad. I wondered if he was drunk, but he didn't sound any different or smell bad. He was whispering stuff in my ear, and that was nice. It felt warm, but the bed was just a single, and he was pressed against me all down my back and legs, so I turned a little. I wanted to ask him why didn't he get help for his sadness from Juliet, but then I remembered that I hadn't brushed my teeth, which was especially uncool, because at that time I wore braces, so obviously I didn't want to open my mouth, so I didn't say anything.

"He did it to me from behind—"

"*Ob-jec*tion!" Doc's counsel is on her feet as soon as Doc has whispered something in her ear. "Your Honor, please!"

But Laura doesn't know what an objection is, so before this legal argument can be absorbed and settled by the court, she pushes ahead:

"I don't mean in my butt, not that night."

"Please stop," says the judge to Laura.

Amen to that, Maisie thinks. She glances at Edward, thinking he must be staring at her, but he's not. Nobody's looking at her. Nobody seems to be looking at anybody.

"I don't understand," Laura says.

"I want you to be quiet for a minute," His Honor says, "while I hear arguments from counsel."

These are impassioned from the defense, a plea for a modicum of decent privacy for her client. "How does it serve the state's interest to have the most intimate details of my client's sexual preferences inventoried in open court?"

"Closed court," the prosecutor argues.

"Overruled," His Honor says, turning to Laura. "Tell us in your own words what you think we should hear. Continue, please."

Laura smiles. Maisie thinks she looks like a kid who's just won a game of blindman's buff. For an awful moment, Maisie wonders if the girl is enjoying the attention.

"I guess I was still talking about that first time. It hurt, even though he'd brought some grease or something. I guess I should say here that it was my first time. He didn't say much I could understand after he said he was sad, I guess because he was scared of waking up Becky, and even though it was so dark in there, I kept staring at her in case she was awake. I could see a pale patch—her face, I guess—but not her eyes. I didn't say anything, and as soon as he shot off in me, he lay there, inside me, and stroked my breasts. I kissed his fingers, and as soon as I did that, I heard him sigh, and then Doc said in my ear, 'You're *good*,' and that made me want to die I was so happy. I mean he's cute, and then it was over and then he left and it was really over. And after that it really began. But you know about after."

Laura, with whom Doc's counsel wishes no further conversation, is excused. At first, His Honor takes the high road, reading from a sheaf of notes. Looking at Laura, he quotes *The Tragical Historie of Doctor Faustus*: "Cut is the branch that might have growne full straight . . ." Looking at Doc, the judge alludes to "these tragic events," invoking Thucydides. "Some men," he declares, "will voyage to Troy even as they know they sail to their ruin."

Maisie can see that the judge doesn't enjoy the sound of his own speech. He puts away his notes, stares at his hands for a moment, then at Doc. The judge seems angry, not that there was anything in the Victim Impact Statement he can't have imagined, excepting the lurid details. He explains now that he has seen the DA's evidence that Mr. Halliday bought that ticket to the site of the young baby-sitter's corruption at the same time he bought tickets for his wife and daughter and the unfortunate girl, to save a buck with the advance-purchase discount rate. He's offended by such cheap calculation. And even though he knows state of mind is irrelevant in this case, "While I cannot base my sentencing decision on unconfirmed rumors of Mr. Halliday's previous behavior . . ." He lets the sentence trail off.

Maisie wonders if the judge now will look her way, and she feels almost disappointed when he doesn't.

"In fact," the judge says, "I wouldn't at all mind throwing the book at Mr. Halliday, but I'm limited in my options by the refusal of anyone other than this one victim to testify against our lover boy here."

Finally, the judge says a deal's a deal, so he reads Doc the riot act and specifies the conditions on his three-year sentence, time to serve suspended unless and until he is charged with another offense against a child.

"A word here," defense counsel says. "Surely Your Honor means *convicted of* rather than *charged with.*"

"Let's cross that bridge when we come to it," says the judge.

"You've got nothing to fear from *me*, Your Honor," Doc says.

Maisie can see that the judge is irked by the self-righteous demeanor of this debauching hippie, so he seems to tack on another condition during the term of the sentence: that Mr. Halliday is not allowed any unsupervised meeting with anyone under the age of consent.

"This wouldn't include his own daughter," declares defense counsel.

"It would," says the judge, watching with transparent pleasure as the smirk disappears from Doc's face. "Mr. Halliday's wife has obtained a legal separation and has custody of the child, and until the state is satisfied that Mr. Halliday has successfully completed a course of therapy, the state will not entrust any young person to Mr. Halliday's unsupervised devotions."

"Therapy?" asks defense counsel.

"Sex-crime therapy," says the judge.

"Let me understand the conditions," says defense counsel. "*No* unsupervised association of *any* kind with *any* woman younger than—"

"Any *person* younger than sixteen. Yes."

"You mean no boys?" Doc says.

"I'm coming in loud and clear," the judge says cheerfully.

Maisie realizes that the judge is beginning to feel that this morning hasn't been wholly wasted. She's not so chipper. Doc is on his feet, trying to speak, and Maisie doesn't want to hear it. She knows this was supposed to provide an epiphany.

Seriously, why else would she have journeyed here? Isn't she supposed to want to climb in a shower, to clean the filth off herself? Isn't this, then, the proper outcome? So why does she feel so tired? What this mostly reminds her of is the end of a bad play, just before the curtain falls, when she worries about fetching her coat and hailing a cab. What she wants is to crawl into bed. And not alone, not alone.

"Let's get out of here," she says to her brother.

"Shhhh," says Edward, holding a finger to his lips, staring at Doc's back.

Doc is asking permission to speak, but the judge shuts him up with a wave of his hand. His Honor has a nice sense of timing, Maisie thinks. He seems to be pondering whether he hasn't already found the exact high note on which to end sentencing, with "loud and clear," but he can't resist the impulse to make one final observation: "You have behaved execrably, sir. You are pathetic. You make me sick. Have you anything to add to this proceeding?"

Doc says, "I'm a good person."

"Golly," says His Honor.

The Nuclear Family

Jinx skipped the courtroom but spent the night before with his son and daughter in their old house. They sat out on the deck quietly, taking in the lake, the mountains, all those soft, sweet colors, grand-scale stage sets for noble acts.

"How could anyone make a mess of this?" Edward asked, thinking he was asking himself the question.

"I didn't do a very good job up here," Jinx said.

"He wasn't accusing you of anything," Maisie said.

"I know that," Jinx said.

"Mom made mistakes, too," Edward said.

Jinx looked up the lake, away from the mountain. "She was wonderful," he said. "I was lucky. God, she used to make me laugh."

"Mom?" Maisie asked.

"Sure," Jinx said. "Don't you remember how she was?"

Maisie and Edward stared at each other, as though they were remembering.

·   ·   ·

The afternoon of the sentencing they're together again. Ann flew in this morning from Chicago, where she has settled with the older brother of a doctor she met years back at Maisie's rehab clinic. Ann has confessed to Maisie that she feels strangely young for her elderly friend, but Bob's generous and warm, and a real power in the office-supply business, small stuff like rubber bands and staplers and file folders and memo pads and paper clips. This has been going on for a year now. Jinx, tipping off his jealousy, has nicknamed Bob "the Magnate." Ann claims her husband-to-be has the same immoderate laugh as Jinx. Maisie, who's met him a couple of times in New York, says she's prepared to like Bob. Edward's talked to him once on the phone, and he's reserving judgment.

The Jenks family has gathered in the conference room of the Valley Trust Company in the presence of lawyers and bankers to sign the papers selling their portion of whatever parcel of dreams made up this place called Blackberry Mountain. The meeting is amicable. Jinx takes his ex in his arms, kisses her cheek, and holds her at arm's length, examining her face. "You look like a million."

Ann thanks him, smiles, and claims she's happy. Maisie's mother fusses with her daughter's hair, admires it. "You smell like baby powder," she says.

"Ma!" says Maisie.

"Well you do," says Ann. "I always loved that smell."

Edward clears his throat. "Mom, I think they want to get started on this."

The house has been dumped at a fire-sale price. Ann and Jinx have come to the closing to look out for their individual interests, but few interests remain. The ski boom is flat, despite a wonderfully cold winter, and empty condos are on the block throughout the northeast. Houses are poison. Who wants to shovel snow and spend half a year's salary on a Subaru 4X4 to get up that bitch of a driveway for a night or two in the second home? Besides, the Jenkses' house has been empty except for Edward's occasional visits, and he's not an avid housekeeper; the pipes burst back in March, the water stains are depressing, and the view from the crow's nest is compromised by a thick layer of dead cluster flies annealed to the panes. The Jenkses reckon they're lucky to bail out at any price, even though they've lost their equity in the property—or rather, *her* equity, as Edward is reminded at the closing. He is relieved to notice that Ann flinches at the humiliation of his father by this accounting of bleak numbers and facts.

The buyers are newlyweds from northern New Jersey who have been given the place by her indulgent father to use as a "ski chalet," as he terms it. The solemn father with the checkbook says "ski chalet" as though he has just now heard the phrase for the first time and has yet to learn its meaning. This man responds to every aspect of the transaction—"Just sign right here. . . . I'll need your John Hancock on the bottom of this page . . ."—with a studied frown, followed by a conclusion: "That makes sense." Edward doesn't dare catch his sister's eye, because he can see that she has begun to anticipate the responses; her lips are subtly miming the declaration "makes sense."

The newlyweds are euphoric. She tells the Jenkses that their house is "an artistic statement." She's pregnant, and Edward thinks she's simply lovely. His heart goes out to her without condescension; he sees her husband smile at her, sees her squeeze his arm. Her husband can't get over how stimulating it will be to live in such a community, "a regular utopia."

Well, the community now is more fission than fusion. Many Blackberry Mountain players are looking at their hole cards, rethinking the postulates. If the Jenkses couldn't get even a percentage of what their place was once worth, at least they're getting something: They're getting out.

After the closing, the family goes through the civil gesture of celebration with a late lunch of soup and sandwiches out on the back porch of the Raven Kill Country Emporium. The river, fed by the stormy winter's runoff, thunders by the deck; water overruns the banks, slapping violently against the supports of the covered bridge downriver from the store, half a mile upriver from the falls and swimming hole.

"Well," Jinx says, "at least we don't have to worry about running into him here."

"So you've finally turned your back on him?" Ann says.

"Don't start," Jinx says, taking his sandwich from his mouth. "You don't want to get into this, believe me." Jinx bites in again, wipes the corner of his mouth against the sleeve of his sweater.

"Folks," says Edward. "Please."

"I was just wondering," says Maisie, staring at the swollen river. "Just curious is all. When did you figure out about me and Doc?"

Edward, despite his alarm at the turn this is taking, smiles at this childlike idiom coming from the big magazine editor.

"Who do you mean by 'you'?" Ann says.

"Well *you*, for one," Maisie says, turning to her mother.

"When did I know what?" Ann says.

"For the love of Mike!" Jinx says. "You know what she's talking about. I'll tell you this, I knew plenty about Doc and his girls. I could write a goddamn book."

"Don't do this," Ann says. "I'm leaving for my flight home in a couple of hours, and I don't want to say good-bye remembering you this way."

Edward feels his face flush at his mother's emphasis on the word *home*. How could this have happened?

"Why not say it?" Jinx says. "Maisie has a right to know.

Maybe she thinks she was the first woman in our family to roll in the hay with our maximum leader."

"Jinx!" Ann says. "Don't do this!"

"Remember the goddamn ski house?" Jinx says.

"The Seraglio?" Edward says.

Maisie stares at her brother. "What's going on here?"

"Please don't," Ann says, to all of them.

"The frigging Seraglio is right," Jinx says. "Your mother," he says, staring at Maisie, "got caught in the sack there with Doc. I mean caught literally, trapped in there."

"When snow collapsed the deck?" Edward says.

"How did you know about that?" Jinx says as his ex-wife stands to leave.

"He told me."

"About Mom?" Maisie says.

"About the design flaw," Edward says. "He was talking about the house, the cantilever effect."

"That motherfucker," Jinx says.

"So how could you be his friend?" Edward asks. "Mom?"

"Ask him," Ann says.

Jinx shrugs. "It's complicated. He was . . . I don't know, is *interesting* the word? I was flattered to be his friend. He was fun. I was scared; he wasn't. I needed a friend."

"He wasn't a friend," Edward says. "Did you owe him money? How long have you known about Maisie? Jesus! About Mom?"

"You've got to understand," Jinx says. "It was different up here before you kids started running all over the place. It was hard-core, and we tried new ways of doing everything. We had a rule: No rules. For example, anything that anybody did from the day before Independence Day through the day after was a free pass. It was against the rules to talk about divorce, whatever happened around Independence Day."

"Whose rules were those?" Maisie says.

"What Mom and Doc did they did in dead of winter," Edward says.

"I'm leaving," Ann says, and she leaves.

"How long did you know about this?" Maisie says.

"My whole miserable fucking life," Jinx says.

Ice

Edward is busy clearing out the house so the new owners can move in. This is a modest chore, since Maisie took her stuff away in a rented car. He wanted her to wait for him, wanted to leave with her. He proposed a life, had ideas for them, together maybe, so why wouldn't she give it a shot? She explained that this was over now; at last, one part of her life was finished. This was the end; they had to get on with their futures. She was gentle. Edward knows nothing of their futures, only that there's no break with their past. He knows that she'll work for that magazine, sleep in that apartment, feed those cats. He'll teach school somewhere. Not here, of course, but somewhere: He knows how to go to school. He tried to reason with his sister, and he begged her. Then she was gone.

The furniture is mostly built-in, and the appliances stay. Edward is boxing up books and records and framed photos and odds and ends when Doc climbs to the second floor, carrying a couple bottles of Molson ale. Edward looks up from a carton of broken toys he can't bring himself to throw out, and Doc signals with one of the beers. Edward responds gingerly. This was not foreseen. Doc approaches him cautiously, slowly, the way an animal trainer works with an unpredictable predator. When he's within touching range, he offers the frost-covered bottle again, and Edward warily takes it and drinks from it. Doc makes a toasting salute with the remaining bottle before he drinks, but Edward does not answer the gesture.

Doc takes a book from a carton, examines it, digs deeper into the box and removes another, then puts it aside.

"What are you doing?" Edward says.

"Picking up any stuff of mine that might be lying around."

"There's nothing for you here," Edward says.

"Well," Doc says, "*this* is mine. This book of poems. Baudelaire. I loaned it to Maisie."

Edward reaches for the book; Doc reaches to stop Edward's hand but pulls back when the younger man's muscles tense. Edward opens the book to a handwritten inscription: " 'What do I care that you are good? Be beautiful! and be sad.' I agree—Your Doc."

"You're full of shit," Edward says.

Doc shrugs. "Maybe poetry's not your bag."

"What else have you left lying around my house?"

"I was over here a lot," Doc says. "I guess you must wonder what to think."

"Not really."

"It must be confusing," Doc says.

Edward shakes his head.

"Have you talked to Maisie?"

"Of course," Edward says. "She's my sister. Why wouldn't I talk to her?"

"I mean about me," Doc says.

"I know what you mean."

"Meaning?" Doc says, squatting Indian-style, just beyond Edward's range, facing the picture window overlooking Blackberry Mountain.

Edward notices the man's hands, discolored with grease, as battered as old tools roughly abused. He thinks of those fingers at Maisie's lips, inside his mother. "What do you want from me?" Edward says.

"Your understanding. We've meant a lot to each other."

"I don't think so. You've got a flock of devotees, what con artists call pigeons."

Doc shakes his head sadly. "You're not expressing what you feel. You're saying what you think you should feel."

Edward laughs an ungenerous laugh. "What a crock!" The words aren't coming easily to him. He suspects himself of playacting, posturing. A mistake, a false show of emotion one way or the other, could cost him dearly, and he wants Doc to leave.

"I've got a proposition," Doc says. "It's really a favor I'm asking. I want you to listen to me. I want a chance to tell you what happened. You know what I am, what I'm not. If you still want to hate me when I'm finished, I'll leave you alone. How about it?"

"Forget it," Edward says. "I'm not a priest or a prosecutor. I don't take confessions."

Doc stands. His face is red. He runs his hands through his thick black hair.

Edward stands, walks up to him. Their faces are close now.

Doc and Edward stare at each other. Edward blinks, averts his gaze. He knows that he has already surrendered something to Doc: priority, maybe, timing or advantage. Doc takes Edward in his grasp and pins Edward's arms to his side, hugs him, says, "Teddy." He says, "Teddy, I know you know, you understand. Maisie told me everything. We're like brothers."

Edward pushes himself free of Doc's embrace. "I don't

have a brother. I'm not looking for a brother. I've got a sister. What more do you want from us?"

"Nothing. Almost nothing at all. Just for you to hear how it was."

Edward doesn't want to hear how it was. Not with his student when she wore braces. Not with Maisie when she wore lipstick and no underpants. Not with his mom when she laughed in bed.

Doc pleads with Edward to climb Blackberry Mountain with him. His voice is serene; he makes good eye contact, knows not to blink. He can do all this in his sleep—he's a master. "You've never made it to the top; I've never made it to the top. We'll do that together, then you can leave. Then I'll leave, too. I've done what I came here to do."

Edward says what he has to say. "Of course."

They leave as once before Edward left, on the dark side of dawn, carrying light backpacks and climbing ropes. It is the second Sunday in April, and fog rises in gauzy sighs from the lake. As the climbers begin to rise, finding their way with miners' headlamps, Doc talks. He warms to his sermon, telling the story of how he found this land, what it cost him to own it, what joy it was to share it. "I never wanted any of it for myself. It wasn't about me." He must know none of this is new to Edward; but if he can just get the boy to listen, he believes he can make him understand he's got the wrong idea. If Doc can just keep talking, he *knows* he can straighten this out. He knows this boy's too conservative to waste what they have in common—territory and memories, these explorations together. Like this one.

Edward doesn't speak as they climb, except to answer "I get it" in response to Doc's question, a refrain of "Do you follow me?"

They make quick progress until they hit crusty snow heaped under the trees. The sun breaks behind the peak, and they look down at the fog burning off the lake. Doc points out the papery delicacy of the bare-limbed birches all around them and seems disappointed that Edward doesn't marvel at his prose poem to the mysterious loveliness of this world. Instead, Edward is deliberate. They fasten their snowshoes in silence, and as they move out for the traverse across a switchback ridge to the ice shaft below the summit, Doc says, "I want to tell you what happened with Maisie."

"I don't want to hear."

"You've got to know what we had between us," Doc says.

"Just be quiet," Edward says.

"No, I've got to get this off my chest," Doc says, and Edward knows that here it is. This is Doc's moment. Doc's got great timing, the gift of seeing the crack in the barrier. Now he tells everything, without stopping. What Maisie said when they lay together, what Maisie told him about Jinx and Ann and about her brother, and what she said—laughing— had happened that night in the tent on the mountain. Doc explains what Maisie did, what he did. He tells how she smelled, how she tasted. "She's quite a woman," Doc says.

Leading the way, Edward says nothing. He hears, but by now the words have no power. This surprises him. By now he's learned all he needs to from this man. Now he needs to learn from himself what happened to them all. This must be knowable. Was it carelessness? Recklessness or courage? No, he imagines it was a matter of character, of will. Their parents, but Maisie and Edward, too: it was what they'd wanted, every step of the way. They set in motion what they wanted, and when they didn't want it anymore, it was too late to learn a new thing to want.

"Did you hear me?" Doc says. "Your sister was quite some girl."

Why won't this man shut up? Edward knows that blame is beside the point. Anger can peel the pretty paint right off you. It's seductive. And Edward is ready to seduce himself with it. They are out of breath now, standing side by side on the precarious shelf ascending the face of Blackberry Mountain. Edward notices something move, and up the path he sees a black bear cub. The cub is looking at Doc, and Doc smiles; then the smile dissolves as he realizes that the cub is probably not alone.

"Bear," he says.

Edward, looking down, has seen the bear. Not just the cub but the sow. And she's on Doc's right, crouched, moving toward her cub, close enough now for Edward to smell her, and Doc's eyes are getting wider and wider. The sow sniffs the air, and her cub bleats pitifully.

In a motion so quick Edward hardly registers its grace, Doc puts himself between Edward and the sow. "Careful," Doc says. He reaches out to touch Edward's arm, to calm him. This is what Doc was born for, taking charge. The sow draws nearer. Edward sees her ears laid back against her head. She's underweight after her hibernation and must be cranky. She smells awful, like rancid grease, so close that Edward can smell her sour breath and see her purply black gums. She's even closer to Doc. She's in attack posture, sniffing the air; then the cub scampers toward its mom, and she growls, studying Doc and Edward, studying the route past them to her cub. And then, squealing from fear, the cub scoots past the men to its mother. Now the bear's attention is on her cub, and she cuffs the youngster and they lumber away, leaving Doc and Edward to themselves. The bear looks once over her shoulder and growls a hoarse warning, then disappears.

"That was close," Doc says. "I mean *close*!"

"It's not over yet," Edward says.

"Sure it is. She's just interested in her cub is all."

"She's interested in us, too," Edward says.

"Don't flatter yourself," Doc says. "Anyway, I'll take care of you. What instincts! Now that's a mother for you. No way is anybody going to harm that baby. She's all mama. Your mother was like that once. Ferocious. A real handful." Doc studies Edward to see how this is working, but he can't seem to tell. "I remember—"

"Save your breath," Edward says. "We've got a climb ahead."

Doc looks up. Thirty feet above them the path dead-ends at the foot of a chute of blue and green and white ice rising straight up to the summit's shoulder. Beside the ice chute they can make out tenuous toeholds. This will be a technically exacting ascent.

"Let's go," Edward says.

Doc looks unsure—a new look in Edward's experience— as he stares at the ice. "I'm not that great a rock climber."

"This was your plan," Edward says. "So see it through. You can do anything you put your mind to, right? No limits, Doc. Just like you taught us. Perform—right to the top. Fuck gravity. Fuck prudence. Do it."

Edward looks at him and knows his mentor's mind. Doc studies the muscular boy he taught everything to. Doc must believe he knows Edward's every secret.

"You lead," Doc says.

Edward understands that these are exactly the right and only words to say. Doc must be picturing them standing together up there, Doc's arm draped over his shoulder, looking down on the entire known world.

Edward leads with the rope coiled around his shoulder and tied in a bowline around Doc's waist. He's good at this, and he keeps the rope free of slack but just loose enough to allow Doc freedom of movement. Doc, in his worn leather hiking boots, is wary as he tries to follow the course of Edward's quick ascent. They've inched parallel to the left of the ice chute, nearly to its top.

"There's ice on some of these toeholds," Doc says.

"Yes," says Edward.

"Hold the phone; I can't find the way up." Doc is fixed by his hands and a foot, and he's searching for a dimple in the slick rock with his free foot.

Looking down, Edward says, "A little above where you've got your boot. Just to the left there." While Doc looks for a toehold, Edward drives a piton into the rock face and secures the belaying rope to it.

"I feel like a dog on a leash," Doc says. The frozen waterfall is to Doc's right, and as he looks over at it he begins to slip. Edward watches the tired man losing his grip. Doc is in a kind of grotesque cruciform, arms and legs spread-eagled like a snow angel, stuck beside the ice chute like a cutout on a bulletin board. Paralyzed, he looks up and sees Edward looking down. Edward is almost all the way up. Doc doesn't see Edward unhook the rope from his waist, then pull the loose end of the belaying rope through the eye of the clamp he has hammered into the stone face above Doc. He doesn't see Edward let the heavy coil fall, but he feels the weight of Edward's freeing act as the rope—dangling below Doc—suddenly hauls at Edward's old hero, and he digs his fingers into the side of the rock. This is not going Doc's way; he's losing it here. Edward watches as he lets go with his right hand and lunges toward the ice chute. Doc grabs the chute with his bare hands and wrenches his torso to the right, clasping the ice shaft like a fireman shinnying up a pole.

"Teddy!" Doc shouts. The cold is like fire on his ungloved hands and between his slippery legs.

"What can I do for you?" Edward says.

"Jesus, man, help me!"

Edward looks down from the comfort of the shoulder just beneath the summit. He climbs higher, where it's safe. He's made the summit of awful Blackberry Mountain. Not so awful after all, maybe just a bump on the planet, higher than some, lower than many. Edward can see everywhere. The back side down to the next valley is a cakewalk, a stroll in the gentle hills.

"Please!"

Edward looks down at the man just barely holding on. "Spring's on the way, Doc. Take my word for it, that ice'll melt. Trust me." And then he turns away.